THIS AGE WE'RE LIVING IN

David Wilson

LARGE PRINT

Oxford

First published in Great Britain 2007
by
Black Swan
a division of Transworld Publishers

Published in Large Print 2007 by ISIS Publishing Ltd.,
7 Centremead, Osney Mead, Oxford OX2 0ES
by arrangement with
Transworld Publishers
a division of The Random House Group Ltd

British Library Cataloguing in Publication Data
Wilson, David
    This age we're living in. – Large print ed.
    1. Journalists – Fiction
    2. Lifestyles – Evaluation – Fiction
    3. Consumer behaviour – Fiction
    4. Life change events – Fiction
    5. Middle-aged men – Fiction
    6. Large type books
    I. Title
    823.9'2 [F]

ISBN 978–0–7531–7936–9 (hb)
ISBN 978–0–7531–7937–6 (pb)

Printed and bound in Great Britain by
T. J. International Ltd., Padstow, Cornwall

"This day and age we're living in
Gives cause for apprehension . . .
So we must get down to earth at times,
Relax, relieve the tension."
                    "As Time Goes By"

"Only two big facts are known for certain: you are
on a large, spinning rock that is hurtling through
lonely space at about 67,000 mph, and one day
your body is going to die. Will a new pair of shoes
really help?"
                    Worth's 12th Rule of Shopping

For my family

Contents

CHAPTER
ONE

NEW SHOES FOR CHRISTMAS

Anti-Style
by George Worth
21 November

Women say special, unique things that men can never say. A man hears these things and realizes that he simply does not understand and that no one will ever be able to explain them to him.

For example, women say: "I can't walk in these shoes."

This remark alone can kill a night out. You've been for a meal or watched a show, and you fancy going on somewhere just down the street, or maybe it's time for a taxi and there's a rank only a few hundred yards away. So the man says: "Let's walk there, it's a fine night." And the high-heeled, pinch-toed woman says: "No way, I can't walk in these shoes."

Now, to a man, the concepts of "shoes" and walk" are inextricably linked. They sort of go together, they are made for each other. If you are wearing shoes, you can walk. If you are going to walk, you wear shoes. The idea of buying and wearing a pair of shoes *in which you cannot walk* is as bizarre as, say, buying a raincoat that can be worn only indoors.

But only a foolish man would say: "Why the hell are you wearing a pair of shoes that do not enable you to put one foot in front of the other in any comfort?" This can bring two killer ripostes from which there is no recovery. The first is: "Well, at least my shoes are fashionable/smart/less than ten years old." And the second is: "I am wearing them because I thought you'd like them."

These thoughts ran through my mind in the human misery of a local high street at the weekend, as I passed the window of a shoe shop which displayed a large poster with the words: "New shoes for Christmas!" Naturally it was over a display of women's footwear. A woman sees that sign and thinks: Yes, of course, there are parties coming up, lots of good times. I need new shoes.

A man sees that sign and thinks: Er, why? I've got shoes. They're broken in. They're comfy. Why do I need to change them for Christmas? What's next, new underpants for Easter? A new jacket for the third Sunday after Epiphany?

I suspect that, like many things, this difference between us is inborn and goes back to the Stone Age. Selfishly, ancient man took the best available foot-covering materials, all the good animal skin, tied together with all the best hemp, so that he could go out for a long hunt without the soles of his feet being ripped to shreds and without tripping over just as something large and fierce decided to chase him. Meanwhile back at the cave, his woman was left with a few scraps of fur trim, a bit of bone and some wood that wasn't good enough for the fire. So she whiled away her time making something that looked good on her feet for when he came home.

But when he returned, he didn't even notice her shoes (because normal men just don't). Instead, he grunted to her: "Hey, come and look at the woolly mammoth we killed, it's only just over the hill from here." And she grunted back: "You're kidding, aren't you? I can't walk in these shoes."

It all helps to show that, if you look back far enough, it's always the man's fault.

"George, are you thinking of asking someone out?"

"I'm sorry?"

"Your column tomorrow, third paragraph. It reads to me like you've been imagining yourself going on a date."

That's Joan speaking. She's my boss. She's also one of the most good-hearted and one of the sharpest executives in national newspapers where, believe me, those two attributes don't always go together. Somehow she still sees the good in me and I owe her a lot.

Her comments, spoken from her desk diagonally opposite mine, were loud enough to carry round the small section of the office where we produce an endless, daily parade of drivel for what are laughingly known as the lifestyle pages.

"No, Joan," I answered firmly. "I am not dating. Like most of the writing round here, it was all based on memory, exaggeration and hearsay."

"Well, that's a shame." She sighed. "Anyway, let's get on with next Tuesday's pages. Sadly, I think it's time for the annual articles about the party season and how every woman needs her little black dress. Any ideas for a new approach?"

I was ready for this. I reached for my cuttings file, where I keep articles from other publications that contain old nuggets we might recycle into new-looking stuff for ourselves. "There was this actress from one of the soaps. She said in an interview that she had a lucky black dress that she'd worn everywhere. How about, you know, getting her to talk more, getting some pictures, calling it Memories of My Little Black Dress?"

"Do you think she would pose for pictures?"

"A soap actress? Try stopping her."

And so it goes on.

Joan, who is Features Editor (Lifestyle), is long-term married and thinks that I have the potential for romance now. This opinion is set against some quite simple views about men, so her argument goes something like this: "Look George, admittedly you have some primeval views about life, you prefer history to the present day, you dislike fashion, shopping, mobile phones, computers, and almost anything else that's modern, and you once wrote an article titled What Is the Point of Young People? You don't even drive a car any more.

"But let's not forget that in the world of romance you'd be competing only with other men, and that's not hard even for you.

"For a start, you've got a steady job and you're not a pisshead, so that puts you in the top fifty per cent straight away. You've probably read a book in the past month and you don't think you're wonderful, and that puts you in the top twenty per cent. You have an approachable face, you are not overweight, you don't smell and you're not actually bored by women's company, so that's more points." Etc., etc. One of these days I wish she would use this line of thought for an article titled something like: Twenty Reasons Why Some Women's Expectations of Romance are too High. Except that our lifestyle pages are built on our readers having ridiculously high expectations of love, of life, of anything really, and we don't like to let them down too much. The idea is that you too can be more beautiful, happier, healthier and generally more wonderful if you can only find the right clothes, diet, vitamin supplements, home decor and attitude guru. This is not just about needs or wants, but passions, fantasies, cravings, temptations, indulgences, greeds, curiosities, fears and insecurities, all bundled together.

Astonishingly, this sort of thing never goes out of style, it just gets repackaged now and again. A little modern irony here, a little old-fashioned sentiment there, some mild male scorn (that's my contribution in my weekly and weakly Anti-Style column, on top of my other duties helping to organize the pages). Mix in some honest self-mockery at the height of the fashion weeks, and we can go on for ever.

Does anyone normal have a lifestyle? I don't just mean a way of living — like supermarket on Sunday, wash clothes on Thursday, watch a video on Saturday night. That may be life, but it's not *lifestyle*. Lifestyle suggests that everything in your life matches perfectly, as if it was all bought from the same shop on the same day. Isn't everyone a collection of different ideas and things they have acquired along the way, that somehow go together in just that one person, making them who they are?

If everyone really had a complete lifestyle, everyone would find themselves out of date every few months, and then what would happen? (OK, OK, they would just shop even more.) Supposedly, when we go shopping, we are not just looking for things, we are shopping for our lives.

Most of the people who work in the lifestyle trade are young: the young do not appear to have yet worked out the total falsehood of it all, and they can still seem endlessly enthusiastic about silver being the new gold, or gardening being the new sex, or toes being the new cleavage, or whatever. The luckier lifestyle youngsters get jobs on newspapers or magazines, or write freelance articles from home. There are now hundreds of good young brains wasting their talents on this stuff, which is a thought to chill the soul.

The unfortunates get jobs in public relations, and spend their time trying to persuade us that some new product or service is worth writing about. They jam our fax machine and emails with desperate drivel that takes hours to sift for the rare good idea. The lifestyle staff of one tabloid grew so tired of sorting this out, they notified the worst offenders that from now on their material would be handled by a special editorial assistant by the name of Candida Thrush. To their delight, the most stupid ones actually began faxing Ms Thrush. Their stuff went straight in the bin.

But if the lifestyle teams are usually young, the readers are not necessarily so. Most definitely not. This was proved by One of the Biggest Controversies in Lifestyle Journalism, when another paper ran a sneering double-page spread featuring middle-aged actresses and female TV presenters trying to look sexy at premieres and showbiz parties, all with backless dresses and plunging necklines, with the headline: Mutton Dressed as Lamb. This produced a sackload of angry readers' letters, and virtually all carried the same message: "I am a middle-aged woman who has spent twenty years putting my children first, I have just started to be able to afford the time and money to jazz up my appearance, and I aspire to be like the very women you are insulting. Are we supposed to wear sacks after we are forty? Who do you think you are?"

It's just possible, hopefully even probable, that a lot of readers know it's all drivel and read it as a kind of harmless fantasy. (Is lifestyle the new porn?) But it's getting harder to defend. Previously, my defence of popular journalism has always been this: in a free society, the media are holding open a door for information to pass through. Ninety per cent of the stuff that gets through may be junk, but if we didn't keep that door open, keep producing newspapers that people actually want to read, then important stuff such as real news would have no way out into the world.

Lately, though, it seems like the junk has been taking over the real news pages too, because it's as if everything is now about lifestyle — the housing boom, health discoveries, shopping trends, diet discoveries, showbiz developments, opinion polls on the most unlikely things, and endless stuff about sex. Words such as sperm and orgasm get into news headlines now. It's amazing. Sometimes it's a challenge to find any drivel left over for the real lifestyle pages. But somehow we manage.

This is twenty-first-century Britain, once the land of Shakespeare, Newton and Churchill. And for some time now the favourite national pastime has been shopping. The whole economy seems to depend on it. It's like a giant party, a spree that everyone knows must end at some point but not just yet.

So this is our job. We tell people that it's never too late to catch their dream. We suggest the dream and say where to buy it. Do we follow the dream ourselves? Not really — we're too busy filling these pages to do much of this stuff, and some of us haven't got the inclination either. Are our lives in the same mess as everyone else's? You bet. It's all, well — what's that word some of the girls use to describe rubbish? Pants. That's it. It's all pants.

Am I happy here? Of course not. This is my personal, comfortable, meaningless hell. And I deserve every minute of it.

People have been very kind to me since I killed my wife.

That thought is in my head every time I walk into the pub after work. No one turns around and says, there's that selfish, stubborn bastard who beheaded the love of his life. They say, there's George, he's harmless, probably a bit lonely sometimes, amazing how he manages to be even remotely cheerful, considering. Hey, George, come and have a drink.

Tonight, our pub was divided into the two usual groups: in one group were the would-be movers and shakers, and in the other were the people who merely get moved about and shaken. The first lot were clustered around Clive "the Hound" Basset, the serial adulterer and ageing smoothie who rejoices in the title of Assistant Editor (Features). Lifestyle is part of his empire. He sometimes goes out of his way to knife Joan in the back, just for sport. Behind my back, I know that he calls me George Worthless. I do not drink with Basset.

Around the other end of the U-shaped bar are the people who have no ambition, the people who do not like to admit that they have ambition, the people who do not understand why they are not getting anywhere and the people who know very well why they are not getting anywhere and are quite happy about it. These are my people.

It's not a great pub, stuck between the era of the real bar and the era of the wine bar, but it's nearest to the office and does a decent glass of red, which is what I should be drinking for my health these days, according to our own pages.

In Basset's gang, someone is usually muttering into a mobile phone. Sometimes they all seem to be on their phones at once. (For all I know, some of them may be phoning each other.) Among my drinking companions, even the few who carry a mobile like to leave it switched off. We prefer to speak to people who are actually present. In general, we are not great fans of technology.

I was just settling into a quiet rant about the eccentricities of our latest editorial computer system when I noticed one of the younger Basset acolytes detach himself from the rest and wander over to stand beside our group. He had an owlish face, brown hair, brown glasses and a black suit and tie. He also wore that slightly anxious expression of his kind, as if worried that his suit might have gone out of fashion in the past five minutes.

He stood near me until there was a lull in the conversation at my end of the crowd. Then he spoke.

"Kirsty MacColl," he murmured to me, conspiratorially.

"I'm sorry?"

"Kirsty MacColl. The singer. She did 'In These Shoes?'. I was just reading your piece in the first edition. I thought you must know that song."

"Er, no." His face fell. "But I know of her, of course. She's my generation. Or she was when she was alive. I quite liked 'Fairytale of New York'."

Pause. I was thinking, first, why do Young People think that mentioning something like a pop song counts as conversation? And second, I know of Kirsty MacColl but I don't know you, do I? Then he introduced himself.

"I'm just starting in features. I'll be doing a bit of everything in each section. I'm Justin Smith."

"Great byline."

"So I'm told."

"Justin for trendy and upmarket. Smith for British and classless. By Justin Smith. It has a certain something."

Some of the others smiled and, for the first time, so did Smith. Questioned by the others, he revealed that his byline had yet to grace our paper because he had only just moved down from Manchester. His girlfriend was still working up there. This was his first go on a national newspaper and, even though it was only a six-month try-out, he obviously felt so lucky he hardly knew where to start.

Then he turned to me again and said, "You know, my mum is a big fan of yours. She always looks out for your column."

Sharp intake of breath all round, and much amusement. Here's a thing: media folk, even minor executives and bottom-of-the-page columnists such as myself, like to think that they might appeal to a range of readers, maybe even a few of the younger ones with the high disposable incomes that our advertisers crave so much. We do not really like to be popular with people's mothers. This was disarmingly naive of him.

"Well, thanks. You know, you have just revealed a lot about yourself."

"No. Why?" Shocked look.

"If your mum reads the paper, it means that's the paper your family got at home. You grew up reading it. So now you've come to London, you're going to prove yourself on this same paper. For you, this is the real thing."

"Damn," he grinned. "You've found me out."

"Actually, George," said one of the very oldest news sub-editors, a man on the brink of retirement. "I have to tell you something."

Expectant hush.

"What's that then?"

"My mother really likes your column too."

Much laughter, including from Smith. Another round of drinks, with Smith included this time. Then it was time for me to get the Tube, as I had a friend waiting at home.

Ben was reclining on the sofa in my flat. Ben is always pleased to see me, whatever he is doing. I know that. Ben will listen to me talk about nothing, Ben will watch with admiration as I prepare dinner in the kitchen. Ben will eat pretty much anything I make, share a walk beside the Heath in the dark, then settle down with me to share my choice of the television programmes without challenging for the remote control.

As I closed the front door, I could hear his tail thumping on the sofa cushions to greet me.

"Hello Ben. No, don't bother to get up. I've only been working all day. I suppose you'll be wanting me to make you some food."

The tail thumped louder. Ben knows sarcastic wit when he hears it. He is pretty smart and sophisticated, even for a Labrador.

Ben belongs to the hospital sister who rents the flat downstairs. When she is on night shifts she doesn't like him to be on his own, so she has my key and leaves him in my flat before she goes to work. I offered this arrangement in the spring when she found herself working regular nights. Ben already knew me from the occasional coffees and chats that pass for neighbourliness in London flatland. Like me, Ben is in middle age, likes his comforts, can't be bothered to get into fights and is happy having someone else around so long as they don't cause too much fuss. We get on famously.

I had picked up my post from the entrance hall on my way in. Among the junk mail there was one actual letter, which was one more than usual. I opened it, saw who it was from, sighed and left it on the kitchen table while I made Ben's dinner. I have learned that he likes a mixture of food rather than just the contents of one tin. Tonight he had canned tripe, a dash of leftover tuna for his joints, a weekly egg for his coat, a sprinkle of bits from the fridge, a dash of cold gravy and a mix of crunchy filler for his teeth. I like to look after him.

The letter was from my "grief counsellor". I read it in the kitchen, with Ben grunting and slurping in the background.

"Dear Mr Worth,

It is now more than six months since you kept one of your monthly appointments. I read your column every week so I know you are still at work. You do not answer my notes or my secretary's messages on your telephone, so I must assume that you do not want to attend any more although you are not actually prepared to cancel.

"Since your GP referred you to me over a year ago, I have continued to be concerned about your feelings of guilt over your wife's death. I am well aware of your pain. Grief takes time to work through and it is not unusual for it to become arrested in a depressed phase.

"If you still have concerns, I wonder if you have thought any more about my suggestion that you should at least keep a journal of your feelings? This would not need to be kept daily. How about weekly, or even monthly at the very least? If you record any events or conversations that leave an impression on you, it may help you to take stock of yourself and examine your emotions. This can be a very effective form of self-help.

"Please give this some thought. I am here if you need me, but I can no longer keep your appointments available unless I hear from you."

This was a new low, to be dumped by my grief counsellor. Bizarrely, I found myself wondering if I had made him feel depressed or rejected, and if I should try to cheer him up by letting him know that I would at least start to write his damn journal. He was an earnest, bearded sort. Every time I had been to see him, his face was bright with care and concern and sympathy.

The thing is, not many conversations leave an impression on me these days. And I do not really seem to have feelings any more. None that I care to dig into, anyway. I've got opinions. Occasionally I even have thoughts. I can be annoyed. But feelings? They are not much use to me right now. Mostly I'm just numb. It's the sort of numbness that leaves me looking at the world rather strangely most of the time, as if I am seeing some of it for the first time and I do not like it very much.

I can live with numbness. It's a holding position. It allows me to keep my distance. It's better than some of the alternatives. However, a monthly journal of numbness may not be quite the adventure of self-discovery that my counsellor wants.

How could I have disappointed him so? Certainly, there was no way to tell him that, in so far as he had ever been any use to me, he had been replaced by the comfort of a dog.

CHAPTER
TWO

SPONSOR A MILLIONAIRE

Anti-Style
by George Worth
26 December

Christmas is a time of music and giving. That's a nice idea. Somehow this has created an annual ritual that I call Sponsor a Millionaire. That is not good at all.

It works like this: children hand over their pocket money, grannies dip into their pensions, everyone gives generously as they support their favourite runners in the race to get to the top of the Christmas music charts.

The only real beneficiaries of this unique frenzy of record-buying are the millionaire pop singers and music moguls who churn out the repackaged greatest-hits albums, theme compilations and a few novelty singles.

There hardly seems to be a new tune among them all, yet this stuff has become a tradition, like Christmas trees and tinsel. It gets more coverage than the best-selling toy, the winners are heard more widely than the Queen's Christmas message, and the whole event is more slickly prepared than anyone's Christmas dinner.

And it's part of a trend that affects the background beat of all our lives, whether we like it or not.

We all know that a lot of pop music is trash, little more than nursery rhymes for the barely pubescent. Not surprising really, as the pop industry targets ever-younger age groups. You can't blame the music moguls. Children make the ideal consumers: they are up for any craze, they can be defiantly and irrationally loyal to the brand they choose, and it's not even their own money that they are spending. Besides, it slyly gets them used to participating in the mass market while deluding themselves that they are somehow rebelling. Catch 'em young, eh?

There has been some talk that downloading music from the Internet might change all this and really broaden things out a bit, but nobody knows how this will work out. Children can download as much as anyone.

The trouble with this youth market is that, too often, pop lyrics have gone into a kind of arrested development, a perpetual adolescence that affects us all because this stuff is played wherever we go. The songs are all about first love, first lust, youthful rivalries, introspective trivia or just annoying the neighbours, instead of relatively grown-up stuff like, well, family life, lost dreams, long-term love, and death. In America, that sort of thing is left largely to the country and western charts. In Britain, men of my age and ilk stick gratefully to the likes of Van Morrison and Chris Rea.

The teenage mentality of popular culture is part of the backing track of all our lives, and it strays beyond the charts to infect television, movies, books and so much more. Sometimes it feels like being a Young Person

17

is no longer meant to be just a phase but a way of life to aspire to, with endless rebellion and constant stimulation replacing any idea of people just getting on with reality. It's a bizarre world when adults feel obliged to aspire to youth culture rather than see it as something we have outgrown. Why should the young call the tune?

The winners in the Christmas charts get no mention here, you'll have read about them on the news pages. Maybe, just maybe, one single track will last beyond this Christmas — in retrospect, all pop songs acquire some of the poignancy of life because a generation remembers what they were doing at the time they heard the music. Hopefully, most will just fade away.

But if you are really looking for rebellion, I've got an idea for next year, something to think about as we gaze around at the anticlimax we call Boxing Day and start thinking of New Year resolutions. Instead of sponsoring the pop millionaires for Christmas, next year let's all take just one per cent of the hundreds of pounds that each of us is now estimated to spend on Christmas, and instead give it to a deserving charity. Sponsor something worthwhile.

Even the pop industry manages to do something like this now and again. Records such as "Do They Know It's Christmas?" have done rather well. But why do we have to buy a record at all? Why do we want something for ourselves even when we are being generous? Why not just give?

We will still have music. There are plenty of old hits, and Christmas has always had its own tunes, after all. There are carols, and Sally Army bands playing on street corners. There are trips to the *Messiah*, or pantomimes with fairy-tale endings. You still believe in happy endings, don't you?

Festive greetings, and a happy new year.

"It's not very cheery, is it?"

"Sorry?"

"I don't mind the message, there are just not many smiles."

"Look, it's for Boxing Day. No one is smiling then, except with relief."

And I can't always try to be jokey, Joan.

Joan is on the phone from her home. I can hear her family celebrations in the background. It is Christmas Day and I am in the office with Justin Smith. We are the skeleton staff of the entire features department, just in case anything happens that makes it necessary to change the pages that were put together days ago. Joan has been glancing through the proofs again, discussing what might be dropped in case we have to clear space as the knock-on effect from some key event such as the outbreak of a war or the death of a minor celebrity.

"Anyway," she says. "How are you two getting on?"

"Oh fine. Justin is down the other end of the department, surfing the Net and phoning his girlfriend. I'm watching *It's a Wonderful Life* on the TV and hoping no one actually realizes that we are here. We had mince pies from the canteen. It's great."

"I'm sure that Basset put you two together as a joke."

"Maybe."

"Well, don't stay beyond the first edition. And try not to frighten your taxi driver on the way home. He won't know how you feel about cars. Happy Christmas, George."

"Yeah. And you."

I don't tell Joan that I have also been occupying my time by doing a bit of idle research on a theme that matches my mood about the year ahead. She would only worry and, anyway, she'd never publish it.

Justin doesn't want to be here today. His girlfriend chucked in her secretarial job in Manchester this month and moved into his London flat, looking forward to Christmas as a live-in couple. She's at the flat now, pining for him. One of the older male writers had volunteered to work instead of Justin to escape the torment of a big family Christmas. ("Sorry, darling, I would love to be with all your relatives but I'm needed at the office.") But there was no escape for anyone. Justin must be here because, well, in large organizations it is deemed to be right that Young People should suffer as part of gaining experience. (Seems OK to me.)

I should have avoided this too. One of my colleagues, my gently ambitious sidekick Arabella, who helps me as Joan's joint deputy, volunteered to come in instead of me. This was also vetoed by Basset. He wanted me to be in.

It is known in the office that I am quite terrified of cars these days. And a car is the only way to get to the office on Christmas Day. Ho ho ho.

My Christmas Day so far: Get up late. Breakfast. Open my two presents: a history book on the British

20

Empire from my former in-laws, and a joke book from Joan about the views of Grumpy Old Men (the third copy I have received in recent years). Start to watch some old film on TV, interrupted by the taxi driver ringing the doorbell.

Unusually for London, the driver is full of festive cheer — well, he is on triple pay and escaping the torture of Christmas telly — so we are a few minutes into the journey before he gets the message that I do not want to talk. There are a few clues that he might have picked up: I had opened the rear door as if opening a coffin lid, clipped the seat belt as tight as it would go, sat hidden behind a newspaper for the entire journey, only grunted in reply to anything he said, and whimpered slightly at tight curves. I am sweating and taking deep breaths at the end.

Out of the taxi and into our barren, open-plan office, which looks even more barren than usual because today it is not only devoid of decoration and natural light, it is mostly devoid of people. Entire rows of computer terminals are unoccupied. No phones ringing. Hardly anyone shouting in the newsroom. Round the corner, in the features area, nobody is ripping up a page with frustration at an idea that just does not work, or on the phone trying to persuade a freelance to accept a dull commission that no staff writer will touch. There's not even the background chatter of our ever-changing array of lifestyle girls as a distraction. (Yes I know I should not call them "girls", and I don't say it to their faces. But the funny thing is that even a right-on woman such as Joan, who hated being called a "girl" in her young

21

days, now refers to them privately as girls herself. It's the price of pushing fifty).

It's only in the past couple of decades (and you have to be pushing fifty to be able to use a phrase like "only in the past couple of decades") that Britain's national newspapers have come out on Boxing Day, requiring a small team of news staff to come in on Christmas Day to try to scrape together a few pages from the least eventful day of the year. There's the Queen's message, the Pope's message, the Archbishop of Canterbury's message, a major house fire that always seems to be in Glasgow for some reason, and, er, usually that's about it. Most of the specialist correspondents try to dress up a story left over from earlier in the week to make it look topical. That's the paper, really, just Christmas leftovers. And a lot of adverts for the Boxing Day sales, which are the real reason for the papers coming out, so everyone can go shopping again.

Features staff didn't need to come in at all, as all our stuff is done in advance. That all changed on Christmas Day 1989 when, just for once, something actually happened. Few now remember that date, but that was the day when the good people of Romania rose up and gave the dictator Nicolae Ceauşescu his rightful fate — taken out and shot — in one of the most dramatic moments in the collapse of the Eastern Bloc. This was a terrific, real story, requiring large numbers of feature pages to be ripped out of newspapers — how can you justify two pages on what to do with a half-eaten turkey when you have got a good running event plus pages of hastily arranged background articles? Next day, news departments moaned that they'd had to do it all themselves and that some features staff should actually be on hand, rather than on call, in case something like that ever happened again.

At the very least, newspapers now require the presence of a minor features executive with a minimal knowledge of production and layout (that's me) and a capable youngster who can turn out a few hundred words on anything (that's Justin). The two of us are stuck on standby in memory of the last day of a Communist lunatic, rather than the first day of the Christian faith. Thanks, Ceauşescu, may you rot wherever you are.

Is this the kind of stuff for a journal? What if nothing is happening, like right now? Do I just write about nothing, like the diary of some drippy adolescent girl? It's not like writing a column. That's easy. Take one of the rants in my head and tidy it up into a seemingly fluid thought. People read columnists because we can shape things into some sort of temporary sense. We are millionaires in opinions, rich in rants. Read us, we cry. We are controversial. We are like you. We express the things you didn't even know you thought. We can ridicule anything and anyone, without courtesy or compassion. Like pop music, we are part of the background fuzz of life, we help to set the mental rhythm. Read us.

But real life is bits. It's contradictory. It's not fluid. Predictable sometimes, maybe, averaged out across the population. But not an individual life. That's bits.

And this journal isn't doing me any favours. It makes me think about what I'm doing, and how I am.

People seem to be aware that I am becoming grumpier than usual but they don't enquire much about it. One of the advantages of being my age is that you can be grumpy without having to explain why. If you are in your twenties and you are in a bad mood, someone will say, "What's the matter with you today? Has something happened?" In your late forties, they say, "Oh don't be so grumpy, George," and they don't ask any questions. It's sort of expected.

While I am here today, I am supposed to be checking some of the material for New Year week, style tips and forecasts about what the year might bring. Round the corner, in the news section where I once worked, there are more certain and harsher elements of the year ahead that they can forecast too. And not just the fixed events of the year, such as bank holiday traffic jams or the Oscars or the opening of Parliament, but the real yearly trends of the human race. In hard news, there are seasons of death.

It's sad and obvious stuff, mostly, a sort of depressives' calendar of the year. It's like a gigantic crash you know is going to happen, but you just have to sit and wait to discover the names of the dead.

This outlook of gloom is the subject of my research today. No particular reason, just curious. Amazing what you can find out by browsing a few official sites on the Net. (Yes, I can surf too if I'm bored or curious enough.)

24

I know death is out there. Of course, we would never print this in all its starkness, even in the days when people accused newspapers of printing only bad news (as compared with now, when we are accused of printing only trivia). But this is the truth. This is the year ahead.

Festive season: yes, let's start right here. Well, it's the peak time for calls to the Samaritans from the lonely and suicidal, up 20 per cent on the rest of the year. And the knock-on effects of the "festive season" stretch for months . . .

January: peak month for male suicides (the aftermath of Christmas disappointments, or maybe they have just seen their credit-card bills). This is also the peak month for natural deaths, especially among the over-forties, as the British winter chill tests our ageing bodies to the limit.

January to March: the young are suffering too. The aftermath of all those festive parties is a tide of unexpected pregnancies. These are the peak months for abortions.

Easter: grand opening of the DIY death season, as the great British idiot reaches for his ladder, power drill, lawnmower and chainsaw, and generally starts several months of accidental electrocution, fatal falls and severed arteries.

May: peak month for suicides in general. It is theorized that too many bank holidays give the unhappy too much time to think. Or maybe it's just the change in the weather.

June to August: time for the Brits to go abroad to die. Like lemmings, drunken youngsters topple off their hotel balconies in Spain, crash rented scooters in Greece, lose their grip on paragliders just about anywhere, and drown everywhere else. Back home, a light plane crashes almost every weekend with an amateur pilot at the controls. (I know a news sub-editor who jokes that he does not feel safe to leave the office for home on Sunday night unless he is reassured that the weekend's death plane has already plummeted to earth, otherwise he feels that it's still up there, circling, waiting to fall on him.)

August: a peak month for road deaths, especially motorcyclists. Ambulance staff have a nickname for motorcyclists — they call them organ donors.

September: the second peak month for suicides in general. (Oh I don't know why. The evenings drawing in, perhaps?)

Autumn: starting the build-up to the great winter indoor death season, known by officialdom as "accidents in the home". House fires, fatally faulty heaters, kitchen disasters. It's the price of people not really getting out enough.

November, December: another peak time for road deaths, especially pedestrians and car users. Then it's the festive season again. Such fun.

And that's not counting the supposedly definite but so far undated events such as the likelihood of us being decimated by bird flu, fried by global warming, sabotaged by terrorists or shut down by the imminent dwindling of fuel supplies, clean air and fresh water. If that sort of stuff happens, all we will have left is each other, and then where will we be?

The amazing thing is, against this pattern of apparent Armageddon, most of us will survive the year unscathed, get on with life and await our turn with fate. If we do not actually hasten it somehow.

Down the ranks of empty desks, I can just see the top of Justin's head. Really I should wander down and have a chat with him. There's just one problem. My conversations with Justin don't go anywhere. It has taken me a while to realize this and it isn't helping. I have always tried to get on with new staff, I really have. (Our lifestyle pages say that one of the roles of middle life is "mentoring" the young, but there are limits.) Justin and I don't seem to have anything in common that either of us wants to talk about. We've done the social chit-chat and the usual male stuff — a brief mention of us both fancying some actress to show that we are both heterosexual; a raising of the eyebrows during a pub conversation about football, to show that we are not that anorak-serious about it; a mutual scorning of some male pin-up to show that we have our own way of bitching, despite working in a department mostly composed of women. But that was it.

Justin's work is good. He has done minor interviews for showbiz, a housing-trends background for the property page, a little research for the main features pages and a personal view on men's fashions for lifestyle. He has a sense of humour. (He wrote a funny piece about how the men who design fashions for women are clearly gay, otherwise they would put all the zips, buttons and clasps at the front, where men could get at them without fumbling, rather than hidden away round the back.) He gets on fine with the younger girls, to whom I am fairly invisible or at least harmless.

Justin has youth, looks, probably a degree, and an appreciation of all things modern, but nevertheless I should be able to find something interesting about him.

There's less than an hour to go, so I risk buying him a coffee from the vending machine in the hope of a limited chat. Here's a thing: our vending machine doesn't take cash any more. We work in a cashless office, presumably to reduce the risk of the lowly paid catering staff skimming off the loose change. Instead we now have "cash keys", little plastic things that we have to load with credit by putting change into another machine before we can buy anything. I keep my cash key on my key ring along with my flat keys. I reflect that, if you can judge a man's life by the size of his key ring, mine has only three keys and one of them is plastic.

"How's it going?" I put the coffee in front of Justin. He breaks off from a website.

"Fine, just thinking of a holiday in America. Looking for ideas."

"Great. Where to?"

"Boston, maybe, then travelling round New England. I've got this ambition to go to every state of the US, and there's a lot of little states in that area."

Sigh.

"With your girlfriend?"

"Yes, but she's got no job at the moment so it'll have to be a cheapie."

"The travel editor may have some trips on offer from the airlines. I'll ask him."

He beams. Young People with glasses often seem to do that. They beam.

"Could you? That would be great. I thought I would settle in before I tried anything like that."

"Yes, sure. Basset takes a lot of the best trips. That's how he tops up his permatan. But there are still a few left for the minions. You never know."

We talk a bit about America, and about his widowed mum, who is also spending Christmas alone. Then we run out of conversation so I send him home. He is away in seconds. I'm staying behind just long enough to print out these ramblings as my journal for this month, make absolutely sure there are no spare copies, totally destroy the original in my personal computer file, then call my cab to go home. Ben will be waiting for me to share the last of Christmas Day.

Back home again, late in the evening. That was a nightmare. I don't want that again.

In the taxi I pretended to doze as a way to avoid conversation (and as an excuse for keeping my eyes tightly shut). The city roads were empty so I was home in no time. I was calm. I was free of cars again.

I paid the cab driver and watched him drive off as I reached into my trouser pocket for my keys.

And realized that they were not there.

I knew I must have left the key ring in the office. Probably in the damn coffee machine. In my mind, I could see the keys dangling there.

So there I was, in the street in Highgate outside my flat on Christmas night. The last of Christmas was ebbing away, there was this large lonely dog waiting for me, probably with a bursting bladder. Nobody at home to let me in. Nobody I knew well enough to give me a lift back to the office. No buses, no Tube, no passing taxis. Nothing.

Part of me just wanted to give up, go to find a pub that was open, or just sit on the Heath and look at the stars. Anything. But I owed Ben.

I could have hiked to the hospital and tried to track down Ben's owner, to borrow her keys to the house and to my own damn door. But I didn't fancy the humiliation of bothering a casualty sister to tell her about my stupidity, or wandering back and forth with her key to the main entrance, because I'd have to return it to her so that she could get into her home at the end of her shift. Too complicated. Besides, she might have thought I was too stupid to be trusted with Ben ever again.

(Also, OK, I don't like calling for help. One of my few self-discoveries is that when you are depressed, you tend not to ask for help very much. Having to ask just makes you feel worse. Anyway, I can cope alone. All right?)

Then I remembered there was a minicab office down on Kentish Town Road, so I set out to walk along the dark streets to find it. Through the big windows of large houses I could see Christmas celebrations, families eating and partying and watching the telly. I was on the outside of everyone. For me, it was a glimpse of Christmas past. I have not felt much more outcast than this.

It made me think of that scene in *It's a Wonderful Life* where an anguished Jimmy Stewart walks unrecognized and unloved down the main street of his town, in some parallel existence where he has never been born. In the film, the whole town was worse off and more depressed without him having lived. In my reality, everyone seemed to be managing just fine without me. Of course, Jimmy Stewart had Clarence the trainee angel to help him. It seems there's no angel to sponsor me.

The cab company was open. For a generous fare, I got a taxi back to the office that I had only recently left, found the keys just where I had left them in the features coffee machine, and then came home again. On my return I was totally shattered, a nervous wreck. It's been a blur.

I don't want to dwell on this, the fear of being trapped inside a car, the feeling of what might happen. Four car rides in a day is something of a success, I suppose, but I don't want to think about it.

Surely things cannot go on like this, but I cannot see how anything can really change, God help me.

When I finally got in to see Ben, he welcomed me profusely. I hugged his thick black fur and I cried. I actually cried.

"Oh Ben, my old mate. What am I going to do?"

CHAPTER
THREE

EVERYTHING MUST GO

Anti-Style
by George Worth
23 January

This is a joke, isn't it? A great big practical joke that gets us every year.

Not long ago we were fighting each other to pay the full prices for all the wonderful things in the shops in time for Christmas. Now the shops are full of much the same things — often the very same things — and they're all cheaper. We could have saved a fortune. (Next year, tell the kids that Father Christmas has been delayed for a week due to bad weather in Lapland. Just see how much you could save. Father Christmas is a lie anyway, so what's the matter with another?)

And everything must go, the sale signs say. Really, everything must go, to make way for a whole lot of new stuff that's coming soon, very soon, for the new spring season.

There is so much that I do not yet understand, earthlings. I do not understand this "season" thing. Spring is months away. The trees are bare. The ground is wet and often frozen. It is cold outside and it has not stopped raining for days. What is this hurry to get ready for spring? Why are we being rushed all over again?

Let us imagine a man who goes out to the shops at this time of year. They are big shops, the very biggest, for this man lives in London and he has gone out to the department stores in the heart of the West End. Let us imagine that he wants to buy, oh let's say a warm winter coat, a new hot-water bottle and some spare bedding for a house guest. It is a cold and windy day. Surely this centre of consumerism will be able to provide his needs?

This is not a stupid man. Admittedly, some of the more recent technological inventions have passed him by — musical mobile phones, say, or online shopping (which seems just a modern form of shopping from a catalogue, once considered to be rather naff even without having to send your personal details into cyberspace). But he copes in the world fairly well. It's OK, really.

All right, I admit it, the man is me.

That winter coat? "Sorry sir, we do not have that style in your size. Will we be getting more in stock? Er no, we are clearing space for the spring fashions, like those over there. Who buys lightweight coats and shortsleeved shirts in January? You'd be surprised. People like to be first with the new range. Oh yes they do."

A hot-water bottle? "We had some but they all seem to have gone. Not a very fashionable item really, we only get a few and they go very quickly. Yes I can see that the fact they go very quickly might suggest that

33

they are still fashionable to some people. I'll make a note of it for next winter, sir. Yes I know it's still winter now sir. Have you thought of an electric blanket, we may have one left. Yes I know you cannot hug an electric blanket, or grip it between your feet, or whatever. How I keep warm in bed is none of your business. There is no need to take that attitude, is there?"

Bedding? It's a miracle, they've got bedding. Spring colours, whatever that means. (Who on earth changes the colour of their sheets with the seasons? You do? Wow.) Anyway, they have piles of bedding. This is bedding city. I have not bought any bedding for a while but I would not have imagined it had changed very much. Then I see the sign promising: non-iron pillow-cases. And I know that this is one of those moments that divides up the human race.

I know that one half of the human race is thinking: Great, at last, what a good idea, non-iron pillowcases, what took them so long? Let's throw out all our old pillowcases and buy a stack of these.

And the other half of the human race, the half that includes me, is thinking: You mean, we were supposed to *iron* our pillowcases? Surely all pillowcases are non-iron, as there is no point in ironing them. We are talking about the same thing, aren't we? Sort of large fabric bags that we put our pillows into and scrunch our heads against all night? What's the point of ironing them?

But OK, if that's what you're selling, I'll buy them.

Actually, there is probably another group, people such as my old mum, who truly enjoyed ironing, who would have been really disappointed about having one less thing to do. Give it here, she'd say, I'll give it a quick going-over. It's no trouble. You can't be too careful.

She also used to say that spring was like a miracle, proof that we should not imagine that we know everything about life. Imagine if you didn't know spring was coming, she'd say. In winter, you see the bare trees and muddy ground and if someone told you that in a few months the trees would be leafy and the very earth would be full of flowers and fresh grass, you would not believe them. And yet winter is just nature's clearout, ready for the spring season. And everything must go.

But it would just be nice if we did not try to get so far ahead of ourselves. It's still winter where you are, isn't it?

"I don't believe it," said Joan. "You've revealed something really personal."

"I'm sorry? Oh, you mean my late mum."

"No, you've used her before. I mean you've mentioned that you have a house guest."

She was looking at me with a smile. So were a couple of the girls nearby. This is a bit of an office joke.

My house guest is Justin. My spare room is occupied by Mr Groovy. We are the odd couple, old fogey and bright young thing, Mr Grumpy and Mr Happy, Eeyore and Tigger, ancient and modern, tortoise and hare.

"Yes, well." They were all looking expectantly. "I can't say too much about the hot-water bottle. It's just that when we go out on the pull, we like to know the beds will be warm."

"That I would like to see," Joan said. "If only. Anyway, I need to get the spring fashion previews organized. And ideas?"

Well, yes, we could tell people not to be so silly, that it really doesn't matter if yellow is the new blue, or that stripey is the new plain, and the stuff that they had last year will be fine. But that wouldn't keep our fashion writers in clover, would it? (Oddly, most of the girls in the office just wear black suits all year, whatever they advise the readers to do.) Anyway, I have my own fashion consultant now. He lives in my flat and looks quizzically at everything I possess. It's bloody weird, I must say.

How did it happen? It was a Friday, the week before last, and Justin was sitting at work with a suitcase under his desk. Stylish suitcase, of course, all black and strappy. The girls had not questioned him too closely about the bag, perhaps assuming he was going away on an overnight job, or for the weekend, which he didn't deny. Then at lunchtime, when everyone else was out, he appeared beside me.

"I don't suppose you know a cheap hotel where I could stay for a few days, do you?"

"A cheap hotel? In London?" I looked up at him and realized he was very unhappy. And embarrassed. Mr Happy, unhappy. It wasn't right.

"What's happened, Justin?"

"It's Sandra. She wants some time alone."

Silence, then a bit of a rush of words as he pulled up a seat. Sandra, his girlfriend, was upset about something, he didn't know what. She wanted Time to Think. She wanted Some Space. It was all too much. Early that morning, he had himself offered to move out for a while. And she had said quietly: That would be very kind.

"But it's your flat," I said.

Silence.

"I mean, you pay the rent. You found it. You partly furnished it."

Silence.

"Are you still paying the rent?"

"She hasn't got a job down here yet. And she doesn't really know anyone."

"She could go back up north."

"She says that if she did that, she might not come back. This way, there's chance."

"What about you?" He looked very sad. I realized I was only rubbing it in. "I mean, haven't you got anyone you could stay with?"

"No. There's not many people I know in London and they are in studio flats or shared houses."

"Well." Then I heard myself say it. "Well, if it comes to that, I've got a spare room you can have for a few days. You're welcome to that."

His face brightened a little. Mutual embarrassment. From a girlfriend to spare room with the office grump. Poor chap.

"Really?" he said. "Could I? That would be good."

All afternoon I could see him at his desk, struggling with second and third thoughts. Neither of us told anyone else. We didn't even speak to each other. At the end, after everyone else had gone, I nodded to him and we walked to the Tube. On the way, I described the advantages of the flat: lower Highgate, a short walk from the Heath, late-night supermarket, pubs, cafes, lots of local greenery, a top-floor flat in an old house, so no noisy neighbours upstairs. He tried to show an interest but couldn't get away from the fact that this was not where he wanted to be.

It's a big moment when someone half your age appears in your home one evening without time for preparation. I know colleagues who have dropped in on their student offspring unexpectedly and have been appalled at the living conditions. This was like that, with the generations reversed. I felt like I was being judged. It was just as well that Ben was not there that night. A long hugging session with a Labrador, watched by the bereft Justin, could only have made it worse.

Once in the door, taking in his new surroundings, Justin's face took on a bemused expression that has pretty much been there ever since. At least the flat was tidy. I am a tidy man. But seeing it through his eyes, I could appreciate that it seemed a little spartan. As he looked around, asking questions, he gradually took in the absence of certain things that he clearly regarded as normal. Broadband? No. Any Internet link? No. Email? No. Digital TV channels? No. DVD player? No. Phone messages? Er, I've got that free BT answering service.

"Well, that's something," he said.

Then he fell silent. In the kitchen, he was looking at something with a kind of awe. I realized it was my washing, hanging on the frame in front of the radiator. More specifically, he was looking at a row of Y-front underpants. I am not sure that he had even seen Y-fronts before.

"Right then," he said. "I'll get my stuff sorted out."

The spare room: an old single bed, an old wardrobe, a few boxes I keep meaning to put in the attic, some rudimentary spare bedding. I don't get many guests. OK, I hadn't had any guests since I moved in more than a year ago. I left him to it while I went to sort out a shelf for him in the bathroom. And another in the kitchen. Somehow I thought that even his food might be different to mine.

After a while he emerged in jeans and a T-shirt. I gave him a spare set of keys and a cup of coffee. I was still in my shirt and suit trousers. I don't really bother to get changed before bedtime.

"Come and go as you like. Treat it as home. I know this is difficult for you. Take some time to think."

"Can I pay you?"

"No. First, because you can't really afford two lots of rent. Second, I don't need the money. Third, because this way I can throw you out whenever I like."

Our looks connected that time. We were coming to terms.

"I don't think this will be long. I just don't know what's happening."

"Well, what's happening now is that I am going out to eat at the Italian place around the corner, then I'll have a drink at the pub. You could come with me, except that we would probably have to talk and I think you don't really need that at the moment. You can stay here, raid my fridge and my food cupboard and watch some rubbish Friday night TV. There are some videos on the shelf. Mostly old movies."

"I'll stay here, thanks."

The people at work had clearly not yet briefed him about my life. As I was putting my coat back on, he said conversationally, "Who's the woman? In the picture on the mantelpiece?"

"That's my wife. Annie. She's dead now." And I went out of the door.

When I got back two hours later, he was watching one of the reality TV shows that encourage fools sitting at home to pass judgement on other, more publicity-hungry fools on screen. We spoke briefly, then I went to bed to read and sleep.

He was gone when I got up. At first I had half forgotten that he had been there at all until I saw his toiletry bag in the bathroom. On the kitchen table there was a note on a page torn from a reporter's notebook. It said, "Gone shopping."

He returned in the mid-afternoon just as I was going out. He was carrying three large bags. One was full of food in various exotic and healthy styles. (I have never understood this. The brighter Young People seem to eat healthily, drink water by the gallon and even go to gyms, at a time when their bodies could probably withstand anything, while unfit middle-aged gits like me eat lots of stodge, live on coffee and never do more than walk.) Justin's other two bags were full of home comforts he could not do without even for a few days. These included some sort of attachment to link his iPod to my hi-fi, several thick magazines, a poster to hang on his wall and some new shirts. He was not going back to his flat until summoned, it seemed.

"I'm just going out," I said. "I've got to walk the dog for the woman downstairs while she's out."

"There's a dog?"

"Yes. He sleeps here some nights. Do you mind about dogs?"

"I like them. We had a dog at home when I was growing up. A spaniel. I still miss him." Pause. "Can I come too?"

Ben was waiting for us, ready to go, not really caring about a stranger joining us, three males setting out for a walk without any womenfolk. Circumstances had made Justin and me equals in that respect.

That first walk, we just took in the views of London from the Heath, watched Ben romp with an assortment of fellow canines, and filled in a bit of basic biography. Justin from the north, me from the south, me an only child with no parents left, him an only child with just his mum. Me starting work on a local paper at eighteen, him joining a provincial evening as a graduate trainee. That sort of thing.

Over the next few days, we worked out a pattern of giving each other as much space as possible. Justin left for work before me and came home later, usually after a trip to the cinema or an Internet café or a drink with one of his London friends. One night I was delayed by work and Justin came home to see to Ben. When I got back, they were both on the couch, Justin reading a book and Ben dozing. Ben wagged but didn't get up. I didn't mind. Maybe Ben was the first real sign that we could share things.

So it's been nearly two weeks and Justin is still here. He has been no trouble really and I suppose that, like Ben, he's a bit of company sometimes. But I remain wary.

We have been circling each other, observing each other like anthropologists from different cultures. He put up with my Radio 4, I put up with his music channels. I examined, without comment, the gels and smells he kept on his bathroom shelf. No doubt he did the same with my aftershave. He was impressed by the number of old LPs I possessed — apparently it's now fashionable to have stuff "on vinyl" — and I was impressed by his knowledge of seventies music, which was considerably greater than my knowledge of twenty-first-century stuff.

All this was possible because we knew this arrangement was strictly temporary. Lines of communication had been opened with Sandra — she rang his mobile phone about the third night after she threw him out. He went to his room to take the call. He also gave her my number in case his mobile had problems or was switched off while he was on a job. I discovered this one evening as I checked my messages, and a young, feminine northern accent said, "Hi. It's me. Just saying hello. Still job hunting, but I may have to give up and just temp. It's good that you've got somewhere OK to live, it gives me more time. Give me a call. You know the number here. Love you."

She wanted to be alone but she still wanted to talk. I had my theories about Sandra. They were:

a) Moving down from Manchester and living together had been too much and she really did want some space.

b) She was a sulky bitch who wanted to punish him for moving to London without her.

c) She had done something terrible, like having an affair, and Justin had stormed out and made up the whole thing about her wanting some space.

d) Justin had done something terrible, like having an affair, and she had thrown him out.

e) After living together for a few weeks, they had realized that the whole thing was an appalling mistake and neither of them wanted to admit it.

f) They were one of those couples who had break-ups and make-ups all the time, and I just didn't know it.

Now it's been nearly three weeks. Lately I have glimpsed a little more of the inside of Justin's head — and I'm not sure that was entirely a good idea. We didn't discuss Sandra, of course. Nor did I join in the office speculation about her. It was none of my business. I suppose Justin and I could have gone on not discussing anything very much, just tolerating one another, except that by chance we stumbled on a formula for talking safely as sort-of friends. The formula was $c = t + p$, where c is conversation, t is discussing utter trivia and p is just happily taking the piss out of each other.

It began like this: Justin was out one evening and there were a few of his men's monthly lifestyle magazines lying around the lounge, the sort with titles made out of initials or words that subtly suggested they contained everything a man might need to know. Annie once bought me one of these magazines as a joke. (An Annie memory. Stop now.) I had not bothered to read them before or since, because frankly I felt too old for them. The covers always featured half-naked actresses of whom I had never heard, and whose faces looked so young and unlined I felt like an old pervert even glancing at them.

Anyway, this time, I decided to have a good browse, purely for research purposes. I'm not sure what I was expecting, but what I found was nothing. I could not believe that anything several hundred pages thick could be so thin on content. It reminded me of a line in the film *The Big Chill*, where the magazine journalist played by Jeff Goldblum laments that he is no longer allowed to write anything that could not be read in the time it took the average reader to have a crap. Except that, in these magazines, almost any of the "articles" could have been read in the time it takes to have a wee.

They made our lifestyle pages look virtually intellectual. In between the endless adverts for clothes and smells and high-tech things modelled by glum-looking boys, hardly any of the writing seemed to come in chunks longer than a paragraph or two. Bits about new gadgets. Bizarre true stories. Endless lists — things to do, things not to do, things others have done, odd places to have sex. What women like in bed. How to argue. How not to look stupid. Nothing old, nothing really thoughtful. It was as if the whole world was born yesterday.

When there was a longish article, it was about something so out of sync with the rest, it was laughable. Serial killers and arsonists seemed to be very popular subjects. So did surviving in the wild, surviving torture and surviving dangerous women who advertise on the Internet. Oh yes, and surviving life as a porn star.

The women were often surprisingly demure and only half naked. In this post-feminist world, it seems all right for even semi-serious actresses and TV presenters to pose legs akimbo provided that they have some underwear on. I can only guess the effect on their later careers. (How about: They Died With Their Pants On?)

The only memorable thing was the trivia. Apparently, the average man produces enough sperm in a lifetime to fill a medium-sized saloon car. On the other hand, one fifth of men fake orgasms. One third of men admit to playing their in-car stereos loudly to impress people with their choice of music. (And I thought they were playing it so loud because they had deservedly gone deaf. What's the point of impressing someone whom you are passing at 60 mph?) For science buffs, there was the snippet that all the main characters in *Thunderbirds* were named after the *Apollo* astronauts, the guys who featured in *The Right Stuff* (Gus

Grissom's real first name being Virgil). That's a real guy fact.

Among it all there were New Year resolutions on how to change your life for the better. This came in the form of more lists, of course. Take an adventure holiday. Make an impression at work. Do something you have never done before.

And, my favourite, my very favourite, at number two in one of the lists: "Buy new underwear. Treat yourself and find out how looking smart underneath changes the way you feel about the day."

"Buy new underpants," I said to Justin. "That's a tip for life?"

"Well, why not?" he said. "Or, in your case, Y-front not?"

He was back from having a drink with a mate, bringing a good mood with him. He was amused that I had been reading his stuff.

"As a life-changing tip, it leaves something to be desired. What about, read a good book? Or take an interest in something more than five seconds old?"

"I think you'll find that sort of thing is in the list somewhere, usually down around number fifty. The easy fixes come first."

"Anyway, what's the matter with Y-fronts? They do the job. These days, I would have thought they would be known as design classics."

"They are the underpant equivalent of an old cardigan. They are what mothers buy for young boys."

"So what do you wear, Mr Cool? Novelty briefs? A thong, perhaps? Or do you go commando?"

"Nah, just boxers. Why don't you try a change? Isn't that what the magazine is talking about, really? One small step?"

"By the look of some of the underwear in the adverts, small steps is about all that the models could manage. It's just underwear. It doesn't matter."

"I think that the idea of the magazines is, um, that everything matters. Or might matter."

"In case you get trapped with a serial killer, you mean?"

"Exactly," Justin grinned. "Now, let's have a drink."

We opened a couple of cans. I was slumped in the armchair, Justin sprawled on the sofa, like a teenager. We talked a bit longer, and again the next evening. He said he knew that the magazines were junk, that's why he liked them. Intelligent young men supposedly regard them ironically. And they gave him ideas for work.

Anyway, we began to spoof the magazines, and especially the trivia and the formulaic interviews with halfwits, imagining how we would answer the questions. This became somewhat revealing. If the result was ever written down (which is just what I am doing, of course) it would go something like this.

Interviewer: So, gentlemen, how are your romantic lives?

JS: No comment.

GW: No comment.

Interviewer: Oh come on.

JS and GW: Piss off.

Interviewer: OK, what do you most dislike about each other?

JS: His Y-fronts.

GW: His youth.

Interviewer: And what do you most envy?

GW: His youth. Well, his unused years.

JS: Er, a little of his grey hair. Maybe one or two of his wrinkles.

GW: You're kidding?

JS: No, really. It looks like you've had experience of life. I still look like the worst thing that I've ever faced was college exams.

GW: You realize that? Blimey.

JS: But it's a small price to pay for my youth.

Interviewer: How do you feel about living in London?

GW: It's a filthy, overcrowded, overpriced mess, even though I live in one of the nice bits. If they wanted to build London today, they would never get planning permission. Fancy having the capitals of politics, finance and the media all in one place. It's nonsense and it's always in chaos. The roads are full, the trains are full and the Olympics are going to make things even worse.

JS: I love it. It's a lot of villages, really. The people are a bit odd — most of them look worried all the time and they never seem to go anywhere much. You've got all these galleries and museums and theatres, yet anyone who has lived here more than a few years never seems to go to them. I love the Tube, it's like a kind of time machine. You blast through solid rock and come up in places entirely different to where you just left.

GW: The Tube. I hardly notice it. I've been travelling on it for so long, I automatically sit in the correct carriage to be right by the platform exit when I get off.

JS: And for trivia fans, did you know that most of the Underground is actually overground?

GW: Yes I did. And did you know that the Tube map, which is supposedly such a design classic, manages to have Paddington on it twice?

JS: No I didn't. (Pauses to check map in diary.) So it does.

Interviewer: OK, the big question. What are your favourite mainstream movies?

GW: What does that matter?

Interviewer: Oh go on.

GW: All right. I seem to like small-town movies mostly. *Field of Dreams. Groundhog Day. Doc Hollywood. Bad Day at Black Rock.* That sort of thing.

JS: Frankly I prefer big-city movies. *Fight Club. LA Confidential. Pulp Fiction.* And *The Matrix.*

GW: Really, is this supposed to mean something?

Interviewer: I don't know, it's just one of our usual questions. There must be movies you both like?

JS and GW: Well, naturally, we're both blokes. So, *Shawshank Redemption. The Usual Suspects. Casablanca.* And *Blade Runner.* (*JS:* The director's cut. *GW:* The original.)

Interviewer: Finally, what piece of advice would you give each other?

GW: Stop being so interested in things just because they are the latest thing. People say they go to the latest big movie so they know what's popular. But if nobody went to it, it wouldn't be popular and it wouldn't matter. Same with music. Everybody wants to know what's going on, and that's what drives the market, but it's all an illusion. Does that make sense?

JS: No. My advice — change something. Change everything. At least change your underwear.

For dinner a few nights later, Justin provided a rather wonderful home-made soup in preference to my usual tins, and I provided one of my easy pastas. Ben explored the leftovers while Justin and I finished a bottle of wine.

It seems to me that there is a stage where two men might really begin to talk to each other. This involves each man being reassured that the other is not a bore, a drunk, a con artist or a threat, that there is a mind and a sense of humour operating behind the eyes, that enough time has gone by without either man proving to be untrustworthy and that it is now more embarrassing not to talk than to talk.

The flat felt comfy. The presence of a second human being seemed to have rendered it less spartan, more lived-in. The spare room looked like it had been included in life instead of abandoned. Justin had even found a hot-water bottle at the local hardware store. (I never did find a new winter coat.)

Lately, I had discovered that Justin's university degree was not in that time-waster subject, media studies (a degree in watching videos, wow), which I had assumed he took, but in journalism with psychology. This showed an extra depth, I thought. Not least, it meant that, whenever he felt like it, he could have used the psychology qualification to try to outclass all my babbling on human behaviour. And the psychology explained how Justin had proved to have a useful talent for writing instant psycho-drivel articles about the significance of any new fashion or trend. He was also fairly good at bringing out a telling quote from interviews, or at least making a quote seem important, which is much the same thing these days.

Short of anything else to say, I asked if he had done any specialist area of psychology for his degree. This turned into the first real, interesting conversation I'd had in ages so I tried to remember it to write it down.

"We had to do a couple of specialist papers each," he said. Pause. "I did one on happiness."

"Happy," I said. "Ah yes, I remember that."

He recognized the line: "John Cleese, *Fawlty Towers*."

"So what did you conclude?"

"It's an interesting subject. There's a lot of research on why people are miserable, but until recently there was not a lot on why some people are just better at being happy."

"That makes sense." I thought about my estranged grief counsellor. "There's more of an industry in unhappiness. People seem to want an explanation for all their grumbles."

"As opposed to just enjoying having a good grumble, like in some of the stuff you read?" (This might have been a reference to the *Oldie* magazine. Or the *Spectator*. Or the *Sunday Telegraph*. All right, it could have been lots of stuff I read. I didn't know he had been reading my stuff too.)

I mimicked an old codger's voice. "It was old-fashioned grumbling that got this country through the hard times, young man, don't you forget it."

He laughed. "That's very British."

"OK," I said. "There might be an article in this somewhere. What, if anything, is the secret of happiness, o wise one?"

"Well, o seeker of truth, there have been general studies of people to identify the ones who seem to be happy, and then trying to see what they might have in common. It's become a popular subject. There are some obvious things. Family and social networks. A pet." He looked at Ben, who had dozed off in front of the gas fire. "A modest amount of material comfort. Some sort of belief in things bigger than themselves, usually religion.

"And some people seem to be able to programme themselves into happiness, and not just with little things like watching a TV comedy or displaying photographs of happy memories. They don't dwell on bad bits in the past, but on possible good bits in the future. They count their blessings. They are not always comparing themselves with people who have more than them. They spread out their pleasures and savour them. It's called delayed gratification. And they find their pleasures in the attainable rather than the unattainable."

"Don't you think we sell the unattainable at work?" I asked.

"I know you think we do," he said. "That might be true if people read nothing but the lifestyle pages."

"What a nightmare thought."

"I think it's just entertainment. People aren't stupid. A bit of trivia brightens the day. I like trivia."

This was broken by Ben letting rip an enormous fart, by which he woke himself up. He raised his head with a start, looked around, saw us, wagged, then went back to sleep again. We smiled at him.

"Now *that* is happiness," I said, and poured out another drink. "The thing is, not many of your big happiness factors can really help people who are not happy. You can't suddenly acquire a family, and looking for a religious outlet solely as an escape is what leads people into the loonier fringes. You may not be able to change what you think about the past, or the future."

Justin said, "This is when psychology drifts into philosophy, I guess. It's about attitude. It's Schopenhauer."

"Oh blimey."

"He was a very depressed philosopher. He said that humans can never be happy because of self-will, because whenever they have got what they want, they always want something more."

"Well, that seems right these days," I agreed. "And that's what makes all the lifestyle stuff even worse. There's no end to it."

"But he felt there was a bit of an escape," Justin said. "We had to conquer the self-will. And the best way to start to do that, as far as I can recall, was, um, to contemplate the real world and the suffering of others."

I thought for a moment. "So what he actually said was if you are feeling down, you should take yourself out of yourself, maybe go for a walk in the countryside, and not forget that there are others worse off than yourself. That's what my old mum would have said."

He smiled. "And mine too."

"Anyway, you can't stop the self-will," I said. "It seems to be the only motivation for most people."

He stared at me. "But that's not you."

"Sorry?"

"Well, forgive me for saying this but you seem to defy this whole branch of philosophy. You don't seem to have much real self-will at all. Sorry, I mean you have very few wants, you're not ambitious in any way that I can see, you are not greedy and you are being incredibly helpful to me."

"So?"

"Well," he said. "On these terms, just on getting by from day to day, you should be at least reasonably content. Are you?"

CHAPTER
FOUR

A MAN TALKS PANTS

Anti-Style
by George Worth
20 February

I have a secret. I have made a change in my life. You can stare at me as long as you like and you would never be able to guess. Yet, for a bloke, this is a very serious change.

This is a subject that British men don't talk about very often. Yet when they do, it is an area of very strong opinions. In the locker rooms of Britain, perhaps after great sporting events, these opinions become apparent. In olden times, when women were sent out of the room after dinner so that the men could talk alone, maybe this was one of the areas for discussion.

We are talking underpants.

When you're a bloke, you don't have much choice in the fashion department, compared with women and their clothes. Consider just the outer layers. Women have skirts and dresses with various lengths of hemline, plus trousers and long tops and short tops and very very short tops. So much choice. Maybe that's how women learn to be able to think about several things at once and make everything happen.

Blokes have trousers and shirts. OK, there are also jeans, but they are just trouser-shaped really, and there are also T-shirts and pullovers, which are just shirt-shaped. The options are basically the same. That's why choice confuses us, but that's also why we get dressed quicker. Simple.

In underwear, it's even simpler for us. Women have bras and knickers and thongs and tights and stockings and garters and basques and, oh, all sorts of endless delights. Men have only one main area for underwear, and the choice is boxers or Y-fronts or some sort of briefs. And even then, I like to think that real men — well, real British men — don't wear briefs. Briefs are more for those Continental types who like to wear next to nothing on the beach or under their trousers, even at the price of stopping their blood from circulating in crucial areas.

So that leaves Y-fronts or boxers. And I have always been a Y-front man. But I have crossed the line. Count one less vote for the Y-front brigade and one up for the boxers. Designer boxers too. Oh yes. The world has shifted into a new shape, and it's rather snug.

There comes a time in the life of, shall we say, the more mature man when he realizes that he might have a little catching up to do. Nothing too serious, of course. Not like changing his haircut or his newspaper. And nothing too visible that might get mocked. Gentlemen, this is it. The designer boxer has been road-tested now for several years by Young People — they have a passion for the new so they can try out all the stupider things that we haven't got time for, then we can see who or what survives.

The designer boxer is now past the stage of strong young men being so proud of the brand names that they walked around with the rim of their underpants showing above their belts. The designer boxer, cotton with a dash of Lycra for, um, support, is now available in every department store. I'm still experimenting, but they are as reassuringly strong as the Y-front yet roomier and lighter and free. And remarkably comfortable. Once tried, you may never go back.

In the changeover period, you have to be careful that this does not affect the way you walk — a little more strutty — so don't go for too much Lycra. This feels like a total stranger has grabbed hold of your buttocks from behind and is propelling you forward. That may be one reason why athletes prefer Lycra for their Olympic outfits.

I have only one fear, which is that one change may lead to another. This is a fear in the heart of the mature British male that applies all the way from clothing to do-it-yourself. In your home life, you just know that if you give a fresh coat of paint to that scratched skirting board it will make all the other skirting boards seem dull by comparison, so that you have to paint them too, which makes the walls look faded, and before you know it you are having to decorate the whole room, and then the room next to it, and eventually the whole damn house.

Will my boxers be like this? Am I doomed to start looking at snazzy socks? Then something less conservative in the trouser department? And onwards and upwards, so that none of my old clothes work together any more but I keep them at the back of the wardrobe just out of nostalgia and faithfulness to something that once served me well.

I shall resist it. And if you see me browsing near something loud and strong in the shirt section, just lead me gently away.

"Is your boyfriend around?" This was Basset talking, on an unexpected visit to our section.

"I'm sorry?"

"The boy Justin? You're living together, aren't you? Do you know where he is?"

Some of the girls nearby were glaring at Basset. Maybe they have learned not to like A Man Who Fancies Himself, of which he is a prime example.

"I really don't know, dearie," I replied. "And anyway, he is taken."

This was spoken as banter. In my gender, apparently, friendships across the generations are subject to suspicion. Women have it better. Maybe that's one reason why they have more friends.

So far as I knew, Justin was outside somewhere having one of his long mobile conversations with Sandra, maybe trying to find out if she's having second thoughts about him or London. Outside offices like ours, the city pavements are blocked by two kinds of loiterers: smokers, who have nowhere else to go, and people having mobile-phone conversations that are too personal to share with their colleagues but are presumably all right to share with the complete strangers walking and smoking around them. Joke: Why do the users of mobile phones walk up and down when they talk? Because they can annoy more people that way. (I have this idea of how to help the poor, demented care-in-the-community souls who wander the streets of London, scaring everybody by talking to themselves. Just give them each a fake mobile phone to talk into, and they will look normal.)

Basset had wandered down the office, stopping to talk at the desk of a new temporary assistant — Pauline, Doreen, some name like that — then wandered back to talk at me again.

"You know, your columns are getting a little too weird lately."

"Really? The feedback from my postbag is quite positive." (Well, so Joan tells me. She reads my office mail. She says that it helps her to keep in touch with the thoughts of our readers, but I suspect she's afraid that I might be tempted to write back in strong terms to any crackpots or critics.) "A lot of people seem to think I am refreshingly normal," I lied.

"Well, I for one find that quite terrifying. Perhaps we're attracting the wrong sort of reader. We've got another reader focus group coming up later this year. I must remember to ask about you."

Then he left. A couple of the girls gave me the kind of smile that they might reserve for an old dog who does not have much time left. Basset's visit had created a bit of an atmosphere that I did not understand. But I knew that he would forget our conversation by the end of a long lunch. Men such as him like to keep an old dog to kick now and again.

Have I no pride? No, not when I'm working on this stuff. On my computer screen was a page about the spring fashions in shoes. The headline said: "Put a spring in your step." Could I let this go in the paper? You bet.

Joan had been out of the office trying to get the picture desk to find some images that seemed to have been filed under something totally bizarre in the new computerized digital picture system. In the years BC (Before Computers), when newspapers stored photographs in filing cabinets, they were physical things and you could find them yourself with a little effort. Now all the images are in a computer database and like all new systems it's only as good as the weakest link, usually an eighteen-year-old trainee who encrypted them with no sense of the English language or logic. We once traced a picture of Tom Cruise filed among holiday liners.

When Joan returned, she heard of Basset's visit and went into a bit of a huddle with the lovely Arabella by the coffee machine. I wandered over and they quietly explained the situation. It seems that the search for Justin was a cover story. Basset was having an affair with the new temp, Pauline, that's her name. She's just his sort. Thirtysomething, rather older than the other girls, maybe unaware of his reputation, maybe just vulnerable and flattered. She had been promised a six-month contract soon, with Basset's blessing. By the time Joan had found out about the romance, it was too late to warn her. Usually Basset picked his extra-marital fancies outside the paper, though sometimes he would bring them to office parties. His latest choice meant that all our office gossip might get back to him. Time to be careful.

Back at her desk, Joan had a message to call one of her friends — she has friends everywhere — who works as a producer of one of those radio talk-about-nothing-much talk shows and was wondering whether that columnist, er, George Something, George Worth, could be a guest on the panel this evening?

Sorry it was such short notice, the message said, but they were rather tickled by that morning's item about underpants.

"You're kidding," said Justin. "I know you just thought that trying the boxers would make a funny article, but have I helped to make you a star?"

"Er, no, this sort of radio thing happens about once a year. It means that a planned guest has dropped out at the last moment. They get a newspaper columnist as an easy fill-in. It's one of those shows with four or five guests who all try to talk at once. I'll say about two sentences but the paper will get a plug."

"You want any tips on what to wear?" Justin's attempts to ridicule and restructure my lifestyle from the inside out had become a joke between us. Just between us.

"Justin, this is radio, for heaven's sake."

"You're going straight there after work, right? So you won't be able to change. So just take off your tie."

"Justin, it's radio."

"But this is about how the other guests relate to you. A suit without a tie, that says mature but casual."

"OK, I won't wear a tie. In exchange can you . . ."

". . . get home first and look after Ben. Yes, of course. You want me to tape the programme for you?"

"No. Yes. Maybe. I'll hear it as it happens anyway."

"All right. I'll do dinner. And George, try not to sound too . . ."

"Grumpy?"

"No, grumpy is fine. Hey, people make a career out of sounding grumpy on the radio."

"Well, what then?"

"Try not to sound too much like a guy who normally wears a tie but has just taken it off."

Six of us around a small round table: myself plus a young actress, an author, a painter, a celebrity chef — each with some new show or book to promote. (I can't be bothered with their names. In my early days, there were only about fifty celebrities in the world. Now there are hundreds of them to help fill all the magazines and television channels. I can't remember them all.) Finally there was the hostess, yet another woman who knows Joan from wherever Joan seems to know everyone. Fortyish, nice warm face to bring out the guests and put them at their ease during the pre-show natter, nice warm radio voice to keep the listeners listening. She seemed especially smiley towards me.

I suppose the idea of these shows is that they are like an interesting dinner party, the sort of dinner party that seldom actually happens, so that people sitting in their kitchens or cars can listen and feel involved without having to invite anyone home or watch them eat or do extra washing-up. There are never any real, ordinary people on these shows. That would be too messy.

We were gathered in a battered studio in a labyrinthine old building and the theme for discussion was The Importance of the New. This had the illusion of being relevant while still being vague enough to pull everyone together. As I suspected, another guest — a pop psychologist, no less — had dropped out, pleading pressure of work and clashing dates. I think I was there as a token menopausal man. I guessed this because the hostess introduced me as: "George Worth, whose Anti-Style newspaper column has made him something of a spokesman for the menopausal man."

"Good grief, has it?" I said. "You mean everyone doesn't think like me?"

Laughter round the table. I can do bumbling innocence quite well.

"Actually," said the young actress, "I know my dad reads you every week and always agrees with you. Except maybe not about the underpants."

The underpants turn out to be a real ice-breaker, a safe talking point, seeming slightly risqué and intimate and yet very safe. The painter has a lucky pair, the chef wears none at all as it's so hot in his kitchen — I'm never eating in his restaurant — and the actress says how awful men look when they take off their trousers before removing their socks, because socks with underpants really aren't sexy, like a character in a scene in her new play which, by the way, starts previews next week.

"But how important is it," asked the hostess, "for the over-forties to keep up with new fashions? George?"

"Well, simply, the answer is that there are no new fashions. One of the pleasures of being, er, a little older, is that you see all the same stuff coming round over and over again and you realize that it's not important. I've seen Young People wearing stripy T-shirts or beige shorts which my parents had to force on me when I was a kid. The hard thing must be to have a job like an artist." I look at the artist, desperately trying to pass the conversation to him. "Artists are always trying to come up with some new vision, which must be really hard."

The artist was too slow.

"But you can't say that nothing is new?" the hostess asked.

"Oh yes you can," I said. "Look at the past hundred years. We think we are all tremendously modern, but there's hardly anything today that would seem totally unknown or inconceivable to an educated person living a hundred years ago."

Much spluttering around the table. How did I get myself into this? That was just the sort of off-the-edge statement that a blundering middle-aged man would make at a dinner party and then spend the rest of the night trying to justify. Sure enough, for the rest of the programme, the other guests would interrupt their own self-promotion to hit me with possible exceptions.

"What about films and photography?" said the actress. You could see where her ambitions lay.

"No," said the painter. "They were both nineteenth-century inventions. But how about the car and air travel?

"Karl Benz 1885. Wright brothers 1903. Both more than a hundred years old." I knew that much anyway.

"Votes for women," said the actress, triumphantly.

"First introduced in New Zealand in 1893."

"This is interesting," said the author. "It puts the modern in its place. But you can't overlook computers. Or email."

"Well, the first mechanical calculating machine with cogs and things goes back to the seventeenth century, although I suppose we have developed them some-what," I said, getting a little desperate. "As for emails, the ability to send words instantly across the globe goes back to the telegraph, which was something that really changed the world in the nineteenth century. Then telephones arrived in the 1870s. And before anyone mentions the Internet, that's just a glorified book. Although with a very large index, I admit. It's just something you sort through and read, although some of the pages are written by idiots."

Cries of, "Oh come on."

"Look, the Victorian age gave us the railway network, gas and electricity, radio and the cathode-ray tube, along with public sanitation, anaesthetics, mass education, mass-produced books, popular newspapers, department stores, proper holidays and democracy." I counted each example on my fingers. Really good for radio. "That was progress. All we've done is try to improve what they did and make it more widely available. In the case of the railways and the sewerage systems, we've hardly managed to maintain what they created."

"So you think there is nothing new?" asked the hostess. "No new ideas, no new vision?"

"Well, OK, we've got the atom bomb and the microchip. We're faster at communication and war. We're faster at destroying things like the countryside and nice buildings. We're faster at change, but really it's the same things that keep changing."

"Anything positive?"

"Well." Thinking frantically now. "There's medical stuff like organ transplants, and maybe DNA research. I could say they are also just things being swapped around. But, look, nobody has mentioned space travel."

"Ah!"

"It had been imagined before, but the real thing gave my generation a vision that no one else had ever had. A vision of the world from space. How the world actually looks. No one else had seen that before. It took us all the centuries just to see how we really look. I find that quite moving, although of course the Earth is rather old and not anything new."

The artist picked up at last and, soon after that, it was all over and my heartbeat went down by about half. Afterwards, over post-programme drinks, the hostess and the producer buttonholed me in a corner and told me I was excellent. Privately I swore that I would never do this again. All the way home, I wondered just how bad I had sounded.

"That was amazing," said Justin. He was especially impressed because he had actually heard of all the other panellists. He played me the tape. I really had dominated the whole thing.

"It was worse than I expected," I said. "Your fault for my not wearing a tie. I sounded like an opinionated fart."

"No, you sounded like you knew what you were talking about. How did you know all that stuff?"

"It's just modern history. You know my bookshelves."

Or maybe he didn't know them. I had noticed that in weeks of browsing his way through my music and my videos and a few of my books, Justin had not drifted into the history section, nor the old thrillers or the few classics. Musically we had compromised our occasional background-pop listening to greatest-hits stations and the likes of Springsteen and Sheryl Crow. Also, I had somehow introduced him to Beethoven, which was playing as I came home. (By happy coincidence Ben also likes Beethoven, some of the lighter classics and Enya. He is a dog of taste.)

This was our interplay so far, after five weeks. We had moved on from swapping magazines and got to books and music. I had switched my underpants, he had borrowed some of my ties. I cooked Italian, he did Thai. He showed me what excited him about newspapers, I told him what I thought was crap, and pointed out how any half-decent idea in one paper was nicked by all the others within a fortnight.

We didn't talk about our own personal lives but we talked about Basset's affair. Some basic things about people still puzzle Justin. Generally he's very adept at fitting in. He manages to mix with both the rival groups of drinkers in the pub. His accent is already drifting from being vaguely northern to vaguely London Estuary. (He has taken to calling me "Guv" occasionally.) Much of the time he seems to be a young man of the world, but then he'll ask a question that shows a certain naivety. Like, why do people such as Basset do this stuff? Justin couldn't really understand why people got married and then still had affairs.

I said that men divided into three groups of about equal numbers. The first were the sort who would always be faithful. People such as us. The second would never cheat in normal circumstances, but if the chance came up and they thought that they could get away with it, they would be tempted. And the third just bonked everything they could, any time.

"And Basset is group three?"

"With knobs on, if you'll pardon the expression. His wife must know and just put up with it. Trouble is, the rest of us end up as part of the conspiracy whether we like it or not."

"But what's his attraction?" He was genuinely puzzled.

"I don't know. To a certain kind of woman, he must mean excitement. You can't always tell what attracts women. It's a mystery, isn't it Ben?"

Ben wagged by the fire. He had got used to our talking, and the silences as we got on with our own stuff.

Justin said, "There's this theory in psychology that men's brains are really wired differently because of our prehistoric past as hunters and loners. So we want to scatter our seed wherever we can. It's also supposed to account for the way that men are more inclined not to show weakness or talk about their problems."

I said, "Really?"

Pause.

"Er, any news on Sandra?" I knew that Justin had received a Valentine's Day card, which seemed a little strange, given the circumstances.

"Not really. She's still temping, and she always sounds tired. There's some news about my mother, though."

"Your mother?"

"Yes. I've been trying to put her off, but she's coming down for a visit sometime soon."

"Ah."

"She thinks she's staying with me and Sandra. I haven't actually told her that we're not together at the moment. I've told her always to call me at work or on my mobile, so she doesn't know I am not in my flat. I'm running out of excuses why Sandra is never around."

"I see."

"So what am I going to do?"

Really, I did not yet have the heart to tell him that the travel department had finally come up with an offer of a fly-drive deal to Boston for him in the spring. A romantic trip for two.

I didn't know what he should do. I hardly know what I am doing about my own life, though he had been taking my mind off that for a while. I suppose events were getting near the point when someone should issue some kind of ultimatum, but that might go terribly wrong and I didn't want responsibility for it. I've realized that so long as I let him stay here, so long as he remains in this limbo and doesn't give up or move on, then at least for him there is still some sort of hope of getting back to the life he wants.

When I first started coming to the Heath, the bit near the foot of Highgate West Hill, there was only one local cafe with a pavement table where you could have a coffee sitting outside. Now they are everywhere and the tables are seldom empty. Terribly cosmopolitan, I suppose. Instead of having a lonely cuppa in your own kitchen, feeling that life is passing you by, you can go outside, walk round the corner and pay nearly £2 to sit and actually watch life passing by.

The life passing by is usually just other people like yourself, looking for a spare table to sit at so they can watch other people also looking for a table.

I quite enjoy it, really. It gets me out of the house without having to go too far. I watch the dogs bringing their owners back from walks on the Heath, and I consider how strange it is that in this neighbourhood of the mainly well-paid and powerful, the dogs are usually the floppy, daft sort of breeds, as if compensating for any ruthless behaviour by their owners at work. It's in

70

the neighbourhoods of the poor and powerless that you usually find the terriers and large bitey dogs.

At lunchtime on a Ben-free Saturday, a weak sun had struggled halfway up the sky, and a very casual-looking Justin was drinking a latte with me before going off to spend most of the weekend with friends, as usual. I was wondering how young men manage to look faintly groovy when they are unshaven at weekends, while unshaven middle-aged men such as myself just look like tramps. I had the time to think about this because Justin's mobile had just rung for the second time since we sat down, and he was talking into space again. At last the call ended.

"Justin, you know that I operate a strict policy of three calls and you're out."

"Guv, why does this annoy you so much?"

"Look, we were talking. It's like someone who is a total stranger to me has come up, made a strange beeping noise to interrupt us and make me lose my train of thought, and you give them your total attention and ignore me."

"But it's not just phones, is it? It's stuff in general. You just don't get it."

He was smiling. This is why I remember this conversation. Six weeks into his stay, Justin probably had every right to think of me as some prematurely boring fossil from a lost age, but he still seemed to regard me with a tolerant, amused curiosity rather than actual derision. We find amusement in each other's differences. He is a rare thing for me: a new friend.

I remembered his amazement at the lack of modern technology when he first saw my flat. I suppose he thought a man my age might have everything. I've noticed that when two young men are chatting at length in the office, they are often going into raptures about "stuff". Computer thingies, mostly. Hand-held, portable gizmos. New attachments and websites (like in my day we talked about cars). But Justin and I tackle stuff from opposite directions.

"I don't get it? Well, OK, I don't buy stuff that I don't really need. I suppose that's my upbringing. In those days, we didn't go to the shops for a day out, we went to the countryside or visited relatives. My parents grew up during the war and rationing. If my dad suggested buying some new thing, my mum would always say 'Do we really need it?' That's just old working-class caution, buying the big stuff only when you feel that you might deserve it.

"And I don't like being hustled. I remember being fairly happy with, what do you call it, vinyl, when we were all pushed into buying tapes, and then CDs, so we had three different sets of stuff and our hi-fi systems looked like mission control. The same thing with TV. First came the video recorder, which I liked, but now there's the digital stuff and the DVD player. I like to hold back. I'm not stopping anyone else."

Justin said, "You'd like to stop the mobile phones, though, wouldn't you?"

"I know they are sometimes useful in emergencies," I offered. "I'd just like to stop the ringtones that don't let me sit in peace with my own thoughts. I'd like to silence the people who blare out one-sided conversations that I can't stand but can't ignore, in the street, in shops, even in the bloody gents' toilets sometimes. And I'd like to liberate your generation from feeling always on call. You've grown up in a world of constant change so you are forever worried that you are going to miss something unless people can always phone you, text you or email you. It's more communication, less content."

"So," he said, "mobile phones are the work of the Devil, the destruction of free thought and human patience?"

"No, that was TV remote controls."

His jaw dropped. Actually I was quite surprised myself. If you settle into conversation with someone, you can find yourself saying things that you didn't know that you thought until you've said them.

"TV remote controls? The humble zapper? This is amazing, what's the matter with them?"

"Well, once upon a time, if you wanted to change channels you had to get off your bottom and go up to the set to turn a dial. Simple human inertia meant that you learnt the patience to sit and watch one programme and give it the chance to develop."

"And now that we can hop between channels at the push of a button . . ."

"I read somewhere that the programme makers reckon they have ninety seconds to grab and keep your attention. That's every ninety seconds all through the programmes. No wonder they are all so endlessly loud and lurid and stupid and full of people arguing and even the best new stuff is so quickfire and slick that real life is bound to seem dull by comparison."

Damn, that sounded old. I'm never saying that again.

"I remember something from university," said Justin. "There was a psychological study about the mood of TV viewers over an evening. It averaged out as mild depression."

A second coffee was ordered. Justin looked thoughtful. "Do you think it's possible you'd like modern stuff a little bit more if you didn't love history so much?"

"You make me sound like the last of the Mohicans. Some aboriginal tribesman lost in a new world." (Which is just how I feel sometimes. And yes, OK, I play this up a bit.)

"And . . ."

"There's a quote from some classic writer," (Cicero, I think, but I'm not saying that) "to the effect that to be ignorant of what happened before you were born is to remain always a child, because you don't know where anything comes from or why anything in your culture is worth saving. It's about a sense of identity that you don't buy at the shops and change every month. It's a story that we are all living in. It's a reminder that something is not automatically better just because it's new. It helps me to put modern life in perspective."

Justin thought this over and said simply, "George, I really don't know anyone else who talks like you."

"And, all right, I like the feel of history, I feel comfy there."

"Aha."

74

"When I was a kid at home, on my own, I liked to read the adventures in history books."

"I suppose I played computer games instead, and listened to lots of music."

"Justin, can I ask you a question? About all your communication stuff?"

"Go on."

"You're going to a party tonight. If you, er, meet someone there, how do you arrange to make contact again? In my day, you just gave a phone number. Do you swap mobile numbers, office numbers, home numbers, emails, the whole lot? Isn't it overwhelming?"

"Nah, people usually just start with mobile numbers. Or just the emails. And it's not overwhelming to me, George, it's just normal. All this stuff you hate, I suppose it makes me feel independent. I can go anywhere and keep in touch and find out anything."

Pause.

"And one other thing, George. We never talk about it, and I sort of appreciate that, but for the record: I may be going to a party tonight but I am not planning to meet anyone in that way. I am still waiting for Sandra."

And it occurred to me that we were probably unique for two heterosexual men sitting at an outdoor cafe watching life go by. There was a reasonably steady and varied procession of London women along the pavement, but neither of us had given them a second glance. Justin was stuck on his future, and I was stuck in my past.

★ ★ ★

Early evening, Friday, six days later. All change. We were in the kitchen and Justin's mobile phone rang. It was Sandra. He went into his room to take the call, then came back wearing a puzzled smile. She wanted him back. Tonight.

I didn't know what had happened, I am not sure that Justin did, but she was making dinner, and she was sorry for all that she had put him through, and she would explain Everything. And then they would work out a plan, but really it wasn't fair that he was not living in his own flat.

Well, yes, I thought. That was true seven weeks ago. Has it really been that long?

"So this is it then?"

"Yes," he said. And then he was putting some things, all his things, into a bag.

"Well," I said. "I suppose I'll miss you."

"Nah, you'll get your privacy back. But I've enjoyed this. I didn't think I would, but I have. In the circumstances."

Silence.

"Can I still come round and walk Ben with you?"

Ben heard the word "walk" and barked.

"You can come with us now if you like. As your final domestic duty."

He looked at his watch and said, "Oh, what the hell. She made me wait all this time."

So we walked out to the Heath and up Parliament Hill in the half-light, looking out on London and breathing in the first possible hints of spring. Ben was sniffing all the bushes, Justin was Mr Happy again and I didn't know what to talk about.

From the top of the hill, you can see the whole of central London lit up, and hear a hum like the throbbing of millions of lives. I sat on a bench and looked at the city where I have lived and worked probably for too long. Justin looked at the city he wanted to make his life.

"Will you tell me what it was all about, when you know?"

"With Sandra? Yeah, maybe. You interested?"

"Of course. Well, maybe. If it's not too complicated."

Silence.

"Try to get it sorted, Justin. And then, well, look after each other."

He turned to look at me just as I realized that I might be about to cry. Damn.

"I didn't look after my wife," I said. "I killed her. It was all my fault."

And I was thinking, I wish you weren't going quite so suddenly, mate. You've got me through what could have been a bloody awful winter. And, OK, we've talked a bit but in some ways, on some subjects, we have not really talked at all.

And my shoulders were heaving. I do not make much noise when I cry, just occasional gulps for air, but my shoulders shake. I was crying now. Not in private, but in public. Not just with a dog, but with a human. With a Young Person, a bloke, someone from work. Damn, damn, damn.

And Ben was sitting at my feet with his paw on my knee, and then resting his head on my thigh. And then there was the silence again, and then the beep sound that Justin's mobile gives out when he's starting a call, and I heard him say, "Hello, it's me. Look, I'm going to be late. Something's come up. Yes, I'm sorry too. I'll call you back later."

CHAPTER
FIVE

THE RULES OF SHOPPING

Anti-Style
by George Worth
20 March

In some ways, shopping is like life. We keep forgetting the rules, so we keep making the same mistakes. We set out bright with hope, but it's only when disappointment strikes that we remember: Oh yes, that's what happened last time, how could I be so dumb?

So here they are, 25 rules of shopping, compiled at last into an easy guide to cut out and treasure always. Or at least, to stuff into that pile of cuttings and special offers that you keep meaning to sort out. Remember, you read it here first.

1. When you finally find a product that you really like, it will have been redesigned or discontinued the next time you go to buy it. Or the shop that sells it will have closed.

2. When you finally get used to the layout of a store, they will rearrange all the sections so that you can't find anything you want. This is intended to make you wander around and notice all sorts of new stuff so that you buy more, but in fact you just end up without some of the things that you usually buy.

3. When you pay a lot for something on impulse, you will see it cheaper in a sale within two months.

4. When you postpone buying something so that you can think it over, you will never find it again. Instead, you will find something not quite as good but more expensive.

5. More choice means more decisions. When you see an advert offering more "choice", just insert the word "decisions" instead. It is always said that people like having more choice. Do you want more decisions?

6. When you have more choice (see rule 5 above) you will always be left with the nagging doubt that you made the wrong decision and that there was something better that you have missed.

7. When you finish decorating a room and go out to buy the furniture for it ready-made, it will not be available for delivery for two months, so that you sicken of the whole idea before it even arrives.

8. If you buy a flatpacked self-assembly kit, you will never be absolutely confident that you have assembled it correctly. (This is because anarchists have infiltrated the flatpack factories. The junior anarchists work on the assembly line and they always make sure that they omit one part in each pack, or they add one extra. Senior anarchists write the assembly instructions. Their plot is to undermine our confidence in the consumer society. The plot is succeeding.)

9. Helplines often don't.

10. All machines go wrong. The more functions a machine has, the more it will go wrong. The newer the design, the more it will go wrong. The best machine

has one fault which you know about and can always fix.

11. When "comfort shopping" for yourself, remember: a packet of Jaffa Cakes is often just as good as shoes or jewellery.

12. Only two big facts are known for certain: you are on a large, spinning rock that is hurtling through lonely space at about 67,000 mph, and one day your body is going to die. Will a new pair of shoes really help?

13. Remember that even though you are looking round the shops, *it is not compulsory to buy anything*. Deciding that nothing is good enough for you is a triumph of self-will and taste, and saves a fortune. For this reason, no one should ever mock a spouse who returns empty-handed from an epic shopping trip. Wise spouses encourage it.

14. The ability to go shopping without buying anything can be doubly fulfilling if you can think of moral objections to a product or its country of origin. (This tactic is especially favoured by impoverished intellectuals.) For example, at Christmas we buy loads of stuff made in China, but China is run by atheists who burn down non-approved churches, lock up people for their beliefs and beat up Tibetan monks. By not buying, you would be observing the true spirit of Christmas.

15. The newer the till, the smaller the brain of the shop assistant operating it.

16. When you are in a hurry to pay at the supermarket, you will find yourself standing behind: a) a garrulous man who is paying by chip-and-pin in the Ten Items or Fewer queue but can't decide which card to use or

whether he wants cashback and all the while he is jabbering on his mobile phone; or b) a woman who seems surprised to be asked for money at all, so it's only when she is told the amount that she rummages in her shopping bag to find her handbag, then rummages in her handbag to find her purse, then counts out the money penny by penny.

17. When you get angry, think before you tell the manager of a local shop that you will never set foot there again. You will spend years going miles out of your way before you finally make a humiliating return, only to find that the manager left some time ago.

18. Never believe that anything is going to be the Next Big Thing. They said that the computer was going to replace the printed word. If this was true, why are there so many computer magazines?

19. When you want to buy something complicated or technical, there will be no sales assistant available who can answer any questions. When you want something simple, a sales assistant will pounce within seconds and talk for hours.

20. The last thing that the world needed was a choice of musical ringtones for mobile phones. Naturally this was invented before lots of stuff we really need.

21. The simpler the product, the more ridiculous the safety warnings. A bag of peanuts has a warning: "Contains nuts". A can of paint has a warning: "Not to be taken internally". A snazzy car will not have the warning: "If you drive this badly, you will kill someone."

22. One of the biggest lies in the world is on small packets of ready meals. It says: "Serves two".

23. With any publication, whether it is an electricity bill or a magazine or an instruction booklet, there are always at least two enclosures telling you about other things that are somehow connected in ways that they do not make clear. You will always throw away the important ones.

24. The most important information in any glossy publication is usually unreadable. This is because a new generation of young designers think it is groovy to put white lettering on a yellow background, or red on a pink background. They think it's still readable because they have the eyes of hawks, albeit with the brains of sparrows.

25. No, you don't need another credit card.

"Are you all right?" It's Joan on the phone from the office. I'm at home. She goes on, "I wasn't sure if you were coming into work or not. You never called."

Me: "I'm sorry. I just forgot. It's the anniversary. You know."

Joan: "Yes I know. Two years! What are you doing?"

Me: "Just hanging around till it's over. Remembering stuff. It doesn't get any better."

Joan: "It will, you'll see. Do you want company?"

Me: "Not today. Maybe tomorrow. I'll come in tomorrow."

Joan: "You got extra space so we could run the whole list of rules. Everyone loved it. They're all making up their own. And you know readers will write in."

(Look, I thought, some of that list came from listening to you lot anyway. I've been adding to it for months, saving it for a week when I couldn't be bothered to write something else.)

Me: "Yes, that'll be good. I'll get an extra column out of that, it'll save me thinking."

Joan: "You're not running out of ideas?"

Me: "Heavens no. You know it's work that saved me. The subject matter is pointless and ludicrous, but I can always get grumpy with something."

Joan: "That's my man. You are essential, you know that."

Me: "So was she."

Joan: "Just take it gently. Remember she was my friend. I loved her too."

Like many damaged men, work is my hiding place, but not today. I was standing aimlessly by the lounge window, looking out towards the Heath, and I remembered that I had never finished writing about that evening with Justin. He's a good listener. He got a lot out of me. It just poured out as I sat on the bench, in the darkness, as Ben lay down and waited. Heaven knows what passers-by thought. We went on to the pub, I had too much wine, then Justin stayed the extra night to make sure I was all right. He left in the morning.

"They say it's good to talk," he said.

"Sorry you got all that. I'm all right, don't worry. And don't . . ."

"I won't mention it to anyone. I've got my own nightmares now. With Sandra."

"Tell her it's my fault you're half a day late. It's Saturday. We can all spend the weekend getting over things."

"I'll call you tomorrow, Guv. And I'll see you on Monday."

"Sure."

We had a sort-of hug, more of a close-up shoulder pat, then he handed over the keys and went back to his real life. Sometimes I have quite missed him. There are no surprises in the kitchen or on the hi-fi. There's no one trying to serve as my resident guide to the twenty-first century, though he still attempts that at work.

Speaking to him that evening had felt like a release. It fell out of me just like a story, not scrambled up like it was when I first used to tell it, before I stopped telling it at all. Time has passed. I suppose it's clearer now. It's a story that's over but I'm left here waiting for the sequel. I don't want a sequel, though, I want the old story back with no ending.

Trouble is, the ending overshadows everything, all the other memories. I can't think of the happy memories without the image of the ending instantly clicking in. That's why it's hard to think about Annie at all sometimes. Mostly, Justin heard the ending, over and over, with just enough of the start for it to make sense to him.

The beginning of the story is great. I can write this. I can try.

I was about Justin's age, maybe a bit older. There was a party, one of those Saturday parties of the old Fleet Street days, lots of media people packed into a big house somewhere in Kentish Town, people arriving late after shifts on the Sunday papers, people leaving early to start radio shifts or to get some sleep for dawn duties. Music and chatter and arguments about things that seemed important then. And in my mind, the crowd parts and there is Annie waiting for me.

She wasn't waiting for me, of course. At least she didn't know that she was until I told her. She was with a couple of girls from the City pages and they were waiting for a drink in the kitchen. She was laughing when I first saw her, just talking to her friends and laughing. I always loved her laugh.

And then, well, it's a cliché. All the big moments of life are a cliché because you have seen them in films and on television, maybe that's how you know it's a big event because you feel like you are in a story. We got talking, and we talked for most of the night. I walked her home, which wasn't far. She wished she lived a little further away, up by the Heath, but she couldn't afford it yet. We had our first kiss on the steps to the flats where she lived and I left because I knew, just knew, that there would be plenty of other nights when I would do more than kiss her and that this was right for now. And that I had been waiting for her too.

I was a general reporter in those days, shouting at politicians, doorstepping the famous, chasing the grief-stricken, and just starting to get my fingertips on the chance of a job on the newsdesk, filling in sometimes for the real guys, dreaming up new angles on the day's news, being ambitious because that's what you're supposed to be, isn't it? I actually cared about the news in those days. Annie was working in admin at the investment department of a bank. That's how she met the City reporters at some promotional event. She made friends easily. She had the gift of friendship. Serious, trustworthy, but a great streak of gentle humour. Slim, with dark hair that framed her face, and that smile. We got married within six months. I had never really imagined myself married, never looked for it, never sought it, but I wasn't stupid enough to avoid it. Not with Annie. Goodbye to the single life, with no regrets.

It was a simple rite of passage, a big bit of growing up. Books and films about rites of passage are usually about Young People. That's because they can always contain a bit of hope. When you are young, every goodbye brings a hello soon afterwards. As you get older, more of the changes are just goodbye, goodbye, goodbye.

It's like an address book that you try to keep up to date. When you are young, any changes of address are for people moving on, going to new jobs, shacking up together, moving to a better house. After a few years, some of the changes and crossings-out are couples breaking up, or jobs going wrong, or some dream that's gone bad. And a few years after that you find yourself crossing out a name and address and putting nothing in its place, because people, real people, people you knew and loved, people who were not especially old, have died. They have not changed to a new address. They have gone.

Back then, when I was a Young Person, I cannot remember what I thought about the middle-aged, those greying plodders ahead of me. But I can say now, we have earned these wrinkles, they are our stripes of battle. We've got a past.

Annie and I dreamed of living somewhere like Highgate — many of our first dates were spent wandering over the Heath — but we couldn't afford it, so we bought a house further out in North London. At the back of our minds, it was to be a house for children. The children never came. I didn't really mind, not at the time, not for me. She was sad when the tests and treatments showed that she couldn't have them. We looked into adoption but there were so few babies to adopt, and we were well into our thirties by then and felt likely to lose out to other couples.

There were consolations. If I let myself, I can display reels of happy memories in my brain, snapshots of happiness. Annie with her assorted godchildren, because all her friends wanted her to be godmother to their kids. Annie and I on holidays in France, or Italy, or Spain, the whole Continent really, and beyond. Nights out, weekends away, nights in. Annie holding me in the night after we made love. Annie making our house so great that we never left. Our whole life was comfy. In our street, most of the other houses seemed to change hands every few years — with a new kitchen installed each time — but we stayed put.

Annie became friends with Joan, who was always ahead of me at work. Joan and her family lived nearby. Sometimes I would find the two women in our kitchen, laughing and talking about nothing much. It was a good friendship, graduating through dinner parties, chats in the street and sometimes babysitting Joan's children. Joan was already a junior features executive, and she would take Annie on "research trips" to the big new shopping malls, a day out looking at what the people were buying, and they would return with a few purchases, hooting with laughter at the giant absurdity of it all. Annie wasn't a big spender. As she said, she would look around at people fussing over some bit of frippery in a dress shop or a furniture store, and want to shout, "For God's sake, there's a whole world out there. Does it matter if something is ecru or sandstorm, or fuchsia or cyclamen? There are jumbo jets and giant freighters orbiting the planet to bring us all this stuff. There's so much, what more do you people want?"

Basset was around Fleet Street in those days too, though not yet on our paper. He once made a pass at Annie at a party. Nothing too serious but unmistakable, she said. By way of reply, she spilled a glass of red wine over the crotch of his white suit. He went home. The story gradually worked its way round the newsrooms. Total strangers would come up to me in bars and pat me on the back. Basset never forgave me, of course. Strange how a serial shagger can resent a man he tried to cuckold, as if it was me who did something wrong, but that's the way it is. Maybe he just didn't like losing. Maybe he resented Annie preferring me to him. Maybe

89

he thought, because I never tried to thump him, I was an easy target for an idle kick now and again. I don't know. We never spoke about it.

Why do some marriages keep working into middle age while others don't? Around us, couples were breaking up all over the place. We learned of each divorce with a kind of weary amazement. By now, I could not think of a life without Annie, and for no reason that I could really work out, she never seemed to stop loving me. We never became one of those couples who bicker at each other at dinner parties. She never got the disappointed look that some attractive women acquire as they approach middle age, when the world becomes less kind to them. We could always talk. She could always make me smile, and I could usually make her laugh.

When I spoke to friends who had drifted away from their wives, they would say that they no longer felt their house was their own, they no longer looked forward to going home, they often sat in their cars for an hour to put off the moment of arrival. Their wives had become cold or angry or simply never hugged them. I never had those complaints.

Pause. I've been remembering and writing all through lunch. I haven't been out so far today and I don't think that I will. It's one of those grey March days, like winter is making a comeback to have one last moan before spring. I'll stay here. I'll finish this story.

Death got closer. Here's a true rite of passage: clearing out your old family home after both your parents have died. It's not like leaving home when you are young, when you know that you can always go back there. It's like leaving your childhood for ever. It's like having to grow up all over again.

We were in our forties now, the time when you have to admit you are not young any more. Then came the deaths. Deaths are so ageing.

Annie and I lost all four of our parents in less than three years. My dad (senility/pneumonia), my mum (stroke), her mum (cancer), her dad (another stroke). All lingering deaths, endless visits to hospitals, in between trying to live a normal life and trying to keep our minds on work after another bleak prognosis from some junior consultant. Shuttling down to Sussex when one of my parents took a turn for the worse, or up north when Annie's were lingering, then back home again after another false start. We grew too familiar with the labyrinthine layouts of the hospitals, the long corridors, the chatter of the day and the silent hopelessness of the night shift. The smells. The hunts for coffee machines and telephones.

Here's a thing: all the main, ground-floor toilets of the hospitals had condom machines. And I always thought, every visitor to this toilet is either a patient or visiting a patient. Who on earth thinks, "My dad is dying, I could really do with a shag"?

And yet, here's another thing. On that morning when Annie's brother rang to say that our last parent, Annie's dad, had suddenly faded and died in the night, Annie took me by the hand and led me upstairs to the bedroom and made frantic love to me before collapsing, weeping, into my arms. We lay like lost orphans, alone and afraid.

I once read somewhere that grief takes an average of eighteen months to clear. But that's for one death. How about four? Is it meant to get easier each time, or is there some sort of compound interest that sets in and never gets cleared, like a bad debt? If you have been through a time when lots of bad things happen all at once, surely there should also come a time when lots of good things coincide? But what if I have already had my lifetime's share of luck?

When I was a boy, crying over some cut or bruise, my mum would comfort me and say, don't worry, pain goes away, just think of something nice. But sometimes the pain doesn't go away.

I cleared out my parents' house in one hard fortnight. It took six skips to shift all Dad's junk from the garage and the loft. He was not a man to throw things away if he thought they might still be useful one day. Old timber, broken radios, jars of nuts and bolts, my old cricket stumps, the radiogram we had in the Sixties. An archaeological dig of my past. And a surprise, from a man whom I had never thought of as full of surprises. Dad left me some of his rules of living.

He had a good brain, my dad. It took him from an apprenticeship as a joiner to the head of maintenance for the local factory. This was a man who knew how everything worked, possibly the last generation who could. This was a man who could not only rewire and replumb his own house, but also knew how every piece of equipment operated inside. He was a keen reader, churchgoer and tireless supporter of local charities. When the senility kicked in, when his brain started fading in and out, it seemed that he knew it only too well and wanted to write down his final good thoughts while he could. They were his last words, I suppose. He certainly had nothing to say at the very end, with Mum and me holding his wasted hands on either side of the hospital bed as he breathed his last. (He'd got pneumonia after taking food into his lungs because he was no longer swallowing properly; I did not know until then that when your brain goes, sometimes your body's normal reflexes start to go with it.) Mum went a few months later, having refused to sort out any of Dad's stuff. It was up to me.

I found the first note in Dad's toolbox. It said: "What you do not maintain will rot." I thought it was something to do with his work. Then, on his bookshelves, there was a scrap of paper scrawled with the words: "Life is like a library book. If you want to keep hold of it, you have to keep renewing it." Slowly, the clear-out became like one of the treasure hunts he organized for my boyhood birthday parties. Maybe he had written down his thoughts during flashes of lucidity, but the hiding places became more erratic. They were all on separate bits of paper, some hardly legible, all over the place, in his desk, in his underwear drawer, between pieces of wood in his shed. In his sock drawer was: "If you always keep the score, you always lose." Among his bank books was: "Things don't matter in themselves. Really. Only the living matter." Tucked in with some of his charity files was: "Doing a bit of good is often the best form of protest."

And so it went on. I can quote them because I typed them all up afterwards. "Life is a free gift. Nobody expects that a free gift will never break." "Bad health is quite normal, it happens in all families." "Wherever you are going, you can only make a start at the place where you are now." "When you lose something — a thing, a mood, a memory — go back somewhere you know that you had it, and look there." "The biggest challenges are not the ones that you choose, they are the ones that choose you." "When you moan about the bits of life that are wrong, remember to celebrate the chunks that are right." "Learn to admire without desire." "All the great truths seem trite until you really try to live them." "Don't judge a life by the ending." Some of these were hardly original, but there was a part of his brain that was determined to record them. There were also two biblical references, Matthew 25, 34–46 (What you do for the least of these, you do for me) and I Corinthians 13, 1–13 (Even if you have knowledge, faith and generosity, if you don't act with love, you have nothing).

There was one last note. It must have been the last because it was in the bag of personal effects returned from the hospital, which mum had never unpacked. It was on a bit of paper torn from a hospital information leaflet. Laboriously written in unjoined letters, and just about readable, it said: "I am so proud of my wife and my son."

I think I began to lose it round then. I was losing my edge, my hunger at work. This is not a good thing in a newsdesk executive.

Looking back, I can even name the day when I first knew I was losing it. It was Concorde day.

History records that on a summer afternoon in July 2000, a supersonic Air France Concorde hit a metal strip on the runway of Paris Charles de Gaulle airport when taking off for New York. The strip had fallen from another plane. The Concorde burst a tyre and ruptured a fuel tank, exploded in the air and then crashed onto a hotel, killing all 109 people on board and four on the ground.

Little recorded is the effect that this had on newsrooms, which was simply orgasmic.

There is nothing wrong with journalists getting excited about a disaster. It is not as if they make disasters happen. They are professionals who welcome a big chance to show their skills and test themselves. Doctors prove themselves with their most arduous cases, politicians are tested by crisis, news journalists run in the direction of a big death toll. It's part of the job.

And you could see it in their faces as the news came through. Concorde? Crashed? This was going to be a fantastic death list. What sort of people travelled on Concorde? Movie stars. Politicians. Business tycoons with their mistresses. Pop singers. Aristocrats. Top-level crooks. Clear the paper! This was going to be pages and pages. This would run for weeks.

By this time Basset had joined our paper, and was then in overall charge of the newsroom from on high. He deigned to come and sit on the newsdesk when the Concorde story broke. Showbiz reporters and our French correspondent were directed to find out which VIPs had been in Paris that day and who might be headed for the States. A small team of reporters were ready to bash out dozens of star obituaries. Picture researchers prepared for a hunt for the most moving celebrity shots.

All this lasted for an hour or so. Then the real news came through.

It wasn't a normal, scheduled Concorde flight. It was a charter. The passengers were not the rich and famous. They were tourists. They were not the jet set. Many of them came from just a few small towns. They were Germans.

Germans! Only Germans! And the reaction at the hard end of the newsroom was a big drop in tension, followed by laughter. Laughter at ourselves, I suppose. Laughter at the absurdity of it all. Laughter led by Basset. If you wanted to show that you were one of the guys, you laughed whether you felt like it or not.

I did not laugh. Recent events had left me unable to laugh about death in any form. I just changed gear a little, thought about the next step: that this was still a disaster and it left a question mark over the whole Concorde programme. I caught Basset looking at me as I plodded on with my work. He kept laughing.

It took a while to realize that I wanted to get out, but I didn't know where to go. I thought of leaving for another paper, but I am not one of those restless, job-swapping types. Besides, I could only get the same work somewhere else. And we were just too busy going through hard times with Annie's parents. In the end, it was a couple of years after Concorde that Joan came to the rescue. Her section was getting bigger. Come over to features, she said. There's a well-worn career path from news to features, for the young seeking bigger bylines and the middle-aged seeking quieter days. Joan said, it's lighter, it's about how people really live, rather than all those artificial rows between politicians and whoever. Start with me in the lifestyle section, I'll teach you the practical things. We could do with a man like you. You could even start to do some writing again.

It's evening now. The day is almost over. I was going to take a walk on the Heath but this isn't one of the Ben days and I can't be bothered. There's not much to write now. Everything leads to this, the end of the story, going back to where I was two years ago tonight.

Life had relaxed. It was good working alongside Joan. It was funny to work on subjects that didn't bloody matter. (In news, if you had an idea for a story, you checked the database to make sure that it had not been done before. In lifestyle, you didn't bother because, mostly, it had all been done before.) Eventually I even got my little column, bottom of the page, below the fold, varying length depending on the adverts, but a real column with half a day a week to write it. It was inspired by the junk that I heard Annie and Joan laughing about, and all the girls. A man's voice, something slightly different, a bit of an edge, maybe drawing some male readers towards the pages read mostly by women. In those days, Annie would read my first attempts and soften them as she had softened me over the years.

And still we thought of moving to Highgate. It had become our standing joke, picturing a house then laughing when we saw the prices. It just wasn't worth it. We walked on the Heath quite a lot. By then we had our dog, a soft old spaniel named Sam. We would drive to the Heath and let him run.

We had been through the hard years. I joked to Annie: look at the time, it's getting late, I'm nearly middle-aged. I have to get a mistress, write a book or buy a sports car. That's what men do at my age.

And I saw the car outside a garage showroom one day. An old model, good condition, an older boy's toy. A bit of vanity shopping, just for me. Annie tried to talk me out of it. It's not safe, she said. Where's the air bag? Where's the crumple zone? And I said, come on, let's be daft for once. I'm a safe driver. We've always been careful. We're getting old. Let's do it. It'll be my car, you've got yours, this is mine. Annie looked worried but she said OK. You're not having the mistress. I'd rather you wrote the book, you always said that you would write a history book. But get the sports car, OK.

And then the story just cuts ahead. Nothing else, straight to the end. We're driving back from a day at the coast, a first break of spring air. A fine day, so we had taken my car. Sam was lying in the back, exhausted from a run on the sands. Annie was beside me, listening to some financial news on the radio. Then a sudden downpour. Shut the sunroof, slow down, turn on the windscreen wipers, take a bit more care on the wet country road.

Then a bend, and beyond it a lorry of road-maintenance men who are packing up their equipment. Moments earlier there had been a warning sign on the bend, but they had just taken it down, they are loading it onto their lorry when they see me coming around the bend. They stop.

There's another car coming towards us in the opposite lane. I can't pull out, I can't go straight ahead and I can't brake in time. I hear Annie take a sharp breath and feel her looking at me. I'm braking and skidding, trying to slow and control the skid. Then I see the car in the opposite lane pull away a little wider and I think there might just be a gap between the lorry and the car so I skid towards the gap.

But it turns out there is a gap only for one person and that person is me.

The left side of my dream car slews under the lorry, taking off the roof along the entire side. I don't remember much sound, we just crunch to a halt. And at first I'm elated. We've made it. I'm alive, not even scratched. Then I look to my left. Slow motion. No Annie. Just bright red everywhere. And then noise, howling from Sam, howling of terror and pain, Sam fatally injured.

And I sit there. I sit there, in the rain and the howling, in a shattered dream. I try my door but it's buckled and won't open. I sit there, entombed, lost and useless. That's still the part that comes back in the night.

And the workmen lever my door open and pull me out. And the other driver stops to help and gets on his mobile phone. Then come the police, and the ambulance, and the duty vet to put Sam down. And them all trying to keep me away so I won't see when they take out what's left of Annie.

And then, it's the cliché again. Death is a cliché. The funeral and the inquest and the grief and the feeling that I might wake up from this and it will be all right, but I can't and it's my fault and I have nobody to blame but me because I bought that car, so my grief is my punishment and that at least is right and proper. It's the only thing that is.

And my guilt is a comfort in a way. It gives me something to feel rather than just empty grief. When I allow myself to feel anything at all. It gives me a direction, a focus for my anger. No need to rage against God, no need to sue anyone. I cannot sue myself and I have no need as I have already been punished beyond any court. My guilt is my punishment.

The streets of Britain must be awash with guilt. Do drink-drivers wake up screaming the day after the crash? Do the speed merchants and the careless drivers ever get over the results of their recklessness? There must even be nightmares for the innocent killers, drivers tootling along at the right speed, with full care and attention, then a child runs out, or a forgetful pensioner wanders into their path from behind a van, and then wham, the innocent has become a killer. I checked the figures — nine people die on the roads every day, plus another hundred seriously injured and almost eight hundred injured in a way not deemed serious. Then add the mental wounds of the survivors. And the mourners. If every dead person has, let's say, just ten close relatives, friends, neighbours, colleagues who seriously mourn their absence, that's almost one hundred more shattered lives every day. Broken timelines, day after day. I must pass them in the street, stand next to them in the shops. A stream of mourning.

After the day of the accident, I did not travel in a car again until the funeral. At the crematorium, I emerged from the undertaker's limo more shaken than I could ever have expected, and that was after travelling at about 25 mph. The other mourners just thought it was grief. Poor man, they said, poor George. But it was also terror. I stood before the massed ranks of friends, relatives and Annie's godchildren, listening to Annie's favourite poems and hymns, shaking about having to go back in a damn car.

There were comforters. I drowned in comfort. Great big weeping hugs from all her friends. Many said the same thing — the suddenness of her death made them feel it could happen to them or their husbands or wives. It brought them closer to each other, made them appreciate what they had. People took lessons from grief to make it make sense. They told me, hoping it might provide comfort.

Let's keep in touch, they said. But they said it in the tone of voice that people reserve for divorces, when they are talking to the partner that they will not be seeing again. And behind the grief, I sensed the question: "Why her and not you?" Of the two of us, the better one had died. I could not disagree.

I slowly cut them all off. I did not go to dinner parties any more, as it seemed there would always be a missing guest: my Annie. I did not return calls. I let my few relatives turn into distant relatives. I did not send out many cards announcing my change of address when I decided that I could no longer stay in a house where she was an empty space in every room. I had cleared out my parents' house, now I was clearing out my own.

I sold the house to a nice young couple who were just starting out, and bought this flat. I kept our photograph albums and some of her old papers, a few bits of furniture, but that was about all.

Her ashes are on the Heath. I went out at night and put them there. There's probably a law against it but I can't be the only one who has done it. I like to think she's in the trees and the flowers. She's not with me but she is everywhere.

At first I felt her presence sometimes. Walking out on the Heath. When I sat alone. I thought she was really there and I turned to speak to her. The hair went up on the back of my neck, she felt so close. Then she was gone. But I have not felt her presence for a long while. It's like she is disappointed in me. I don't suppose Dad would be too proud of me now, either.

I'm a bit of a novice at self-pity. I went to my doctor when the nights became worse — I thought I'd get sleeping tablets but instead I got counselling. I used to think that I was a strong person but maybe it was just that nothing really bad had ever happened to me, or that I had never before caused something bad to happen. Once you lose everyone who defined who you are, then who are you?

It occurs to me that this day's journal is pretty much my whole autobiography, apart from schooldays (I was good at English and History, and once lost a fight with the school bully). It's not much, is it?

Much of this I dumped on poor young Justin, while his girlfriend was waiting for him to return to his flat so that she could tell him her news. And the news was none of the six guesses I had made earlier. It was, g) She's pregnant, she has thought things over and she wants to get married.

CHAPTER
SIX

HERE COMES THE BRIDE

Anti-Style
by George Worth
17 April

Let us rise up today and revolt. Let us say we have had enough and it's all getting ridiculous. Let us target our anger on the money-grabbing, smarmy parasites who feed on our finest emotions and leave us broke.

Let us rebel against the marriage business.

Love is meant to be beyond price but somehow they have found a way to overcharge. The average cost of a wedding is now said to be around £18,000. They say that they just want to create a perfect day, then they ruin it with the cost. They are just trying to create the perfect bill.

Spring is the marriage season. All over Britain, young couples have told their delighted families that they have plighted their troth, they are going to get hitched, do the decent thing, make a life together. There are about five minutes when all this seems wonderful and simple, full of anticipation and joy. Then the happy couple lose control of the whole thing as they get sucked into the chaos of planning and the mounting bills.

104

There is not much of a cut-price end of the marriage market. There are few out-of-town discount centres, no special offers, no Brides "R" Us. You pay the full whack or you are a cheapskate, it's not true love, you are trying to spoil The Happiest Day. It's blackmail, plain and simple. The day is somehow not blessed unless the parasites have cast their spell on it.

And they are all in on it. The glossy bridal magazines, the stationers, the venues, the hotels, the caterers, the florists, the photographers, the honeymoon operators. Always there's the subtle jibe: you only want to pay how much? But don't you want the best? You want to do it properly, don't you? As if you are not really married unless your florist's bill goes into four figures.

No other rite of passage is like this. You can have a cheap party for a new baby. You can have an eighteenth birthday celebration down the pub, a few drinks to celebrate a degree or a new job, a simple party for your retirement, even a cheap funeral. Nobody really judges the worth and emotional value of all that on how much they spend. Well, nobody sane anyway. They know it's the feelings that count. Why should marriages be different?

You can't really plan a perfect day anyway. Uncle Fred will still get drunk and embarrass you. A bridesmaid will be sick. And the happy couple will be watching anxiously to check where all the money has gone.

The crying shame is that the wedding parasites are helping to make marriage less popular. People look at the price and say, that's crazy, if that's the price I am not getting married at all, we can't afford it.

But that "average" price is fake anyway. It's put about by the bridal industry, who calculate it by adding up all the "essential" parts of a wedding, plus the luxury honeymoon, and then finding out how much people are getting away with charging.

So let's make it clear that we are not paying it any more. Let's reclaim marriage from business. And I nominate churches to take the lead. They want people to get married, let them provide a full marriage package. The wedding, a bit of a do in the church hall, flowers and a cake from the Women's Institute, maybe some pictures by a parishioner who does photography as a hobby instead of hours waiting on some ponce from the local photographer's studio who bores everyone by getting all the permutations of relatives and friends in focus while the food goes cold. Get the bridesmaids some cheap princess dresses from Woolworths or Disney. Make it fun.

Let's call them Real Weddings. And let the overpriced fakers become regarded as seriously naff. You had a £1,000 gown and a flautist? You poor thing, how could you be so vulgar? All that money, it can't be real love. It's just so fake, who were they kidding? Simple is so much better, don't you think?

Then the happy couple can put their time and their concentration and their money into something that really matters. Such as the rest of their lives.

"You said it all," Justin agreed.

"I'm sorry," I said. "I've been listening to you so much, it just seemed too good not to use it. You don't mind?"

"Mind? It's a revolution waiting to happen."

Then he went to take a phone call about the guest list.

Everyone at work has been getting terribly excited about the forthcoming nuptials, known affectionately as Justin's Shotgun Wedding. The idea of someone marrying a pregnant bride seems to be regarded as rather quaint and chivalrous. Justin is being treated with great fondness by all the women, except possibly Basset's bird who is a little cool about everything anyway. (Maybe she's jealous. Or maybe it's because everyone is rather wary of her.)

The girls quiz Justin about Sandra's health and insist on seeing a copy of the latest scan of the growing foetus, which sends them into a silent wonder followed by proclamations of amazement. I was chastised for saying it looked rather like a seal.

Justin was more amazed by the sound-check on the baby's heart, which sent out a staccato of about 150 beats a minute. It would make a great backing track for some acid house music, apparently.

Sandra will be a June bride. It takes that long to organize, so they may as well do it properly and be able to maintain that they are not rushing into anything. They are lucky to have been able to book any day at all in the next couple of months. The pregnancy will present some challenges over the design of the bridal gown. (Basset's comment: "At least in later life she will be one of the few wives who look thinner than in their wedding pictures.") In any case, Joan has moved into full fixer mode to help out with ideas and cost. There's a bridal designer who owes her a favour after an article on our pages. There's a caterer we are using for a party-food feature shortly. Joan knows them all, and Justin is part of the family now, although he is still waiting to hear if his six-month contract is going to turn into a staff job.

It has taken Justin some time to fill in the gaps of the pregnancy story. In the office, he seems to confide only in me. I didn't ask much at first. He was in shock.

On the Saturday he returned to his flat, Sandra didn't comment about him being half a day late. She seemed to have regarded it as a rightful gesture of independence after all that she had put him through. She sort of respected it.

The baby might well have been conceived on Christmas night, for all I know at the very time that I was getting locked out of my flat. So it's due around the end of September, a peak time for births. Even in something so personal, Justin is still up with a trend.

I tried to make sure he had been through all the options, not rushed into things.

"Guv," he said in the pub. "I lay awake at night thinking of all the options."

"And they are . . ."

"The woman has three: abortion, adoption and parenthood. The man has four — the first three are the same as the woman, plus we have the added choice."

"What's that?"

"Running away to Alaska."

We both smiled.

"And you don't feel like running away?"

"No, that's just it. I don't. When I went back into my flat, it was like coming home."

"Which it was."

"No, not just the flat. Sandra, and the whole baby thing when she told me about it. It was like it had all been, you know, waiting for me."

Pause. A reaching for glasses, a drink. He continued.

"And I remembered what you said."

"Me?"

"About how you know it's a big moment because it feels like a cliché. And you don't mind, because it's your own cliché. It's all been waiting for me."

This was the story of a good-hearted but ruthlessly practical girl who had been horrified and embarrassed to find herself pregnant, who didn't want to talk about it with anyone she knew until she had decided what she wanted to do. She just didn't know it would take so long. Her seven weeks of decision-making had not been an idle time. Thorough research was going on while she came to terms.

She told Justin how she had felt a kind of panic that she had to deal with alone. She knew of girls who felt they had been rushed into a decision, one way or another, by friends, family, lovers, bosses, tutors. Facing the choices, she went into each possibility to see where she might feel that she belonged. There followed strange scenes of a woman alone in a strange city. She sat outside an abortion clinic to watch the faces of the women coming out. She did the same at a maternity unit. She grew braver and started sitting in crowded waiting rooms. She lived in a world of pregnancy, she was an alien on Planet Baby. She started to notice babies everywhere, babies in prams, babies in cars with stickers saying Baby on Board, babies in shops and cafes. She had never noticed so many before. They were, she realized, a normal part of the population, though not yet part of her immediate circle. But still she spoke to no one except a GP who confirmed her pregnancy, gave her advice on diet and asked if she needed any counselling, while she made up her mind. She said that she didn't.

She got a leaflet on adoption but could not stand the thought of her child tracking her down eighteen years later and asking why she had not been able to cope.

And all the time the baby was growing and Sandra didn't know what she wanted. She browsed a book on baby care, which horrified her with details about nappies and sore nipples and battles for sleep. She had morning sickness. She read that miscarriages were most likely in the first three months, and she let that be her deadline. All her choices were so enormous whichever way she turned.

Then, one day, she was passing a mother-and-baby playgroup and went in to look, saying she was pregnant and planning her future. She was welcomed. There were mothers who were little more than children themselves. There were mothers aged forty or more. They were all races and all sorts. None of the babies seemed to mind; they were born trusting their mums. She got chatting to a single mother and asked if she had any regrets. The woman said she wished that the father had stuck around, but added, "The thing with a baby is, it's hard work, but you get moments of total joy every day. You don't get that with anything else, do you?"

Sandra looked into the trusting eyes of the woman's baby and thought, "I can't not do this." From then on, she felt that she had a relationship with the child inside her. Within days, she had decided for sure. She wanted Justin and his child.

Listening to the story in instalments, I've been wondering how I feel about all this. As a bloke. As me. I'm supposed to be writing about my feelings, and this is the biggest chunk of real life that has happened lately to anyone I know. I should be feeling something. I'm fine at passing comment on general things. Specific cases are a little harder.

Trouble is, it's not the ideal subject. I suppose I feel it's wrong that Justin was left in the dark for so long — he might never have known anything at all if Sandra's decision had gone the other way. But this brings me perilously close to talking about abortion, and men of my generation know better than that. It's not a hugely mentionable subject, socially. And I know, I know, that the abortion law can't work by vote when there are two people involved; there might be too many tied results. It's one woman, one vote, one person with the right to know.

The law had only just been introduced when I was in puberty. Really, I have known no other world. Along with other reforms, the view of my generation of young men was influenced partly, to be honest, by the hope that it could help our sex lives. Self-interest was always involved. We mostly favoured the bits of feminism that seemed to benefit us. We adapted to the other bits, like the language thing. (This still goes on today. I hear the young men on the Tube, chatting self-consciously with the studenty girls, making sure their pronouns and their nouns are as non-sexist as they can be, and I know it's just an extra layer of chat-up language, and if they didn't want sex they would be talking somewhat differently. Women should concentrate far more on whether men walk the walk rather than talk the talk, as the Americans say. Actions are far truer than words.)

But now I worry about whether my views are changing with age.

Here's a thing: at a basic level, I'm not the man I was. I was reading somewhere lately, in some piece on diets, the little nugget of information that the cells in our bodies are in continuous renewal, and that not one molecule in any bit of us is more than nine years old. We keep the same shape because our DNA tells the new molecules what to do. But do we have to keep the same opinions, frozen in time all our lives? Are my attitudes stuck in my DNA? Is it so wrong if an older man changes his mind?

And I haven't changed much. In this, as in many things, I don't feel wiser, just sadder. Abortion was to be for desperate cases; we just never imagined that there would be more than 190,000 desperate cases a year. I wonder if it's been affected by this idea that every event has to be perfect — the perfect purchase, the perfect home, the perfect wedding, a baby only at the perfect time, and nothing else is acceptable. Does every damn thing have to be planned?

And I can't forget holding Annie in my arms the night she gave up hope of adopting a baby, and she said, "If there's supposed to be a sisterhood, you'd think more of the sisters would carry a baby for nine months for the sake of women like me."

So how do I feel? It's taken a while but I've realized that: a) in the end, I feel quite proud for Justin and Sandra. After so much death, it's good to have a new life; b) without Annie's care, I must be wary not to sound like a sexist git; and c) even when I think of sexual things, I still feel sad.

Joan has been trying to fix up my life again. After I was on that radio panel in February, the producer was chatting with Joan at some dinner party and said that I would be good as a regular, maybe once a month. At least that's how Joan tells it. I can't believe that it wasn't at least partly her idea, to publicize her section of the paper and help me get out of myself, whatever that means.

"And you know what?" she said.

"What?" I sighed.

"The producer reckons the presenter quite fancies you. She was very curious about you."

Pause.

"Joan."

"Yes?"

"Stop it."

"Oh all right. I just thought that you might like to know."

I finally caved in about going back on the radio thing this week, because Joan tipped them off in advance about the subject of my column. They had lined up a group of guests for me to attack: a society-wedding photographer, the manager of a hotel specializing in theme weddings and the editor of one of those bridal magazines.

This was just the start of an evening that seemed to have been built around me having to meet people. I had also accepted an invitation to dinner with Justin, Sandra and Justin's mum, who has finally arrived for her much-postponed visit. I had a handy excuse to be a little late for dinner because I was going on the radio first. As I left the office, my sidekick Arabella gave me a kiss on the cheek for luck.

On the Tube to the radio station, a strange thing happened. My willy woke up. I'm just logging this as I think it was my first daytime erection in two years. I don't know why it happened. I wasn't thinking about anything much, certainly nothing sexual. It just went up, as if having a stretch, maybe checking what was going on, then went down again. I can just about remember that erections can happen at all sorts of inappropriate times, but it was bloody unnerving. Still, there was one consolation. When this sort of thing happened in the old days, it sometimes got stuck in the Y of my Y-fronts, and I had to perform little contortions to get it comfy. No such problem with boxers. I don't suppose the manufacturers can mention this in their advertising.

"Well, I think you should all be ashamed of yourselves." This is me in full grumpy mode, at my fellow radio guests. The presenter is beaming at me. This is what she wants, I take it. This is lively radio. I have been trying to avoid any direct one-to-one contact with her all evening, not least because I keep forgetting her name.

"Well, I think you are an old Scrooge," says the magazine editor. "You are just a grump who doesn't believe in spending money on anything."

"And that's exactly how you lot bully people into spending too much money, by suggesting they are mean if they don't."

"We are giving people romance," says the hotelier.

"You are giving them romance? You? I rather think you'll find they had romance long before they got to you. Isn't that the reason they're getting married?"

The photographer pipes up. "But it's the celebration of their romance. The chance to be the stars of the show for a perfect day that they can look back on and remember."

"That perfect day now includes over an hour of being photographed — longer than the service itself — while chaps like you boss everyone around. All anyone wants is a few good pictures, for heaven's sake."

The presenter intervenes to stop this getting too stroppy. Maggie, that's her name. Rather shapeless clothes, worn for comfort. Perhaps a little buxom. Tightly cut hair, slim wrists, no wedding ring. A great voice. Not really my type, if I had a type, which of course I don't any more.

She lets the others drone on a bit to plug their various businesses. The editor, apparently, is merely providing a guide to help her readers make their choices, rather than stoking up their dreams beyond reality. The hotelier claims to be relieving the bride and groom of any worries about the big day by taking over all the organizing himself, thus leaving them free to enjoy themselves. The photographer is preserving it fully because not every day can be as wonderful as this and they will want to look back on it.

"But after all this," says Maggie, "isn't there a danger of an anticlimax? If they build up the wedding as perfect, is this any guide to married life? Shouldn't they spend more time thinking about life after the wedding? George, I know you had a long and happy marriage before the death of your wife. What do you think?"

I stare at her. I'm silent. I'm bloody speechless. Did she have to be so direct? She stares at me, realizing that I am upset. Embarrassed silence prevails and no one can find words to break it. Silence on air. This is the nightmare of radio land. It's called dead air. Nothing to listen to. Potential listeners surfing the airwaves will land on the station, find nothing on, think they have been mistaken and then turn the knob to find something else. Five seconds of dead air. Ten seconds. It's mesmerizing.

"Looking back, um, looking back on my marriage, it's not the wedding I really remember," I manage to say. "Certainly, it's all the years that came after it. The

116

wedding is a blur. As for celebrating a perfect day, I think there were many perfect days, but the best days happen by a kind of chance, and the best times were because of the sort of person she was."

And I stop because I can't say any more — it's as if I am defending Annie from an attack that had not been made. And because my eyes have filled with tears. I'm not sobbing, thankfully, and I don't think my voice shook, but this was bad enough. This is getting ridiculous, I am crying every other month, and in front of an ever larger number of people. If this goes on I'll be weeping in front of a whole stadium in the end.

And then the other guests, these people whom I have been attacking, they fill in for me and talk through the final minutes of the show without once putting me on the spot, because they realize that I am upset and this is British radio after all, and we are decent people in our way.

Afterwards, Maggie seeks me out.

"George, I am most terribly sorry. I didn't mean to upset you."

"No, no, really, the question just took me by surprise. You were just doing your job. There I was, talking about other people's weddings, and obviously it's natural to ask about my own."

Actually, I think, we had all been performing a fake rage for the benefit of the listeners, like I do for readers with my column, and I had not thought it would have to be linked to real life. But the question was no worse than any I had asked in my reporting days. I have gone soft.

"Strange," I said. "It just hadn't occurred to me. I must have sounded like a silly old sod."

"Oh no, you spoke with great affection. We don't get, well, real emotion like that very often. Look, you really must come back soon. You will, won't you?"

As I took the Tube back across London to Justin's flat, I counted all the reasons for avoiding having dinner at someone else's home. The slim chances of everyone liking the same food. The opportunities for conversation spoiled by some dominant bore, or a couple who decide it's a really good time to have a row in front of witnesses. Or — and this especially applies to media folk — the flare-up of some fierce argument about a tiny point of politics or current affairs. As if arguing has a point, as if anyone has ever changed their mind as a result of a major debate at a dinner party. As if they are going to concede to a fellow guest, "Hey, you're a total stranger, I've known you for only the time it takes to drink a bowl of soup or eat half a feta salad, but your incisive insults and personal remarks have totally changed my views on one of my core beliefs. Now can you pass the salt?"

None of this mattered with Annie. She always changed it into a game, an entertainment. From the start, even before we arrived at a new house for dinner, we imagined the decor inside, trying to guess if the seemingly ultra-modern hosts would turn out to have antique pine everywhere, even in the bathroom, or if an apparently ordinary couple would have a house that was a riot of modern art, or red velvet like a Viennese brothel. And we would describe it to each other in the same mock-posh voices we used when we read out loud from the more laughable pages of the Sunday supplements.

And now I realized I was having a pure, happy memory of life with Annie. Not just a flash of a smile, but an informed memory that was flowing from me. Why now?

So, out of the Tube station with an A to Z map to find Justin's flat in would-be trendy Highbury. I knew he had rented it from a City couple who had done it up before taking a year's assignment in New York. I pictured a wannabe warehouse effect, but much smaller. The kitchen, dining room and lounge all combined. As it was a rental, the decor would be a few minutes out of date. Vaguely uncomfy modern sofa. Shining kitchen, a hint of brick, a light wood. Some books, Justin's sound-system technology and home computer. A large, vaguely abstract art print. No clutter. A big plant. Light wood flooring and soft beige walls, like being inside a cardboard box.

Justin answered the door and I stepped inside and grinned. Hey, I can still do this. Mostly I had guessed right, apart from a row of family photos on the shelves, and the Chagall poster over the black dining table. And the two big vases of flowers. Maybe that was Sandra's contribution.

At first glance, Sandra seemed a medium sort of girl — medium height, medium build, medium brown hair, medium voice, medium happy. Early to medium pregnant. Justin's mum was about five years older than me, a good northern mum in the nicest possible way. Bright, with a lively mind, but a little woman, making you wonder how she managed to give birth to such a solid-looking son. The mother and her imminent daughter-in-law were busying themselves in the kitchen area, getting stuff out of the oven now I had arrived. They had waited for me.

"Mr Worth," said the mum.

"Call me George."

"Call me Brenda. I always read your bit in the paper."

Justin glared for a moment then gave up.

"Well I've heard a lot about you," I said. "And it's terribly kind of you all to invite me to a family do like this."

Kind? Justin had begged me to come. His mother was down for five days, checking out his flat, his life, his immediate plans and his work. She had to know he was working with normal people. For some reason this was my role. Also, I was the only colleague who knew the Whole Story, so wouldn't stumble in the wrong places.

There was music playing, Fifties ballad stuff like Sinatra, possibly for the mum's benefit, or maybe it was a revival that Justin was into. The food was simple, some sort of bake, lots of salad, gooey pudding. Sandra had an ice-breaker conversation all ready.

"So, where are you going for your Basset holiday?"

Basset had decreed that the annual British holiday section next month could not just be the same old travel writers going on the same old freebie trips. He would get writers from other sections — such as the lifestyle section, business and sport — to visit places in Britain and speak of their love or hate for the old country. It was a good idea, really, but I suspected his motives. Only a couple of days earlier we had been talking in the office, bemoaning how so few all-expenses-paid trips were coming our way, especially as Justin and Sandra didn't feel like flying the Atlantic now that she was pregnant. Maybe Basset's girlfriend had repeated our moans back to him. Basset himself was having a week at a luxury health farm, probably with her.

"I'm still thinking about where I'll go," I said. "I haven't been away much lately."

"Will you go alone?" Sandra asked.

"I don't know."

"Justin's taking me to Manchester for a weekend."

"But that's where you're from!"

"Yes, but we've never been there as tourists. It's got a real tourist industry now and there are places that we never visited while we lived there, like Londoners never go to the Tower. We'll see it in a different way and stay at one of the big hotels where we've never been."

"Good idea. A last trip home before the wedding."

"We used to have lovely family holidays when Justin's dad was alive," said his mother. "We never had the chance to go abroad but we saw all of Britain. Two weeks in the car every year."

"Me on the back seat, asking if we were there yet," said Justin.

"You were no trouble, love," she recalled. "You've never been any trouble."

She looked at me. "He was wonderful when my man died. Twelve years ago. I don't know how I would have coped alone."

Silence. And I guessed they had heard me on the radio.

"I wish he could be at the wedding," she said. Justin put his arm around her shoulders.

"Mum."

"It's all right. It's just that he would have liked to see us all happy like this."

And so we talked, this family and I, of unremarkable things mostly, of past weddings, and dogs, of North and South, and London prices and places to go. And all the time I felt Sandra watching me, and we exchanged a couple of smiles, and that was about all until Justin started to do the dishes and his mother went to help him, leaving us at the table.

"I've been afraid of meeting you," she said. "But I knew that I should."

"Afraid? Why?"

"I don't know what you can think of me, except bad stuff. I don't know what Justin said to you all those weeks."

"Hardly anything deep. Really, we're blokes. I just let him wait and see."

"Well, I should say thank you. Thanks for looking after him like that. It might have been much worse if he'd crashed out the whole time with one of his mates. Anything could have happened, he might have been wound up to dump me, or demanded to come back and have an argument. Anything."

"Really, it was good having him around."

"Please understand this. I don't know if you have any idea what a surprise pregnancy is like."

"Er no, not really. Not personally."

"Well it's terrifying. It was terrifying for me. I wasn't ready. I didn't think he was either. He really wants to get on and enjoy himself. He loves it here, London is all he's ever wanted. I didn't want him blaming me for, I don't know, making him settle down too much. I didn't know what I wanted. I read all the books and there's all this awful stuff with morning sickness, and that's just the start. I even considered getting rid of this and not telling him."

"Have you told him that?"

"George, I've told him everything, along with the fact that I'm very sorry it happened this way." She was searching my face for a more emphatic response. "I really needed that time on my own. I worked out what I wanted, that I wanted my baby and Justin, if he'd have me. It's just earlier than I would have hoped. I'm more old-fashioned than I thought. And it doesn't matter where I live.

"I don't know how other women cope at times like that. But that's what I needed and you helped to make it possible. Other people your age might have fussed or tried to bring us together. A woman would have tried to do that. But not you."

"Er no, it was none of my business."

We were silent for a moment, as if too much had been said. I wondered what Annie would have done right now, in my place. Then I reached out and squeezed Sandra's hand. We looked at Justin and his mum, finishing putting the dishes away.

"He's a good bloke," I said. "He might be a bit more old-fashioned than people think. And patient too."

"Just as well really."

"So, let me get this clear. What you're saying is, I got it right. Not asking about personal stuff and feelings."

"Yes."

"It was the right thing to do."

"Yes." A smile.

"Blimey."

I smiled too. And then I laughed.

CHAPTER
SEVEN

WALKING THE DOG

Holiday special
by George Worth
19 May

It was a perfect day. A gentle sea breeze drifted along a vast, empty beach framed by miles of open country-side. At the shoreline, my travelling companion emerged from the waves after a relaxing swim.

Then he shook himself, sat down on the sand and barked for a biscuit.

Ben is a city dog. I had been unsure how he would take to joining me for a gentle, three-day hike along a nineteen-mile stretch of the Northumberland coast path. But it was worth a try. The choice of travelling companion can make or break a holiday. Couples may fight, families get sick of each other, children sulk, friends want to go different ways. Why not take a placid, middle-aged Labrador who walks at my sedate pace and likes to swim?

"Look, Ben," I had said. "There's a train from London that gets us to the coast path in just over three hours. Then we can keep heading north beside the sea for a few days, between little harbours and castles. Do you fancy a walk?" He liked the word "walk".

And so a good dog and an Englishman went out in the afternoon sun after arriving at Alnmouth station. First problem: the station is not exactly central. We got off the intercity train and, as our link with civilization pulled away, we found ourselves stranded next to a B road that seemed to be in the middle of nowhere. Feeling lost on arrival was not quite the adventure I had planned.

After a mile of walking, the village of Alnmouth finally appeared and Ben proved his worth as we checked into a hotel. (You didn't think I'd go camping, did you?) It turns out that Ben has a previously undiscovered skill — he can charm hotel receptionists in a way that I have never managed. Not all hotels take dogs but, among those that did, he always got us a good room. A wag, an appealing look, sitting down unbidden to show he is civilized. It's a pushover. "Normally, sir, you would have a single room but as you have such a large, well-behaved dog, there is a double/family room that is available tonight. No extra charge."

We explored the beach until dinnertime. Ben minded the room while I ate. Next morning, I smuggled up some breakfast sausages to him. Then we began.

The footpath from the estuary led us around Alnmouth's bizarre golf course, which rises in levels along the cliff. No doubt it's fascinating to golfers but long ago I left instructions that, if I ever show any interest in golf, I should be taken out and shot as an act of kindness. We walked on.

Ah, the joy of the open countryside. Thousands of years ago, after the Ice Age, the first nomadic arrivals in Britain are thought to have made their way north along the coasts, the land being too densely forested to allow any easy progress. Maybe the first Britons took this very path, followed by the occasional tame wolf seeking food leftovers. Man and beast striding forth, just like me and Ben.

Or perhaps not quite like us. I doubt if the wolves required so much luggage. It occurred to me, as I adjusted my rucksack, that much of the weight was stuff for Ben. A couple of cans of dog food, just in case. His bowl. His biscuits. A bottle of water, mainly for him. His towel. His lead. Who was in charge here?

At this time of year, there are signs warning of new lambs in the fields, where dogs must be kept on a lead to avoid worrying the sheep. This was no problem to us. Ben does not worry sheep. Sheep worry him. With humans, he's fine, but he slunk past any sign of unfamiliar animal life.

It's surprising how you can spin out a six-mile walk into a whole day if you start late, finish early and take lots of rests along the way. We lunched at Boulmer and walked above cliffs teeming with bird life to spend the night at Craster, where you are meant to dine on kippers. Ben had the skins. And some sausages. After dinner, we had a late stroll in the darkness and enjoyed the peace and the night stars whose absence shrinks our souls in the cities.

The second day was epic: seven miles along one of the finest stretches of the British coastline. Up the long, sloping path to the fourteenth-century Dunstanburgh Castle, abandoned since the Wars of the Roses. Ben relaxed in the entranceway while I explored the ruins. In return, I spent much of the remainder of the day idling on beaches while Ben paddled in a series of broad sweeping bays. Lunch at the pub in Low Newton was spoiled only by the design of a couple of local stiles, too narrow for Ben to squeeze through and too high for him to climb. Lifting a full-grown Labrador over a fence is not the best way to start an afternoon. (Even here, I am anti-stile.)

Apart from the stiles, everything else in this landscape seems to have been designed on an epic scale — the sweep of land and sea, and the sky. As the afternoon sun hit different patches of high, light cloud, it was if the sky was a vast canvas that had been worked by the brushstrokes of a series of different artists, a bit of Turner over here, some Constable over there, and maybe some Coulson below.

A long sleep in Beadnell, and a long breakfast, and then the final five miles, mostly along dunes where the soft sand sapped our strength. A rest in touristy Seahouses and on to the journey's end at Bamburgh. We both arrived panting.

The village of Bamburgh was once a royal capital city, and it is still dominated by the castle that had been on our horizon for miles before we finally reached it. We were staying two nights here, as I had awarded us a full day of rest. Just as well, as my legs were stiff in the morning and Ben's must have been too — when he saw that I was not packing the rucksack, he lay down with a sigh and went back to sleep.

Much of Britain's early history can be told from Bamburgh. It was a tribal stronghold of the early Britons, and a royal seat of Anglo-Saxon kings when Northumbria was the most powerful kingdom. It was they who invited Celtic missionaries to set up the monastery at nearby Holy Island, later to be sacked by Vikings. This place has survived most things and will hopefully survive us all.

Below the castle is a vast beach where Ben had a lazy afternoon and a light swim.

The next morning, before we caught the local bus to Berwick-upon-Tweed to catch the train home, Ben did a strange thing. He walked out to the edge of the sea, sat down and barked towards the waves. I don't know what was in his mind. Had the city dog become one with nature, or was he just saying goodbye?

He left a perfect trail of pawprints in the wet sand. Soon we would be gone and all trace of our visit would be washed away.

A landscape so vast and full of history is a reminder that one day, all trace of any of us might be gone. But in a fleeting visit, I know a dog who has already been to heaven.

"Good grief, George, that was a bit soppy."

"Yeah, sorry about that, Joan."

"Just as well it wasn't in your usual slot. People want you to be a grump now. They expect it. Tell me you won't start revealing that underneath the grim exterior there's a heart of mush?"

"It won't happen again, boss."

"Better not." But she's grinning. The travel article was accompanied by a picture of me and Ben at his most photogenic. One of the girls liked it so much, she put it on the notice board. For a while, it got more aaahs than any talk of Justin's baby and Justin's marriage.

The holiday was like a glimpse outside my prison bars. It was unsettling. One of the older guys in the pub says that he never takes holidays any more because he hates the feeling of coming back. I know what he means. I feel out of sync with whoever I am meant to be.

It's hot here now. A few days after I returned to grubby London, the heatwave that I had enjoyed in Northumberland arrived here too. The office air conditioning was taken by surprise. We can't open any windows so we have desk fans spinning round the stale air.

It was hell on the Tube today, grimy and stuffy. Many of the girl passengers are travelling with those little bottles of water clutched in their hands all the time as if they are worried that they are somehow about to evaporate, or that the carriage doors will suddenly open at an unexpected stop in the middle of the Sahara.

Also, breast day has arrived. I don't know how this happens every year without us announcing it on the lifestyle pages, but somehow it seems that all the young women in London decide all at once to leave off as much clothing as possible and wear plunging tops tight across their cleavage. (I should use this in the column sometime.) This sudden exposure of chests is a challenge to my generation of men as a) it is clearly not for our benefit and b) we have been trained for decades not to stare at women below the neck unless we have formal permission. It is especially challenging these days as many of the women are wearing tops with logos or slogans written across the breast area, so we find ourselves idly reading the words and then realizing that we are, after all, staring at their chests but for entirely innocent reasons, so we have to look away fast.

Then there are the young men. In the hot evenings, groups of youths hover in the streets and outside pubs, and as I walk by I feel threatened by a faint air of menace. Every few weeks, on the news pages, there are stories about harmless middle-aged men being beaten up by gangs of inner-city youths, just for a laugh or in revenge for some imaginary slight. It's as if they think that the evenings belong only to Young People.

In the city centre, in daytime, life rushes by. People walk in the same way that they drive, crowding each other, cutting in, muttering if someone dawdles in their way. They are even greedy with time. If a customer in a shop stops to chat with the assistant for a moment, like a human being, everyone behind lets out a collective sigh of frustration.

Sometimes lately I watch the crowds with a kind of fascination, as if watching a strange tribe. They surge around with such purpose in the great human struggle for something or other. I resist an urge to tap people on the shoulder and say, hey, do you know that we are all going to die one day? In the mighty city, people forget about death, or they defy it. Something like a bomb makes them feel vulnerable, but only for a while and then they are off again, rushing about, chasing their wants, the desires that get them through the day to beat the sense of boredom or unease. Maybe the girl/bloke at the office will smile at them. Maybe the job will work out. Maybe the shops will have something for them. Maybe tonight's TV will be OK.

This might be the lure of the lifestyle pages. You don't have to worry about the things you can't solve — like existence or world peace or neighbourhood problems — and instead you can console yourself with the things you can choose, like the telly or the right pair of shoes, things you want.

I have few wants but Justin was right, it doesn't make me feel any better. I haven't *chosen* not to want stuff, like some New Age, simple-living type. I just don't know what I want. It's becoming a bit of a puzzle. If the Green brigade are right when they say that the planet won't survive unless we all learn to expect less, then I've got a head start because it seems that I don't expect anything very much.

Justin's long weekend in Manchester with Sandra appears to have gone well. His travel article managed to celebrate the club scene and historic sights, but I get the impression that they spent most of their time just enjoying the rare delights of a five-star hotel before the coming madness.

Planning for the wedding has reached its final stages. They have trimmed it down perfectly by the simple ploy of holding it on a weekday lunchtime in London.

The most determined guests from the north will travel down, but not the freeloaders. And there will be no bridesmaids. The ceremony is to be at St Bride's in Fleet Street, the official journalists' church, with the reception at the nearby hall. There will be no disco. Instead, the happy couple will catch the Eurostar to Paris. At five months pregnant, Sandra has decided not to fly anywhere, not even for an hour.

I didn't know, but there is one gap in the planning. Justin raised it cautiously over lunch in the office canteen.

"Guv, I need to ask a big favour."

"Oh yeah?"

"Is that all right?"

"Is what all right?"

"A favour."

"I don't know what it is yet. I'm not agreeing to anything in advance. Last time you wanted a favour, I had a house guest for seven weeks."

This wasn't going anywhere. I looked down at my meat pie (the menu never identifies the type of meat) and Justin regarded his stuffed pepper. It's amazing when you think that he interviews people for a living. But hey, that's not real life.

"Is this about the wedding?"

"How did you guess?" He smiled.

"Just about everything seems to be about the wedding at the moment."

"'Yeah, I feel like that. Actually, it's about immediately after the wedding."

"Oh yes?"

"It's my best man. He's a good bloke, well organized and everything. I went to school with him. He'll make sure no one handcuffs me on my stag night. He'll get us to the church on time, he won't get pissed, he won't lose the rings."

"But?"

"But he's crap at public speaking. And terrified. Says he can't do the best man's speech. Says it will make him stutter."

"You're kidding. It's the easiest speech. A few embarrassing things about your past, a bit about how you and Sandra were made for each other, a rude joke and then the toast. I could write it myself."

Pause. I had just heard what I had said. This might be something I regret.

"Could you?"

"Could I what?"

"Write the speech." Finally he's getting there. "We'd love you to write the speech. And then, um, we'd like you to make it."

"Make it? Make the best man's speech?"

"Yeah," he smiled.

"You want me to be another best man?"

"Only at the reception. Sort of half a best man, really. You could think of this as a compliment, you know. Sandra really wants you to do it. And my mum."

"I'd be half a best man. That's a compliment?"

"It's not like we're saying you're half a man. Half a best man is still pretty good."

"Thanks."

"So will you?"

"I don't know. I'll think about it."

I couldn't tell him that I was still deciding whether I was even going to turn up for the wedding at all. In case I can't cope. There's a simple reason. Annie and I got married at St Bride's. I'm not sure I want to sit through a wedding there.

Northumberland was Annie's home county. That is to say, she grew up there and spent her youth dreaming of escaping. It left her with an abiding dislike of cold winters, long days of limited choices, and pubs with folk music.

I always liked it — the slower pace, the sense of space, the glimpses of an England we usually ignore in media land. They see things differently there, they have other concerns. I remember, when broadsheet newspapers started to shrink into tabloids to suit the cramped life of city commuters, there were wails of complaint in readers' letters from rural Britain. And one of the main complaints was this: you can't light a good fire with a tabloid, you need a long, rolled-up newspaper to get the flames right into a big hearth. In the country, things have to be useful, and newspapers are for setting on fire.

On trips up north, Annie and I always planned to walk the length of the coast path, but we never did. That's partly why I went there, it was something we had left unfinished. And it was good to get out of London.

Long ago, I liked wandering from place to place. That was one of the joys of my old reporting days, setting off for some town that was completely new to me. (I suppose it was the last time I felt truly myself at work, a nomadic existence before I settled down.) And when I got to each new place, part of me just wanted to explore rather than join the pack of other reporters tracking down the bit of grief or disaster that had brought us there. It was like going out on a hunt, except that by the time we got there the human prey was usually already wounded, or dead. I often thought that it would be nice to have a job where I could wander from place to place with no good reason in mind, but who'll pay anyone to do that?

The other reason for my walk with Ben was that I thought Northumberland might be a good place to think. I'm allowing myself to do a bit of thinking nowadays. See where the thoughts go, instead of blocking them off.

A few things happened that I didn't put in the travel article, and I surprised myself with all of them. First, I admitted to myself that I have not been telling the whole truth in this journal. I suppose I may have been lying a bit, by omission. Second, I actually read a self-help book. Well, sort of. And third, I went to see the other Annie, young Annie, and her family.

I'll take these one by one, the things I did and thought on holiday.

You can do a lot of thinking as you amble along a country path, following the gently rolling gait of a Labrador's rear end, often with no other people in sight and perfect scenery all around. Strange thoughts pop into the mind. I was admiring that wonderful Northumberland sky and thinking how I might describe it. Usually I'm not much into description. I always skip over the descriptive passages in novels. What's the point of them? If it's a sunny day, why can't the author just say so and then get on with the story? I can imagine a sunny day without being told, I've seen sunny days, I don't live in a cupboard. Does the author think that he/she is the only one who has seen the damn sun shine? Even descriptions of people seem fairly pointless. They're just made up, after all. Give me a few details, I say, then get on with it.

But here's a thing: before I left on the trip, I had read the first half-year of the journal and realized what a self-absorbed whinger I seem to have become. Worse, it's as if I don't notice other people, not really. I take them for granted. I don't "describe" them much. At least, it doesn't seem necessary to describe people I have known for ages, because I know what they look like after all, but I've been wondering whether my failure to describe, say, Joan or Arabella means that I have failed to reveal anything else.

And there's Ben's owner, Rosalind. I don't think I've even bothered to name her before now. Caring face, a bit drawn sometimes, boyish figure, thirtysomething, a little stand-offish but kind enough to share her dog. She welcomed my taking him on this break, so she could go away with a new friend until Saturday. It's possibly a new romance but I didn't ask. I seldom even ask her about her job, even though nursing is a proper job that actually makes a difference to people's lives. Maybe I bother with her only for the sake of Ben. What does that say about me?

And Joan. Is it relevant that she is a bit, er, chunky? Not fat, but a bit broad, a bit farmer's-wifey, with curly brown hair that never seems quite tidy no matter what she says to the hairdresser. To her credit, this means that she insists our pages occasionally carry fashions for the "larger woman". It also means that she tones down the wilder fringes of some of our diet articles. She loves to cook, and her husband loves to eat. Hunger, she points out, is the easiest human craving to satisfy fully. You're hungry, so you eat. Simple. Why get guilty about it? (People might wonder how a woman such as Joan found herself running a lifestyle section in these crazy times. The answer is that it was the best available section for an ambitious woman to take over and turn into an empire.) But does her shape matter to me, does it allow her to mother me a bit without me feeling too threatened?

And Arabella? Does it matter that I have not pointed out that she is not only lovely, but actually quite gorgeous and black? In the office, we like to watch the reaction of outsiders when they first meet her after they have previously talked to her only on the phone. Arabella has the poshest English accent in the building. She's a diplomat's daughter and went to a top girls' boarding school. Visitors look for an English rose and then this tall, black vision approaches them. We watch and grin. We are proud of Arabella. Out in the provinces where she started her career, she had a double challenge: her colour upset some, her cut-glass accent upset others. She's on her way up now but she's not pushy about it. Just indispensable.

She is also one of the most fancied women in the building. Men stop talking as she goes by. I've seen Basset stare at her with a forlorn look. Hilariously, I get a kind of kudos from sitting next to her. Blokes say: You lucky thing, looking at her all day. A model's figure, big smile and deep, disturbing eyes. Always a delicate perfume. Always looking cool. And happily married.

So yes, it is significant that I haven't described her. Because, of course, I fancy her too. I would never do anything about it because: I really am not that sort of man; she is a big churchgoer, wears a small crucifix round her neck and, when Annie died, she rang to say that we were in her prayers every day; I have met her lawyer husband at parties and he is built like a rugby forward; and I would fail abjectly. I am a bit in awe of her so we don't talk much about personal things. Arabella's attractiveness is simply a fact of life I live with. I have often fancied other women. Men do. I've just never let it go too far, even in my head.

But the truth is, Joan was right, way back when I first started writing all this, back at the beginning, that first month's chapter. I have been imagining what it would be like to go on a date. I am noticing women more. I could ask a woman out. It's allowed. I don't have to deserve it.

Inside men's minds there is a kind of wild dog living out fantasies of adventure and passion. We walk this beast with care; he could embarrass us. Even the mildest men have amazing thoughts. When the American humorist James Thurber wrote his short story that created Walter Mitty, the timid husband who has endless secret fantasies about heroic adventures, he was asked if he had based the character on anybody. He replied, "Every man I have ever known."

A recent survey has found that many men have three regular, favourite fantasies: a sports fantasy, an adventure fantasy and a sex fantasy. I don't tell anyone but sometimes I still imagine scoring the winning goal in the FA Cup Final. I don't know at what age this stops. Occasionally, in my head, I rescue a child from bullies or a damsel in distress. And right at the back of my mental cineplex, in a tiny studio at the end of all the corridors, there is a soft-porn film on a permanent loop. I don't visit it often, because mostly it just shows fond flashbacks in gentle focus, and the female star is now dead.

I don't look at the women in the office and imagine them in lingerie or bent over a desk, making sounds of passion. (At least, I had not done so until I had to write that sentence.) But I'm a bloke and I'm alive.

My willy is more awake these days. Must be all the damn fresh air and exercise. Maybe recent grief and Y-fronts were better at keeping it contained. It's always up before me in the morning, so that when I go to the bathroom I have to stand about a yard from the toilet and take aim so that an arc of wee will land in the bowl. My willy goes up again a couple of times a day. Fortunately this is not as bad as in younger days when the damn thing was going up and down in my pants all day; you could power a city from the wasted hydraulics

140

of men's unused erections. But it's still a nuisance. Like me, it's not going anywhere. Somehow I am not much driven by will or willy.

On the walking holiday one night, in a hotel bedroom, as Ben snored on the floor, I paused while changing for bed and looked at myself in the mirror. I'm still fairly fit. In the low light, I'm OK. I must be lucky with my genes. I've got no paunch yet. Close up, my face is slightly weathered. I always thought that age might change my looks utterly, but it's only like I've been to make-up. Lines, a bit of grey, that sort of thing. It's still me on the outside. It's the inside that's the problem.

Which brings me to the self-help book.

There's a craze for these books now. It's bizarre. Browsing in bookshops, I have noticed that the self-help section divides into two distinct types ranged against each other on the shelves. There's the career self-help book — how to get ahead fast, be more cunning, shaft your office rivals and kill the competition. Then there's the love/life self-help book — how to slow down, be more lovable, discover the joys of friendship and be more sympathetic to others. And I want to say, hang on, don't these sort of cancel each other out? Maybe if everyone was not so bloody anxious about work, they might be nicer anyway. And suppose everyone read all these books, could everyone get to the top all at once, could everyone be more lovable?

So I hadn't really bothered with this nonsense, except to scorn the occasional reviews and excerpts on our pages. (Seven days to a new life, nine steps to positive feelings, ten laws of a happy relationship, twelve ways to spot a dangerous man and get him out of your life.) I keep suggesting that we should secretly follow one of the shiny-looking authors for a few days, to catch them raging at traffic queues or looking terrible at the newsagents on a Sunday morning, just like everyone else.

Anyway, I had been passing Justin's desk before I went away, and this book was lying beside his keyboard. I skimmed through it and was about to comment when he looked up and said, "Guv, why don't you borrow it and read it so that you can insult it in more detail? I'm supposed to be reviewing it but it's only a reissue. I've finished with it."

The book was about men. Indeed, it's supposed to be a definitive book about men, and it's actually written by a man. I read it during idle moments during the walk. It was not exactly a cheering read.

Men, it said, pretend about life. We want more but we don't quite know what it is we want. We are emotionally timid. We fail to feel our misfortunes properly. We think we cannot live without a woman's love, when really we need more space to be ourselves. We choose our partners before we have worked out where we are going. We need liberating, but we just end up role-playing as vaguely lovable dopes. That sort of thing.

And I was thinking, well, yes, it's a point of view, but what's the answer? Sure enough the author revealed his Seven Steps to Manhood, and I found that I stood no chance.

Step one: resolve your relationship with your father. *I think: Too late!*

Step two: find sacredness in your sexuality. *Hah!*

Step three: resolve issues with your partner. *Too late!*

Step four: engage actively with your children. *Hah!*

Step five: learn to have real male friends. *Hah!*

Step six: find your heart in your work. *Too late!*

Step seven: find your wild spirit in nature. *Hah!*

Well, OK, I suppose I was vaguely communing with my wild spirit by walking the coast path, but it's not turning me into an iron man. I'm not hugging trees or playing the tribal tom-toms just yet.

As for the other stuff, where can I start? For as long as I can remember, people have been slagging off men and I'm sick of it now. (It was OK when I was with Annie, at least I felt loved there.) I wish just once I could read an article by a woman in praise of the normal bloke, the restrained Englishman, who would like to be out exploring somewhere but instead hangs about to listen and lift heavy things when required, in exchange for a bit of praise and some sex.

We may grumble but we don't shout much. That's a strength too. I keep reading articles by women columnists who say how they want their man to be like a best friend, but in the very next breath the same women complain that their men always walk away from arguments. And I want to say, but men don't really argue with friends, that's the bloody point.

We like a bit of peace. We like a few moments of quiet when we first come home. And we like to go and

143

think in silence when there's a Big Problem to solve, and we don't want to sit around and empathize about it until we've got some kind of answer. We talk about it with ourselves inside our heads. No doubt there are a few women like this, but it's mostly men.

This male friendship thing: yes, most male friendships are low maintenance. There are pub mates, workmates. We don't bother each other much and we're fairly tolerant about each other's failings. We don't get too emotional about problems, we offer help — a place to sleep, a career tip — then move on to other things. Sometimes we know there just isn't a solution. We are fairly resigned about life. We really don't expect too much. This is kind of a strength, or at least a self-preservation. I've got a vivid memory of watching the office television back in the eighties, when some feminist spokesperson was being interviewed, and she said, "Women want the chance to have it all, *just like men have.*" And every male wage slave within earshot laughed out loud.

I work surrounded by women and I know that they are different. Maybe they are just better at admitting they need friends. They hang onto old friends and often they seem to be actively on the lookout to make new ones, in a way that a bloke would not. But sometimes their friendships can seem so pressured. They have bigger fallouts. They get together in a crisis but some of them are there only because they are afraid of missing the gory details. And the endless discussions create problems where none existed before.

144

All this is generalizing, of course. Here's a thing: all humans are 99.7 per cent genetically identical. Me, Charlie's Angels, Brad Pitt and the Queen of Tonga. All much the same really. If this is true, then after all this time it would be so good if men and women would agree that we are all mostly well-meaning fools in our way, and that we should stop being snide and instead play to our strengths. Women are good at emotion, many of them are good at caring in a focused sort of way, but when it comes to sheer pointless resilience, someone to keep staggering on alone in silence even when he doesn't have any solution or any idea at all where he is going or why, then it's a job for a man.

Strangely, though, one of the book's suggestions struck a chord. It said that each year, around the time of their birthday, men should go away and spend a few days in solitude. This is just what I was doing on my coast walk. Because the end of the week was my forty-ninth birthday. And that was the reason why I was feeling so introspective. The start of my fiftieth year. I suppose that was the true point of it all. Dig out my battered old hiking boots and have a wander and a think. I'm not sure it had got me very far.

Except that, at the end of the walk, suddenly I felt the need for some human company. I didn't want to spend another birthday alone, or just with a dog. And cunningly, I had allowed myself to be in the very place to put this right.

Annie's brother, Maurice, lives in Berwick-upon-Tweed with his wife and daughter. It's Annie's old hometown and it was only a few miles away. Among all the friends and relatives from my Annie days, they had been the most determined about keeping in touch with me. I hadn't seen them since the funeral. So I telephoned them on the Saturday morning from Bamburgh. As I dialled the number, I realized that part of me hoped that they would not be in, that they would not answer. But I was happy that they did.

Maurice came to meet me at the bus station. As soon as I saw him, I knew that I had missed him these past two years. Annie and her brother were very close. He's a big, genial bloke, as non-London as you can get, really solid. Always looks like his clothes were not quite meant for him, in style or size, and doesn't care. He clasped my hand and slapped me on the back, and I allowed him to load Ben and me into his old Land Rover. I don't know why he needs a Land Rover, as he's a desk-bound council official, but it suits him and I felt fairly safe for him to drive.

Berwick isn't a big place so it was a short ride to their house, the Georgian building that was the old parental home where Maurice and Annie grew up. When their parents fell ill, much of the burden was on Maurice, who still lived nearby. It seemed only fair that, when their parents died, Annie waived her share of the house, and Maurice moved there with his small family. The house is in a lovely spot on the edge of town, overlooking rolling farmland stretching to the sky.

As we pulled up the drive, Maurice's wife Beth opened the front door and greeted me with a smile.

146

"Hello George," she said. "This is a nice surprise. Happy birthday."

"You remembered."

"We've sent you a card in the post. It'll be waiting for you when you get home. But I can offer you a birthday drink."

She stopped to pat Ben, who had approached her with a wag to say hello. Maurice came up with my rucksack just as their daughter appeared at the door.

Annie. Their daughter's name is Annie. In the family, she used to be known as young Annie, to distinguish her from my wife. She was ten when I last saw her, still just a child. Now she's almost thirteen and a faint resemblance to my Annie has become stronger, not just in looks but in how she smiles. This could have saddened me, but in fact she's a cheerful sight.

I hugged Beth. Annie hugged Ben. She wants a dog of her own and has been promised a rescue pet some time after her next birthday. It'll teach her responsibility during her teenage years, according to Maurice.

We sat down for a light lunch. I said that I was just there for the afternoon. They said that I was welcome to stay the night, how pleased they were to see me. Annie took Ben to play in the garden. We watched as he inspected the flower beds, fetched a stick and allowed himself to have his stomach rubbed. Girl and dog lay in the spring sunshine. She talked to him and he listened. He's such a tart sometimes.

"Does she remind you of anyone?" Beth asked.

"It's amazing," I said. "It must be a strong family gene, along with the family name."

My Annie's mother had been an Annie too. She was known as old Annie. Maurice looked fondly at his daughter and said, "I like to think there have been hundreds of Annies stretching back over the centuries, and that there'll be hundreds more in the future."

"That would be nice," I said. "I like that. How's she doing at school?"

Beth, who is a school assistant, said, "She hasn't got your Annie's gift at maths — that'll be where my genes come in, ha ha — but she's happy enough. I'll just be pleased to have a teenager who is not at war with us."

I remembered that giving birth to Annie, their only child, had damn near killed Beth. This must be part of the price of parenthood — fearing rebellion from the person for whom you nearly gave your life.

We took a walk along the river and talked about my Annie. Well, our Annie, I suppose. One reason they were pleased to see me, they said, was that I reminded them of her happy times as a grown woman, beyond Maurice's more personal memories of her early years. I remembered taking this walk with Maurice, my Annie and their parents on the weekend when we came up to announce our engagement. Now we were a parade of survivors.

When we got back to the house, they opened a bottle of wine and the family photograph albums. We looked at pictures of Annie and Maurice growing up, and college days, and my wedding, where Maurice was best man. Young Annie mocked the fashions and the haircuts, giggling, in between stroking Ben who had settled at her feet.

148

I stared at my favourite wedding picture, an unstaged shot, just the two of us looking at each other with utter love, totally happy in our own world. I must have stared for a while, and missed a bit of conversation.

"George, are you OK with this?" Beth's voice.

I looked up to see her searching my face with concern.

"You mean, looking at the pictures? Yes, it's OK. I just haven't done this for a while."

Beth said, "She was very lovely. We all still miss her so much."

Maurice added, "I still reach out to the phone to call her sometimes, then remember that I can't."

We cheered ourselves up. One bottle of wine became two. I agreed that I was staying the night, and rang Ben's owner to check that it would be all right to return him the next day, rather than that night, as I had promised. We closed the curtains, Beth and Annie disappeared into the kitchen and a birthday dinner appeared, with party crackers, and a cake with candles which Maurice had bought in town before collecting me. We wore silly hats from the crackers. Annie read out the jokes. Ben ate the leftovers.

At Annie's bedtime, she said, "Good night, Uncle George."

As she disappeared up the stairs, I said to Beth, "You know, sometimes I forget that I'm an uncle."

And Beth said, "Well, she doesn't. You are her most glamorous uncle, you know. She wouldn't say it, but she's quite proud of you. She tells her friends about her uncle, the newspaper columnist."

Beth and Maurice exchanged looks. I supposed there had been a family conversation about how I could be a better uncle. I just send vouchers at Christmas and birthdays.

"Beth," I said. "I'm not as good at this as my Annie was. If you ever think there is more that I should do, you can always say so."

She patted my hand. "Coming to visit was a good thing, and you did that all by yourself. And Ben has been a real hit."

I looked around for Ben and realized that he was missing. Beth searched all the downstairs rooms, then went upstairs and found that he had gone into Annie's room and fallen asleep beside her bed.

Finally Beth said goodnight, and I sat on the sofa with Maurice. It seemed to me that he was possibly the only man in my world who knew what I had been going through, having once nearly lost his wife, and having lost his parents and my Annie too.

He poured me a whisky and said, "You know, I still think about her every day. And then I think, if it's bad for me, it must be worse for you. I've still got Beth, and Annie has been a terrific comfort. How do you manage?"

I said, "Sometimes I feel like I've been dead myself. It's only lately I've been coming out of it."

We were both speaking quietly, so as not to wake anyone. Maurice now became quieter still, and spoke more slowly, as if trying out a new language.

"Is there, you know, anyone else?"

"Anyone else?"

"A new woman? A new romance? Sorry to ask, Beth just wondered." He looked embarrassed.

"Maurice, there was only one Annie. I was lucky to get her. I don't think there's a way to replace her."

"Maybe so. But you shouldn't feel that you should stay alone. We wanted you to know this. We won't feel bad if you find someone else. We'd be happy for you. Annie would want you to be happy."

I looked at this big man and thought this was one of the kindest things anyone had ever said to me.

"Maurice," I said. "I am so sorry that I lost Annie for you. I was her husband. I was supposed to look after her."

"George, we don't blame you. It was just one of those things."

"You say that I can replace a wife. But you can't replace your only sister, can you?"

"God, no." His voice broke. "No I can't."

He cried a bit then, and I put my arm around his shoulders until the tears stopped. It made a change, me being the comforter. We sat for a while and compared our griefs, and the times when we had to be alone, and how time might yet be a great healer but how we did not want to be numbed of the pain if it also meant losing the sharpness of her memory.

In the night, alone in the spare room, I woke up and had to remind myself where I was. I got that feeling you can sometimes get when you are sleeping in a family home, when you can sense the other people breathing, sense the energy of a child somewhere around the place, and there's a kind of peace. Outside there was a faint breeze rustling a few trees, and it was once again one of those moments where I felt that my Annie was nearby, and that she was not unhappy.

This had not happened for a while. When these moments happen, I stay absolutely still, unsure how to cope. Is it her? Why should it not be her? Then the moment gently faded, and I fell back to sleep.

In the morning, they all came to see us off at the station.

"It's only a few hours to London, you know," I heard myself say.

"Yes, we keep thinking of coming down for a visit," Maurice said. "Sometime in the next year. As a treat for Annie."

"Well, let me know. I'd love to see you all."

On the train back, Ben was lying at my feet as I watched England out of the window: the miles of countryside with Holy Island in the far distance, the bridge at Newcastle, the sudden splendour of Durham and the little figures of people sitting by the river below the giant cathedral. And I was thinking, those little figures are other lives that I'll never know, gone in a glance.

I was also thinking, why doesn't the bloody train inspector stop making so many bloody announcements so we can sit in peace and think? You can't sit quietly with your own thoughts on a train any more. Every other minute they have to announce all the places where the train is going, and repeat it twice (even though the train is travelling at about 125 mph and it's a bit late to get off if you realize you're on the wrong one), then they tell you which bloody tickets are valid on this journey, then they tell you that the buffet is open "for the sale of hot and cold drinks, snacks, sandwiches . . ." (what else would they sell in a buffet? Cattle? Flame-throwers?) then it's time to announce the next stop and repeat that twice, and remind you not to forget your belongings, as if you are a child or a moron.

Maybe people like the reassurance: this is where you are, this is where you are going, this is what you can have along the way. I would prefer to sit in peaceful limbo and just be nowhere.

I was trying to think about my age, my fiftieth year, what I might want and why I feel so cautious and uncertain about change, about doing anything. I guessed that one reason was that with age comes the realization of a terrible fact of life, which is simply this: often in the past you've been wrong, so you're probably going to be wrong again.

You look back and realize that of all the things you have done and believed, many turned out to be complete bollocks — a choice of politician, a point of view about some trend, a choice of car. So you look ahead and realize that, if this goes on, it means that some of the things you believe right now will turn out to be bollocks as well. And yet you must take decisions about the future based on your current beliefs, even though you know that some of these beliefs are bollocks. You just don't know which ones.

153

It's a wonder that I manage to take any action on anything.

But then, I had to take action at York. I had to get off the train because Ben was desperate for a wee. He had been sitting by the carriage door for a while as if asking to be let out, which is rather difficult at 125 mph. So when the intercity finally stopped, I took him out to a nearby hotel garden.

By the time we had picked up another train and then waited for a bus from King's Cross station, we were very late home. Ben greeted Rosalind profusely and then he climbed into his basket. Apparently he slept for twenty-four hours. I went back to my flat and realised that my old hiking boots had nearly fallen apart. The end of an adventure.

That was last week. This is now. Back at the office, Joan is lobbying hard for Justin to be given a staff job. He's in limbo. His six-month contract is over, he's still on the same pay but with even less security, yet he gets married next month and he'll be a dad by the end of the year.

It's like this in newspapers, maybe it's like this everywhere: they expect us to do our stuff pretty much on time every day, but when it comes to managerial decisions about jobs and livelihoods, things slide along for months. Basset has told Joan that he'll do his best, but that she'll owe him a favour if he comes through with a job for Justin. Joan didn't like the sound of that. She doesn't like owing favours to Basset.

154

She told me this as we sat in the office at the end of another day, finishing off some drivel.

"Anyway," she said. "Talking of favours, Justin says that he has asked you to do the best man's speech."

"Er, yes."

"It's quite a compliment, you know."

"So he said."

"He was a bit puzzled about you not saying yes or no."

"You know why."

We stopped and looked at each other.

"I was married in that church. You remember, you were there. I'm really not sure I can go in. I'm not sure I'll turn up."

"Well, you should. You must, George."

"Go on, tell me why."

"Because you can help someone else to be as happy as you once were."

CHAPTER
EIGHT

END OF AN ERA

Anti-Style
by George Worth
12 June

All right, that's enough changes now. I've had enough. My brain is full.

It has been a time of year for launches of new styles, new things, and the relaunching of old things with new looks. So let's do a deal.

They can try to invent new things, and they can pretend to invent new styles. But the old stuff, the familiar stuff, has got to stay the same. Or at least, it's got to keep the same names.

Everyone has moments when the world seems to have changed out of all recognition, and nothing seems quite right. Often it's simply because some tinkering bureaucrat, commercial sponsor or PR consultant has decided to alter the way that something is named, and make the familiar seem unfamiliar.

It's as if they are trying to drive us all mad.

Take a simple thing like football. I lost track of football somewhere around the time that the good old League Cup became, in rapid succession, the Milk Cup, the Littlewoods Cup, the Rumbelows Cup, the

Coca-Cola Cup and, for all I know, the Tampax Cup. It's not just that the game now seems to be played by overpaid boys rather than the knobbly men I remember in my childhood. I am no longer certain what trophies they are playing for.

Familiar shops and businesses rebrand themselves for no apparent reason except to be "modern", and that it's a "new era", thus driving away customers who think that the old store has closed. Even perfectly sensible organizations change their names to things such as Liberty and Relate — as if we can no longer remember more than a single word — and then find that the new name has proved so unmemorable that many years later, newspaper references to Relate are still followed by the words "formerly the Marriage Guidance Council", so that its ultimate title has become even longer and less snappy.

Even in our own homes, we are not sure who is who and what is what. The entire framework of public utilities has changed so much that not only do we hardly remember the names of the companies supplying us with our gas, electricity, water and telephones, but they each compete to supply the other services, so that we can buy our gas from the electricity company, our telephone services from the television company and, probably, our water from Kentucky Fried Chicken (sorry, that should be KFC).

Many of us are no longer even sure which county we live in, after endless tinkering and reforms of local government. Manchester is no longer in Lancashire, though it still supports that county at cricket and

Lancashire's ground, Old Trafford, is actually in Manchester. Middlesex ceased to exist in 1974 yet its name still lives on in local courts and postcodes. Birmingham, the home of Warwickshire cricket, is in a county called West Midlands. And one of the most attractive parts of Scotland was for a while simply called Central Region — how can you identify with a name like that?

And then there are the strange announcements from businesses and banks that say something like: "Blobb Enterprises Inc. is proud to announce that it is entering an exciting new era of progress/customer care/robbing you blind. After extensive refurbishment/a new boss/ mass redundancies, we are marking our new, streamlined service with the simpler name, Blobb! We look forward to . . . blah, blah, blah."

And you think: That's not a new era, it's just new stationery.

What's the problem with all these people that they have to declare the end of an era all the time? It's likely they are suffering from a condition called chronocentrism (yes, it's a real word, look it up), which is the egotistical delusion that you occupy a pivotal place in history that no one has ever experienced before, rather than just the same old company with a new name.

The thing is, I haven't finished with the old era yet. I've been comfortable there. How about you?

(We may, of course, live in a pivotal moment in history if it turns out that we are the generation who finally wreck the planet, but that's more than a bit of rebranding.)

The truth is that just changing a name isn't real change, it's merely another damn thing to remember. We've lost enough of the old certainties. And we've all got enough to remember already, thanks very much, what with pin numbers and phone numbers and computer log-on codes and birthdays and stuff. (And depending on your age, trying to understand weather forecasts in centigrade when your brain is still in Fahrenheit, or trying to stop remembering the value of money in pounds, shillings and pence.)

It's not doing us any good, this steady erosion of any permanence in our lives. People need to identify themselves within a familiar world. No wonder we feel alienated and insecure when so many parts of our internal wiring no longer match up with life outside. If life is a journey, why must they keep changing the signposts?

Real change happens in our own real lives. Real change is things like births, marriages and deaths. Some people still change their names when they get married, and that makes sense. That is a new era for them.

I've been thinking that we should all get our revenge on officialdom and PR idiots by each rebranding ourselves at regular intervals, not just with new fashions and new attitudes but with snappy new names as well. I'll have to run this past a committee, of course, but I've got some nifty ideas for myself.

One-word names with ridiculous punctuation and confused lettering, that's the style. At the very least, it would screw up their mailing lists. If they want our custom, they would just have to keep up.

"Dear Blobb! I am delighted to hear of your change of name. I am also entering a new era due to the lack of any real progress/your useless service/global warming. After minor changes/new underpants/another birthday, I am marking my new life with a simpler name . . ."

It could work. Or my name's not w:@rth!

"Bride or groom, sir?"

"I'm sorry?"

"Which side of the church will you sit on?"

"Oh, I see. Groom, I suppose."

The young usher in a new suit pointed me to the right of the church, and introduced himself as Sandra's brother. I would have met him a few days earlier if I'd accepted Justin's invitation to the stag night. It was a kind thought but I had not fancied the idea of joining a lot of Young People in a bar and then going on to one of the new, up-market lapdancing clubs (to be enjoyed ironically, of course. I was mildly curious, but no thanks). As I had turned down that invitation, I didn't feel that I could turn down the wedding as well.

I arrived for the service with minutes to spare after lurking in Fleet Street for half an hour, looking at old haunts, remembering old days, wishing I could turn back the years to when all the local office blocks were newspapers, when this street was a community of journalists, before the buildings were redeveloped as centres of commerce and we were scattered around London.

At least St Bride's was a familiar face. It is a gem of a church, tucked away down an alley. You don't realize it is there unless you look up and see the white, layered Wren spire, apparently the inspiration for the first tiered wedding cake. It is a church that means something even to godless hacks. There have been a series of churches here since Anglo-Saxon times, and possibly earlier. The City of London's first printing press was established here in 1500. Samuel Pepys was christened in the church that stood here in 1633. Wren's spire survived the Blitz.

The inside seems bigger than it should be. There's a central nave and then two outer naves that are filled only for memorial services to the great and the good. I was hoping to sit at the back so that I could escape if necessary, but Joan and Arabella must have been looking out for me and waved me over to sit between them nearer the front. There was a good turnout from the office. All the girls were there, all in their best hats and frocks, which made a nice change. There was a lot of grinning. People grin a lot at weddings.

The organ struck up and there was Sandra with her dad. Her gown flared out from just below her bust, like a country maid. Her bump hardly showed. There was a garland of flowers in her hair and she was grinning. At the front, Justin turned to see her and grinned too. At this rate, all our jaws would be aching by the time we got to the vows.

All weddings are the same and all weddings are different. The vows and the ceremony are basically the same, so everybody can remember a blur of other weddings going back through the years in an endless recitation of hope. All weddings are different because it's a different couple with their own story. In all the time at Justin's wedding ceremony I did not much remember my own. Something in me accepted that this was their day and not an echo of mine. I felt quite pleased with myself.

I had forgotten how the acoustics at St Bride's are so clear and brilliant. A choir of four can sound like a harmony of cathedral angels. This encourages the congregation to sing along. It helped a lot with Justin's extra twist on the ceremony. Other people might add a harp, a trumpet, a lot of poetic hand-holding or a cute bridesmaid. Justin the media trendy had simply chosen a special song as his final "hymn". Apparently he chose it because it came from his dad's favourite film. As I turned the page in the printed order of ceremony, I found myself staring at the lyrics of that song from *Casablanca*.

In the choir, the soprano did the opening, less-familiar refrain as a solo.

"This day and age we're living in
Gives cause for apprehension
With speed and new invention.
And things like fourth dimension.
Yet we get a trifle weary
With Mr Einstein's theory
So we must get down to earth at times
Relax, relieve the tension
And no matter what the progress

Or what may yet be proved
The simple facts of life are such
They cannot be removed."

The whole choir picked up the next verse on their own, hushed and simple. The organist kept down the scales and the volume so that nobody felt too nervous about joining in.

"You must remember this
A kiss is still a kiss,
A sigh is just a sigh.
The fundamental things apply
As times goes by."

In the congregation, some of us had hesitated at first. But by now we were all up for it.

"And when two lovers woo,
They still say, I love you.
On that you can rely
No matter what the future brings,
As time goes by."

The young guests sang it as a happy song. The older ones were belting it out as an anthem of life. At the front, I could see that Justin's mum had her hankie out, dabbing her eyes as she sang.

"Moonlight and love songs, never out of date.
Hearts full of passion, jealousy and hate.

163

Woman needs man and man must have his mate
That no one can deny."

My tear ducts opened at "man must have his mate".
Joan and Arabella must have seen this coming. They
both put a hand on my back at the start of the line, and
we stayed like that until the end of the song.

"It's still the same old story
A fight for love and glory,
A case of do or die.
The world will always welcome lovers,
As time goes by."

Not a dry eye in the house. Brilliant, Justin, just
brilliant. I wish I had thought of that.

Outside in the rear courtyard we were snapped by the
paper's poshest photographer, returning a favour for
Joan. Then Arabella took a posse of the girls back to
work to keep the office going, while I joined Joan and
the remaining guests to go to the reception at the
nearby hall. I remembered the place — we used to hold
big union meetings here in the old days. Now it was a
shiny venue for conferences and dinners. Before we all
took our seats at a giant U-shaped table, I managed to
grab a few words with Sandra's brother and some of
Justin's friends, to help to fill out my speech.

I'd said to Justin that a wedding speech was the
easiest. Your audience was already happy and willing
you on. Everyone is connected so it's not like a debate

164

when you'll be followed by an opposition speaker (now that would be an interesting idea at a wedding; maybe a rejected lover or pissed-off relative could speak). It's a cinch. Oh yeah.

My mouth still went dry when the master of ceremonies — OK, the head waiter from the caterers — called for silence for the best man. At once everyone looked to the top seats, so they must have thought I was some mad interloper when I rose from my seat at the side. I took a large swig of wine and stared at my notes. They said: Embarrassing moments, Young People, young hopes, job. Much of the rest was barely legible, though it had seemed to make sense when I scribbled it last night.

"Ladies and gentlemen, I have been called upon to speak today as the second-best man. I am told that this is because the real best man, while immensely capable, is too shy to give a speech."

Cries of "No" and "Shame". The real best man blushed bright red.

"I can't believe this to be true. I think the real reason is that Justin and Sandra have wisely realized that if they had a speaker from their own generation, it would be someone who knew all their embarrassing secrets.

"A friend of Sandra, for example, might refer to a certain party during her time in the sixth form, and to events she witnessed at a Club 18 to 30 holiday in Ibiza." (Laughter. Bride and groom grinning warily.) "A friend of Justin might mention certain events at a rag-week disco while he was at university, and the true story of why his interview with a leading stage

165

personality bore no relation to what the man actually said." (As a cub reporter, Justin got drunk on the star's champagne, lost his notebook, and just stole a lot of quotes from clippings of the star's past interviews)

"I know nothing of these matters, so I cannot mention them." (Laughter.)

"Justin and Sandra, of course, are Young People. In the past I have been known to make a few deprecating remarks about the young. This is partly because I am middle-aged, and one of the signs of middle age is that you stop criticizing the generation above you and start criticizing the one below.

"But also there is so much more to criticize.

"I have often asked: what is the point of Young People? They are generally noisy, frequently drunk and make most of our town centres impassable on a Saturday night." (A little jovial heckling here from the younger guests. This is fine, I thought, I can just play the old git. It worked when me and Justin took the piss out of each other.)

"Generally, Young People have all got degrees and yet they know nothing. They all seem to want to be famous but they don't really know what for. They want lifestyles before they've got lives.

"They've got so much stuff but they still want more. Their bodies will never again be so smooth yet they like to pierce themselves with studs and tattoos. They all want cars before they've got anywhere to go. They know the resorts of Spain better than they know most of their own country. They keep wanting new rights like the right to vote at an ever earlier age yet they are more likely to vote for candidates on a reality TV show than at a general election . . ."

Occasional laughter at the start, fading a bit now.

"They eat anywhere and everywhere. They are among the most overweight Young People in Europe. Our mass media feeds them a steady diet of greed and disrespect, so they are also the most debt-ridden, the most drug-addled, the most foul-mouthed, the most sex-mad, violent and drunk. They wave the flag of England at sports matches but have no idea of the essential parts of English history, or of English characteristics such as reserve and duty. They are terrified of being bored. When they get drunk at weekends, they swagger along our high streets breaking windows and attacking strangers in a way that's vaguely reminiscent of the Hitler Youth but without the sense of purpose . . ."

I was enjoying myself so much that it took a while before I noticed that Joan was pulling firmly and insistently at the back of my jacket. I stopped and looked around at the silent faces of the guests. A couple of the older ones had been nodding vigorously in agreement with me, but a few of the others were open-mouthed. Had I gone too far?

"And then . . ."

Get yourself out of this.

And then . . . what?

What had I planned to say?

"And then . . . there's Justin and Sandra."

A few sighs of relief. A few smiles. Obviously, I was going to say the bride and groom were fine examples who totally restored your faith in Young People, blah blah. And really, I was going to say that. It was sort of implied. But as I looked at Justin and Sandra, a flash of my own wedding reception came back to me, a memory of Annie looking glorious, and damn me I started to go misty again.

"It is possible to be too gloomy sometimes. But at my age, there is much to be gloomy about. Bad things happen. You can sit in a church, like we did today, and wrestle with the problem of evil and why bad things happen in a world that's supposed to be good."

My voice broke here, a bit. This was either going to come out as profoundly sentimental or utterly mad. I didn't know which myself. Slowly, hesitantly, I was trying to force words out of my mouth

"Or you can take the grumpy point of view, that the world is simply a sorry and miserable place where you should want nothing and expect nothing, because that way you won't be disappointed. But when you get to that point, the problem is not how to explain the bad things that happen. The problem is how you explain good, how you explain hope.

"Because a bit of hope, a bit of happiness, is a joy and a delight. Sandra and Justin have chosen hope and love and life today, and I can't help but feel pleased for them."

Sandra was listening to this last bit with care and smiled at me. Finally I could remember where I was going. With a flourish, my planned, concluding drivel came back to my mind.

"Young People do have a point really. It's their job to carry on where we leave off and hopefully do things better, or at least no worse. And it's their job to feel their emotions totally and with great certainty. This all starts to make sense at a wedding. And it has been a wonderful wedding today." (Relief all round. Shouts of "Hear, hear.")

"It's now part of my role to read some of the messages from people who could not be here today." I read through a blather of bad puns and jokes about Justin and Sandra's forthcoming first edition. Then Joan handed me the envelope that Basset had given her last night. It takes an old rogue like him to come through with a gesture that had perfect timing, though Joan had taken the trouble to steam open the envelope to make sure that the contents were as promised.

"My final message is from the newspaper. I won't read this out loud, Justin, you can read it yourself later. But I know its contents and I'm happy to say that it is confirmation of a staff job as a general features writer, which is thoroughly well deserved." (Applause, Justin beamed and was hugged by Sandra.)

The job offer was going to be my big finish, but I even managed an ad lib. "This afternoon, I have to say, one of the highlights of the service was us all singing 'As Time Goes By'." (Shouts of "Yes!") "I well remember two lines from that film. One is, 'We'll always have Paris.' That will be true for Justin and Sandra, starting tonight.

"And the last line of the film is, 'This is the beginning of a beautiful friendship.' And if there's one piece of advice that I can give to a couple just starting out, it's that you stay friends, whatever happens, across the years."

An old couple across the room were getting a little misty now and holding hands. I was misting up again myself. Time to stop, especially as I had just remembered that in *Casablanca* the hero gives up the girl.

"I know that Justin and Sandra are good friends, and they have been good friends to me. I would ask you to raise your glasses to toast the future."

I sat down to applause. Joan put her hand on my shoulder. "Well, that came from the heart," she said. "It's a shame you didn't filter it through your brain first."

The end of the reception: all the speeches had been made, most of the drink had been drunk. The bride and groom had wandered the tables, trying to have a word with everyone. Wedding receptions make for hazy memories. Later events of the afternoon have already crowded out my recollection of Justin's speech (lots of thanks, his job, my "memorable" remarks, wishing his dad was there) and Sandra's own speech (she patted her bump and talked of the third person in their marriage).

At the very end, Justin had gone into a huddle with Joan beside the window, talking earnestly over the last of the champagne. Once or twice they glanced at me. I thought they were talking about his job or my speech.

170

Magically, Sandra had managed to change out of her gown somewhere and was now obviously pregnant again in a pair of stretch pants and one of those big floating jackets that look like a leftover from a circus wardrobe. It was time to go.

Nearby a limo was waiting, one of those stretch jobs. A small extravagance. Justin and Sandra waved and were driven off. Some of us hailed taxis to follow them — "Follow that limo" — and in the late afternoon of a sunny day, with that soft glow that can make even London look like a natural place, a small procession turned along Waterloo Bridge and over the Thames towards Waterloo station.

Major railway stations look more like bazaars than transport centres these days. Concourse cafes, shops selling everything from chocolate to handbags, giant posters, ever-changing digital displays. It is as if the trains were an afterthought. Maybe people come to the station for a day out.

I had never seen the Eurostar bit before. They have made it look as much as possible like an airport departure lounge, all steel and chrome and people in uniforms. Through the doors beyond check-in, I glimpsed baggage X-ray machines and passport control.

"Blimey," I said. "It's just like going abroad."

Justin glanced back, his arm around Sandra.

"Yes, you ought to try it sometime."

"Maybe. You never know."

Sandra disentangled herself from Justin and hugged everyone: her family, Justin's mum, friends, me. It's nice to be hugged happily. Perhaps the NHS should set up an extra service, the national hug service, where sad gits can go just for a happy woman to give them a great big hug. It might have a long waiting list but it would certainly make a lot of people feel better. Me, for a start.

"Thanks for everything," Sandra said. "It's been a good day."

"That's OK. By the way, what did happen in Ibiza?"

"You'll never know!" she said. "But you described some of my old friends quite well in your speech!"

Then there were the last farewells and they were off, the doors sliding shut behind them. The rest of us weren't sure what to do so we wandered slowly away, breaking into small groups as we drifted back towards the Thames.

I found myself walking with Joan, chatting about this and that, then we stood with our backs to the ugly concrete South Bank complex and watched the river flowing past. Joan was just in front of me, leaning over the riverside railing, when I saw that her shoulders were moving up and down. At first I thought that she was laughing at some memory of the day, then she turned and I saw that she was crying. What is it with me and tears, has it become contagious?

"You stupid man," she said.

"What?"

Then she actually hit me. Both hands flat out, bang on my shoulders. She was not only crying, but angry and crying.

172

"You stupid, stupid man!" She was shouting.

"What? What have I done?"

"That car? That fucking car! Is that all you're stuck on? Is that why you can't let go? You think it's not just the grief, it's because you bought a car?"

Pause. So that was her earnest conversation with Justin. I felt my face freeze.

"Justin talked." I looked away. "He said that was just between us."

"He spoke to me because we're your friends. Some of the wedding guests had been asking about you, which is not surprising after that bizarre speech. It just came out. Why the hell didn't you talk about this with me?"

"Because it's hard enough not talking about it and just living with it." I was shouting now. "Because she was one of your best friends and I killed her."

She stood about two inches from my face and looked straight in my eyes, then she spoke slowly and carefully as if telling something to an idiot.

"She . . . loved . . . that . . . car."

Pause. *Newsflash*.

"You heard me. She loved that car. The day you bought it she rang me up and told me about it. She was excited."

"No," I said. "It terrified her. I forced it on her. She tried to talk me out of it."

"George, she put up all those objections because she was saying what you would normally say. All your usual moans about doing anything spontaneous and reckless. She couldn't believe you wanted it. She was so pleased.

173

She gave you a chance to back out, to make sure you were sure."

"Bollocks."

Silence again. We both turned to face the river. Time passed. And then, well, I don't know, sometimes it's easier to talk about the serious things when you are looking out at nothing.

"She'd been worried about you." Joan in a quiet voice. *Newsflash. More news. Stay tuned.*

"Why?"

"You were settling into middle age too early. She was worried that you weren't doing enough to stay happy. That there were too many things that you didn't like, and not enough that excited you."

"She excited me. She made me happy."

"George, she knew that. She was happy with you too. All those men at your age who wander off with some young piece or disappear behind a newspaper most of the day, and you never tired of her. Some women were jealous, you know."

"Jealous of her having me?"

"No, don't be daft you old fool. Jealous of the two of you."

Silence again. *More details are now coming in. Live from the scene.*

"Also, she was planning to use the car for a bit of bargaining with you."

"Go on."

"Like maybe, she could treat herself to a decent home computer at last, with a bit of encouragement from you."

"What? She could always treat herself to anything she wanted."

"Oh come on, George. You took the piss when she got herself a mobile phone. She needed a new computer more and more for her work. She was having to go into work early some days just to catch up with emails that could have been done from home."

"But I wouldn't have stopped her."

"That's not the same. She wanted to share with you."

"I thought you said she was happy. Joan, don't do this to me."

"She was happy. But I think you would have gone through some changes if she had lived, you know."

I stared at her. This was getting a bit much. I was becoming angry. Joan led me over to a nearby bench and we sat down, half turned towards each other. She started again.

"Things happen in middle age, George. It's the end of an era. The balance changes. Women get a bit harder and argue more. Men get a bit weaker and confused."

"Like lovable dopes?"

"Yes, quite. Why do you say that?"

"Just something I read somewhere."

"George, I think she would have wanted me to say all this, if it helped." Her voice dropped again. "You know she never stopped regretting that she didn't make you a dad. It would have given you something extra now."

"I'd have been a crap father."

"You would have been a good father. You had a great relationship with your own father. And you are not bad with young people. The girls at the office like you."

175

"Oh come on."

"If they make a mistake, you sit with them and you go through an article saying what you want. You don't rant. You don't lech. You're patient. George, sometimes you can be kind."

I snorted. "Work is all too silly to have arguments about."

Other people must have been walking past us as Joan dissected my life bit by bit, but I didn't notice anyone else. It was like being trapped in an invisible chamber with only the sounds of Joan's voice and my objections.

"George, think back. You'd been a bit gloomy for a while. Before the crash. Before Annie's parents. Maybe when your dad fell ill. A father's death is a big moment for a man. It's possible you never had the time to get over that. You know you'd started to lose some of your energy though perhaps you hadn't felt it so badly."

"Maybe. You know I wasn't happy at work. So?"

"What I'm trying to say is this: maybe this gloom of yours isn't just about the deaths. Maybe if all the deaths hadn't happened, you'd be going through something like this now anyway, though you'd have more support. It's about you. Middle age. Midlife. Weary of life, wary of change. All that stuff. And from that point of view, buying the car was a good thing. You were trying to break out of the run of misery, but you were beaten back in again. Now you are stuck because you blame yourself for the car."

"This is just psychobabble. I insist on buying a death trap and that's fine?"

176

"Annie said that driving with the roof open was like being young again. She joked about the fear thing. It was like you were a young man talking her into doing something reckless, like riding pillion on a motorbike or something. And she knew you were a good driver."

"She was wrong."

"She was right. No one could have avoided that crash. I was at the inquest. I heard it all. You didn't make a mistake. Inquests are full of if onlys and people who made mistakes, mothers who left their toddlers alone for a minute, drivers who looked the wrong way at just the wrong time. You did nothing wrong."

"Bollocks again."

"The only thing you did was that you survived. Stop feeling guilty about it."

She looked thoughtful for a moment and went on, "We're both survivors in lots of ways. Bloody hell, look how old we are in this industry, surrounded by youngsters. Look how many people have fallen by the wayside over the years. The drink and the divorces and the bad luck. The heart attacks and the cancers. We survived. I'm buggered if I'm going to feel guilty. I'm lucky, I'm grateful, I'll try to share my luck and gratitude as far as I can, but I'm not going to go through life feeling guilty because otherwise I'd just end up as an empty shell."

"Like me."

"No, you're on autopilot, George. You are hardly doing anything you like. It shouldn't matter but I have seen you happy and I know that you're wasted." She held my hand. "Sometimes I feel like I'm using you. At the paper. You're trapped in our section because Basset is in charge of features now and he doesn't want to help you. I love you being so grumpy in your column. But you don't have to be like this in real life."

She paused for breath. I stared out at the river again. The sky was starting to darken and the alcohol was starting to wear off. I was feeling hungry and a bit lost.

"Have you finished?" I asked. "Any more advice before I go home?"

"Well, a lot of the girls are of the opinion that what you really need is a bloody good shag."

We both laughed.

"George, you don't have to find someone else. Try just finding you, that would be a good start."

Then she got up, kissed me on the cheek and walked away.

CHAPTER
NINE

SUMMER LOVING

Anti-Style
by George Worth
17 July

Romance is in the air. It's summer and there's a lot of bare flesh about. We are long past that day when suddenly it seems like every woman has decided not to wear a bra. (How do you all know the right day? Is there a formal announcement? Hey, it's National Bare Breast Day!)

People are going on holiday. How do holidays get sold? With the lure of romance. People are buying their annual books at the airport. What are these books about? Romance. At home, we are lured to the cinema with light, fluffy summer films. Naturally, they are romances, with happy endings.

And it's all a load of pap.

Travel can be an adventure for the body and spirit. Books can be adventures of the mind. Cinema can take us to places and situations beyond our imaginations. Why is romance the only game in town, the measure of everything?

Once upon a time, Hollywood made films in which the heroes actually went away at the end *without the girl*. Oh yes they did. The hero might go away nobly, like in *Shane* and *Casablanca*, or sadly, like in *The Way We Were*, or not giving a damn, like in *Gone with the Wind*. But he left all the same. He had some other reason for living, beyond simply trying to impress the nearest hard-to-get bonk.

And there were plenty of television series where the hero was on an endless journey and went off alone at the end of each episode, ensuring that he would be free to have another adventure the next week without ever settling down. From *The Fugitive to Quantum Leap*, these heroes did not get slagged off for failing to commit.

Now it seems that all the mainstream movies are propaganda for romance. If you've got it, you're a success. If you are desperately seeking it, you are normal. If you'd rather go for a walk, you're a failure. Romance and sex are the new religion, the focus of our yearnings, the great mystery. Cinema usually expresses this in the shape of some bone-faced actress whose love is the answer to everything. Well, sorry, but it isn't.

One of my favourite films, *Groundhog Day*, is ruined by its romantic ending. Up to then, it's great. There's this cynical, world-weary guy, Bill Murray, trapped by some strange spell into living the same day over and over again in a small New England town. He rages with frustration, he tries to escape, he tries suicide, but he's still trapped. Gradually he learns to live with it. He gets to like people. He tries to save lives. He takes the opportunity to read great books, to learn the piano and ice sculpture. But he is still trapped. Clearly he has not yet proved himself. There is something he must do to win back his life, something even more meaningful. And what is it? It turns out that he must win the love of Andie MacDowell. And, er, that's it.

I'm still working out the meaning of life, but I am pretty sure it's not Andie bloody MacDowell.

Romance can be one of our highest emotions, but it can also be a cop-out and the lowest common denominator for advertisers seeking to make us think there is something big missing in our lives and that it can be bought. In this, I am at one with the most militant feminist: it's not compulsory for men or women to be having a romance in order to have meaningful lives.

We are all the heroes in our own movies. Sometimes we get the girl, sometimes we don't. Sometimes when we get the girl, we don't get to keep her. Living with that, and trying not to get bored with ourselves, is part of being alive.

That's it, really. I just thought someone should say it.

"Wow, radical stuff," says Justin the married man, back from his honeymoon.

"I'm sorry?"

"Now you're anti-sex as well as anti-shopping. You'd never get this into a novel."

"Sex-and-shopping blockbusters are out, haven't you heard? It's all rite-of-passage stuff now. And romances, of course."

"But who needs sex anyhow?"

"Precisely."

So the girls think that all I need is a good shag? This has been stuck in my mind. Like, that's it? Yet it appears that I am far from the only one in the office with no sex life at the moment. As we churn out the usual summer features — the perils of holiday romance, sexy summer fashions, the right age to let teenagers go on holiday unsupervised — the office positively crackles with frustration. Recently we reported the useful nugget of information that there are 120 million acts of sexual intercourse across the world each day. But none of them involves people here.

There are the girls, for a start. Oh yes! This is one of those times when the majority of them don't seem to have a bloke, so there is a background chorus of lamentations about the absence of spare men in London. Odd, as I have not noticed that the city is suddenly empty of men. But of course they mean *suitable* men. Men of a certain appearance, and occupation, and general acceptability. (The girls are so insulting about men. I blame those women-friendly comedies where all the men are bastards or fools who can be redeemed only by a woman.) Over the past few years I have heard all this before, until one by one they meet someone not previously on the suitable list, such as a football nut, or a plumber, or a childhood friend, or an impoverished East European émigré, and they all go off and redeem each other.

Then there's Basset and his office squeeze. I don't think there's anything happening there at the moment. He no longer steps into our section if she's around. A certain amount of glowering has been observed, some tension has been felt, and possibly there's been some weeping in the ladies' toilet. We are a little worried there might be some general fallout from this. We are hoping that the problem will somehow go away.

Then there are the newlyweds, whose happy honeymoon already seems like a distant memory. Sandra is almost seven months pregnant, which can't be easy in a hot July. According to Justin, by day she likes to lie in a cool bath, her stomach cresting the water like a desert island. By night, she lies in bed groaning with discomfort, padded with an assortment of pillows and cushions, clutching Justin's Highgate hot-water bottle filled with cold water. She occasionally thumbs through one of the rash of pregnancy magazines that fill the newsagents' shelves in between the bridal magazines and the true-life magazines that largely feature marital break-ups.

The lovely Arabella revealed that her husband had been away on a case in the Midlands for several days but is due back the next day. She has remained calm.

And Joan has confided that her husband Matthew has been having checks in the willy department. I don't think she meant to reveal quite so much. It began when she had to leave work early one afternoon to fetch him from a day in hospital. Pushed a little further, she revealed that he was having an internal check on his prostate and bladder, achieved by inserting a camera probe the thickness of a biro up his penis. I cannot even think of this without crossing my legs. Matthew is a lovely bloke, although thirty years as an accountant

183

have left him with a slightly worried expression. I bet he looked worried that day.

The way Joan told it to me the next day, the pre-op involved him lying naked on a bed as two young nurses appeared. One took hold of his penis. That was the high point. The other nurse produced a device that looked like a cake icer, inserted the nozzle into the mouth of his willy, and squeezed the contents into him. This was the local anaesthetic. It felt like he was being frozen. He had dim memories of being wheeled down a corridor, and of lying in near darkness with his legs apart while a man wielded a tube that seemed to be connected to him. The man kept looking sideways, and when Matthew looked he saw an image of a red tunnel that he realized was a projected image of his own innards. Then he recalls lying back in the ward as a doctor told him that he was fine, and that the symptoms that had worried him and his GP were probably just middle age.

This was all a little more than I wanted to know. Age is catching up with my generation. I look ahead and think it can't be long before bits of me start to fall apart.

According to an item in the health reports, the prostate needs to be (ahem) flushed twice a week to stay in good condition. I pretty much managed that in my married life, but I am now some way behind.

For I am the champion of abstinence here. My willy may be awake but I have realized that it will take a certain amount of mental rewiring before I can start waving it around. In my head, I'm sure, part of my brain still thinks that I am married. When you've been married and faithful for a couple of decades, you acquire the ability to fancy other women without doing anything about it, like admiring a work of art yet accepting that it will never be your possession, even on loan.

After Annie died, it was months before I stopped sleeping on "my" side of the bed and allowed myself to sleep in the middle. I am comfy enough there now, though I am bored with sleeping alone. It's not the sex that I miss the most, it's the sense of closeness, the night-time chats, laughing at trivia, easing anger, feeling valued just for me, and not always starting the day with just myself. The idea of plunging back into some sort of active sex life is still bizarre, if it's just for the sake of the sex. When I was last out there dating, it was in the halcyon days between the arrival of the Pill and the big arrival of Aids. It's like I've been in some kind of sexual fallout shelter, safe from all the dangers of the world. And when I stick my head out of the sealed entrance, the all clear hasn't sounded, the alarm is still blaring. What do people do these days to prove they are safe? Carry a blood donor card, or a list of safe former lovers?

I suppose it's all condoms now. And here's a thing: this is a way for a forty-nine-year-old bloke to feel young again — but not happily young. Stupidly young. Embarrassingly, stutteringly, adolescently young. It's simple. Just replay one of the worst rites of passage of a teenage boy — go into a chemist's shop and consider buying some condoms.

I was at a big chemists the other day, buying some multivitamin tablets which may nor may not be a complete waste of time, and I just happened to look at the display of condoms. I knew there had been changes going on out there in the world of latex, but I didn't realize quite how many. I cannot believe the range, not just all the different textures, and the different chemicals, but the ones that glow in the dark. And the flavours, such as banana. What sort of trade-off does that involve? Some women don't like the taste of semen, but they love sucking banana-flavoured rubber? It's not serious. Sex is unreal for me now, and that's a comfort. I think of it like I think of scoring a goal in the FA Cup Final, as a fantasy with no danger of reality kicking in.

Last on the list of sexual abstinence is Ben, who has never had any sex anyway. Sometime in the past, before my neighbour got him from a dog-rescue home, someone had taken the liberty of having his balls removed. If he remembers having them, he doesn't show it. Sometimes he sniffs at a lady dog on the Heath, rarely he half-heartedly tries to mount one but he doesn't know how. Once he tried to mount from the side. He doesn't know what he's doing so the risk of rejection never seems to disturb him.

And it's too hot for him now anyhow. On a summer's evening, the Heath is full of big, panting dogs making their way determinedly towards the ponds, where they stagger in to get cool. Ben just stands there up to his chest in the cold water, revelling in it, then swims for a rubber ball that I throw for him, far into the big pond.

186

A glorious sight, Ben cutting through the water, the trees beyond, the evening light.

After this evening's walk and his swim, we sat in the long grass overlooking the ponds. Ben rolled around to dry out, then just lay there with me, looking and listening. Ducks flew in lazily from the pond higher up Highgate Hill. People wandered past below us. Behind us, fathers and children played with kites.

Nowadays, in these moments, I feel all right, even happy to be alive. I may not deserve it, but how many of us really do?

It's night-time, in the flat, just me. I'm not sleepy. For weeks I have been thinking over the other stuff Joan said after the wedding, about Annie and me. Such as the suggestion that I had long become a bit of a stick-in-the-mud as far as change was concerned.

All right, I plead guilty. Unintentionally guilty. With mitigating circumstances. Like, we had been through so much, losing our parents and everything, I suppose I did not have the energy to change what we had left, predictable as it was starting to become. Our comfortable life.

What makes you feel older, change or the lack of it?

Women prefer the scenery to be changed after a major act in the play of life. Thinking back, I remember a few hints about the need for a proper home computer. And maybe also some extensive redecoration in the house. And landscaping the garden. And one or two remarks about how male fashions had changed lately. And how about us joining a local activity group together, or both joining a health club? Or having a health check? And the computer again.

"A home computer? Not for me," I'd have said, or thought. "I drown in enough emails from the moment that I log on at the office. It's like a fax machine that scrolls out right into your face. It's maddening. There's a word for it now: infomania. The mental distraction caused by too much electronic input. Do we need this at home too?"

If Annie really wanted it, I would have gone along with anything, eventually. We usually managed to negotiate things somehow. But I admit that I wasn't taking up the hints, coming up with my own ideas, worrying about wanting to please her, as I would have done in the early years. I wasn't asking her for directions. (Unfunny joke: why don't men ask for directions when they get lost? Answer: because often they are not really interested in where they are meant to be going.)

So I am guilty of keeping the life we had. There's a good side to that. We were still happy. We were still together. We were still us.

I've tried to think: when did I change from the sort of man who liked being up to date, to the sort of grump who was proud of being out of date? Sometime in my forties, I guess, when there was too much real-life stuff happening, and it seemed like the pace of so-called progress meant it was going to be hard to keep up anyway. Each generation of technology changed so fast, I realized it was possible to miss out two or three changes without it mattering very much, because anything I bought would be out of date within a few months. Somehow I stopped being curious about stuff. And about life.

What was the last new invention I really liked? Can't remember. OK, what were the niftiest things that had come along in my adult life? Cashpoint machines, so you can get your own damn money when you want instead of being broke all weekend just because you didn't get to the damn bank on a Friday afternoon. Those adjustable office chairs with wheels, so you can be comfy and whizz around the desks. Video recorders, so you can watch the few programmes that are worth watching, as they always seem to be on at the same time on different channels. And personal headphones, so you can listen to your own music on a beach somewhere. And, er, that's about it, really.

There was a woman writing on a letters page the other week, about a game she played with her husband. The game was called "When you are dead, I shall . . ." Apparently it's a jokey way of highlighting marital annoyances. When you are dead, I shall . . . be able to find an unsquashed tube of toothpaste, make love a new way, decorate the house with taste and keep it tidy.

What would Annie have said after the dots? Would she have said, buy more modern stuff?

And what would I have said? It's hilarious, but I'd have said, meet more people I like. As a marriage goes along, somehow it's the wife who takes charge of the social life and you realize that most of "our" friends are actually "her" friends. Many of them were fine, of course, but somewhere down the line I missed having more friends that were mine. I didn't like many of her

189

City types, I admit that, but she didn't like some of my old reporter mates either. She said reporters were just glorified ambulance-chasers really. I said that investment experts were just headless chickens, especially after the dot.com bubble burst.

And this was one of the happier marriages, truly.

But maybe we were due for some changes.

And then, there's the car. By Joan's argument, buying the car was not a Bad Thing after all. It was really a Good Thing that went tragically wrong. So this is not all about grief, or guilt, but also some midlife crisis thingy as well. This middle-age I'm living in.

(Secretly at work, I have surfed for details about male midlife crisis. There seem to be two stages. First a crisis of personality when home and work life become predictable. Then a gradual physical crisis as testosterone levels decline. Symptoms can be similar to grief, including depression, moodiness, anxiety, low libido and just generally feeling sorry for yourself, all worsened by the male instinct to deal with problems alone rather than talking them through. Interesting, although I'm not sure how to pursue this further. And, blimey, if this is midlife, how much worse is old age?)

If Joan is right, even just about the damn car, then I've been thinking about this the wrong way, addressing the wrong problem. This is now entering the realm of philosophy — that if you want to think up the complete answer, you first have to make sure that you are thinking about the right question. But then, maybe the problem is that I have been thinking about it all too damn much anyway. Just thinking hasn't done me much good. This is supposed to be a journal about my emotions.

These are late-night thoughts. The sleepless and lonely take refuge in their thoughts. If we are lucky, the thoughts are not too extreme.

So now, er, I have been thinking about emotions. OK, it's still thinking, but at least it's a start. It helps that I have been feeling more of the nicer emotions lately, and actually finding myself interested in the emotions of other people. (I've rung Maurice two or three times since I got back from Northumberland. Just chit-chat, but it must be a good thing.)

There's a definition of depression: it is when your emotions have not caught up with events. You can know something as a fact, even as a great truth, but unless you have accepted it emotionally you don't truly know it and you won't act on it. Like, this is now the twenty-first century. Fact. I am in my fiftieth year. Fact. My wife is dead. Fact. The brain knows what has happened, but the human being can't accept it until he is ready. I'm working on it now.

I can see that there are limits to thinking. There are limits to the intellect. Thought alone can't explain or solve everything, not without feelings or emotions. Our reaction to music, say, or beauty, is not just thought. The great decisions of our lives are emotional — whom we love, where we like to live, what we like to do. We use our intellect to control the excesses, but we remain an emotional lot. Perhaps we even decide our emotions first and then form our opinions around them.

But I am not just my emotions, am I? Just letting rip all my emotions as a way to feeling better would be so self-indulgent, like a kind of comfort shopping in my head. Just let it all pour out, lose control, feel even weaker. (Maybe even a bloke like me has a scared little caveman inside his head, worried about being left behind on the hunt if he shows weakness or fear.)

Anyway, would it make me feel better in the end to become really emotional now? And is that the only point, just to *feel* better? Some people feel better when they go shopping. I could feel better with a bottle of wine. It would not mean that I *am* better.

There is a place where emotions and thoughts meet, and that's attitude. It's a sort of balancing act. Getting the right attitude to life, finding an approach that works, that's you. You think, you feel, you're someone. It's who we are when we are not actually thinking. My attitude needs to change. I'm out of balance, unhinged, the scales are moving up and down and they still haven't settled, the weights have gone.

Yet to have an attitude, you've got to have an attitude "to" something. The job in hand, the thing, the point of it all.

Is that the question I'm really asking: what's the bloody point? Maybe everyone asks this sometimes. What's the point? How should we live?

I'd like to discuss this with someone, face to face. I can't exactly raise it in the pub. "Thanks for the drink, the footie's finished, so hey, what do you reckon is the point of living?" I don't think so.

192

Really, I'd like to talk about this with my dad. Joan was right about one thing for sure. I did have a good relationship with Dad. I was lucky, I got to know the man. He had a kind of wisdom. I didn't always agree with him but at least we could talk. A few times a year, he'd come to London on day trips by train to catch up with some exhibition or concert, and we'd talk about anything and everything. He was not much interested in looking round the shops. He never bought into the lifestyle culture either. He'd always say that when you're dead, at your funeral nobody ever talks about what you owned, they talk about what you were like.

Towards the end, when his mind was leaving us bit by bit, and every visit to him was like another good-bye, those were some of the most powerful emotions I've ever felt. His funeral was packed. People remembered a thousand kindnesses.

I should have more wisdom by now. I should know how to live.

So what's the bloody point?

Here's a thing: I've been reading some philosophy. Well, that might be obvious from the way I have been rambling on. I blame Justin for this, for something he said back in January when he was talking about how to be happy. I blame him for a lot lately.

It turns out there is nothing like philosophy for making your brain hurt and realizing the dangers of Thinking Too Much. Some modern philosophers are clearly strange men — they are usually men — who

Think Too Much. Some of them argue that life is an illusion, that none of us may actually exist, yet presumably these guys still go to the toilet or use an umbrella in the rain like everyone else. Others say that the mind is only a machine and nothing more, and that consciousness is just the machine working, yet presumably these automatons still feel love and watch the telly.

I think we're real. But what's the point, eh? I made some notes. There seem to be three options:

1. *There is no point, it's all a horrible joke.*
Spokesman: Arthur Schopenhauer. I remember Justin mentioned this guy and some theory about the importance of controlling self-will. Having looked this up, I'm not sure whether Justin fully understood it, or even whether he was taking the piss a bit.

For a start, this man was a loner, hopeless at romance, hated noise that intruded on his thoughts, felt that most people were not really worth talking to, and seems to have loved only his dog (a poodle). Why did Justin think of him while talking to me?

Anyway, Arthur was a rampant pessimist from Danzig and had an inherited fortune that left him free to dwell on his thoughts. And these thoughts were: existence is meaningless and our expectations of happiness just make us more miserable as life is really about suffering. Instead of seeking enjoyment, we should just try to avoid pain. We are driven by a relentless will but if we ever found happiness, we'd be terribly bored. Books, formal music and other people's misfortunes can help to put life into perspective. I suppose his modern motto would be: shit happens.

And another thing: he said that romantic love was solely the result of a will to breed, which was all that women were good for. As Annie and I shared romantic love with no hope of "breeding", I distrust this bitter little man. Lately he appears to have become recommended reading for the unhappy and broken-hearted. Frankly, I'd rather go shopping.

2. *The point is to be the best that we can be.*
Spokesman: Michel de Montaigne. Married with a wife and daughter. Inherited a castle and estate near Bordeaux (lucky chaps, these philosophers), leaving him free to spend his days in his extensive library. He liked discussions over dinner, believed in tolerating other cultures, was a bit disrespectful of authority, and felt that animals were often wiser than humans because their instincts were better.

His view: life is subject to chance and the frail unpredictability of our bodies (he mentions farts and willies). Complex intellectualism can be a waste of time, it's better to strive for simple wisdom, which means living happily and morally, and trying to have a beautiful soul. We should be less proud of our achievements and less embarrassed by our failures because in the end "we are but blockheads". In other words: we should not be so hard on ourselves.

View on romantic love: fine as far as it goes, but true friendship is the highest relationship.

3. There is a bigger point, vast and eternal.
Spokesman: er, OK, how about my dad? Nice bloke, worked all his life, married, one argumentative son.

His view: the God thing. An ultimate truth, a reality beyond appearances. We are part of some eternal balance but can't be fully aware of it any more than (my dad's metaphor) an electron whizzing around inside an atom, yet we are vital all the same. Faith means accepting the unknown, revealed in glimpses: human yearning, the religious instinct, music, awe, hope, love, beauty, altruism, connectedness, a miraculous universe. Motto: love and action.

View on romantic love: I remember him saying, after seeing a film with me, that he could not understand how people of this generation were so transfixed by romantic love and yet so dismissive of religious belief. To him they both required a leap of faith that changed lives.

I stopped thinking about all this and started thinking just about Dad instead, because two more memories had come to me, and one was entirely new.

The first memory: I was a teenager looking for something to rebel against, and I picked on Dad's gentle religious faith, which he never forced on me. "The trouble with religion," I said, "is that there are too many rules." Back then I didn't want rules.

He did a dramatic, startling thing. He took hold of a Bible, broke the spine, ripped out the Gospels, handed them to me and said, "Here, show me all the rules in that." Very clever. I read all the way through and found there were hardly any specific rules on what to do. A lot of general stuff about love and forgiveness and belief, but the clearest list of actual practical instructions was the bit from Matthew 25 that was in Dad's final notes. Feed the hungry, help the sick, greet the stranger. That was what Dad's local charity work was all about. Churches needed rules for organization, he said, but religion was really about spirit and people.

The second, new, memory: it was near the end, in the final months, a blur of grief. Now I was a middle-aged son, sitting by my ailing dad, wondering if his mind was with us today or not, wishing for at least one last, clear conversation with him. That wonderful, kind brain, fading away. And I turned to my mum and said something like, "You know, I think he's one of the wisest men I have known. I wish he'd written down his thoughts about life."

I now think he might have heard me. That's what all those bits of paper were for. He did it for me because I asked. Simple rules of how to cope. A little trite, yes, but it was all he could manage, staggering through the darkness of his mind to leave a message. This was his side of a last conversation.

Thanks for the thoughts, Dad. Sorry I took so long to remember. They may not help like you hoped, but the important thing is that you wrote them for me.

Hello, Dad. Thanks for loving me.

Oh shit, I miss them all so much. I miss putting my arms around my wife and telling her I loved her, because that's when I felt most worthwhile. I miss telephoning my mum and telling her that I was all right. And I miss my dad, having someone older and wiser, someone to live up to.

They all live on in me, I know. Ideas, memories, bits of genes, little things that were unique and special. But at some point I should be my own man, not just bits of other people. I wonder what will live on after me.

I don't want to become the older generation, the next ones in line for sickness and death. Bloody hell, I'm nearly fifty.

I feel lonely and scared. Is that emotional enough?

In the radio studio this month, once again they have used one of my columns for the theme of the programme. They keep doing this when I am on. This time Maggie's subject is: Can we be happy without romance? The guests — heaven help us — are a youngish romantic novelist, a thirtysomething lapsed nun, a seen-it-all agony aunt and me. I am the only bloke.

It means that I am going to be talking in public about the possible merits of celibate singlehood, in front of the one woman who might be interested in shagging me.

Just before we go on air, Maggie turns to me and says, "George, I just wanted to ask, is it all right this time to say that you're a widower?"

I say, "I suppose you'll have to. Otherwise I'd just be some sad git who has no excuse for being alone."

The others laugh warily, then we are on. I don't mind this now. I'm up for it. It's like going on trial. I can spot the presenter's tricks, nudging people through the cautious opening, spotting points of controversy in the comments, making eye contact with the person most likely to argue so that they will speak next. Oh yes, I'm a radio pro now.

The novelist says, well, romantic love is a vital life force, it makes the world go round and there's nothing wrong with fantasizing about the perfect romance.

The agony aunt says that the fantasy of fiction can build up false expectations about romance and sex, which life can't always supply, leaving people even more depressed. As for sex, she comes up with a quote from a much-shagged actor who in his later years once observed that sometimes the sex had been very good but sometimes he should just have gone for a walk instead.

The lapsed nun says that she had enjoyed walks herself but in the end she had met the right man and decided she would not be true to her humanity if she did not stop walking and, er, have a lie-down.

"So, George Worth, what do you think?" says Maggie. "In your column last week you said there was a danger that sex and romance had become the new religion."

I glance at the ex-nun. "Well I suppose that one point of a religion is that it should enhance life and not become an activity for its own sake. I don't think romance makes a good religion. Even when you find a good partner, it's not the answer to everything. There are so many aspects to our lives, other relationships, other interests and passions. It seems to me that we are underrating ourselves if we become obsessed with just one part of life."

This is the bit that I had thought up beforehand. I don't know where I go from there. Happily, the novelist cuts in.

"Well, that's something of a male view," she says. "You should realize that the great love stories reach into women's hearts and inspire them towards happiness."

I am just wondering whether I am allowed to utter the words "sexist bollocks" live on air when the ex-nun speaks for me.

"Excuse me," she says. "But that's just not true. The great love stories of fiction are all about misery and emotional enslavement. There are a few moments of delight followed by endless heartache and sometimes even death. Reading them when I was young was almost enough to put me off the whole idea. I'm thinking of stories like *Anna Karenina* and *Romeo* and *Juliet* and *Doctor Zhivago*."

"That's interesting," says Maggie. "Then there's *Wuthering Heights*. And *Antony* and *Cleopatra*. And *Carmen*."

"*La Traviata*," says the agony aunt. "*Aida. Tristan und Isolde*."

"*Brief Encounter*," I suggest. "*Love Story*."

We are all smiling at our cleverness. Except for the novelist.

The nun says, "Yes, all those. It's not exactly happy ever after, is it? Surely the point of love is like the point of anything, it's not just a moment's comfort, but becoming a better person, a feeling of being more connected with the world."

"But all your examples were weepies," says the novelist. "Even the longest relationships must end in death. And anyway, it's good to have a weep . . ."

Maggie interrupts ruthlessly, saying, "Maybe there's a message here, that perfection isn't possible for very long and we're all just setting ourselves up to be unhappy. Does this mean we should all lower our sights a bit and be more realistic?"

I think, well, that's not much of a compliment if she's interested in me.

The agony aunt chips in a bit about how some people now seemed to be giving up on romance completely and just going for the sex, which was not always happy either. And then she adds, "George, you're a widower, this must be something you've noticed about starting again on your own. Once you've had the real thing, a close long-term relationship for many years, it's especially a shock for someone your age to realize just how much people who are dating now see it so much in terms of sex . . ."

"Er, well, it's a shock all round," I babble. "Frankly I'm not sure where I would start."

". . . because, even when you find someone you like, you would start off thinking about the relationship rather than the sex?"

I'm watching Maggie, who is watching me.

"Well, it's not like I'm a teenager . . ."

"That's an interesting comment," says the agony aunt. "I often think, for someone at your time of life, it

201

is a bit like teenagerhood. You are not sure what the rules are, you need confidence, you're afraid of making mistakes, or looking daft and vulnerable . . ."

What the hell is this? A live, on-air counselling session?

". . . it's like coming of age all over again, but in reverse, because this time our natural energies are slowing down rather than speeding up . . ."

I interrupt. "Actually, I rather like to think of myself not as slowing down, but as maturing."

Laughter. And a wink from Maggie. (Did I see that right? Maggie winked at me?)

"Well, good for you," says the agony aunt. "And I do agree that there's more to life than romance. Sometimes just getting through the day is an act of will on its own, without worrying ourselves sick about whether we're going to be attractive to someone or not. And strangely, I think it's when we pursue other interests and other passions, when we are relaxed about ourselves, that's when romance sneaks up without us looking for it."

This is like a reply to the lovelorn. The other guests look at me, as if I'm supposed to comment back again. Really I'm just quite pleased with myself for taking this sort of public attention without crying or throwing something.

"In the meantime," I say, "it's possible to be single and lead a fulfilling life. I just feel that people are being driven into relationships they may not want. Why can't we just like ourselves as we are?"

"Learning to love yourself," says the novelist, "is the greatest love of all. But it can be hard to do it alone." And we never quite recover from that, so it is fortunate that the programme finishes a few minutes later.

Afterwards I am scuttling off when Maggie catches up with me in the corridor. "Thanks for giving us an idea for the show again. You are good at this, you know."

Then she says, "Joan mentioned you might be coming to the cottage this year."

"The cottage? It's the first I've heard of it."

"Oh damn. I've spoken too soon."

Every year in August, Joan and her family rent a large cottage on the South Devon coast and invite guests to join them at some big folk festival that's held nearby. Every year she invited Annie and me, and every year we made excuses not to go as Annie hated folk music. I've been making the same excuses since I've been on my own.

Here's a thing. It's just possible that I am not good at taking advice. Or maybe it has to come at the right time. There's probably a lot of stuff that I should have allowed to sink into my head a bit more over the past two years. Annie used to say that sometimes I listened but didn't actually hear, so it was best to let me get to the point in my own way.

On the way home from the radio studio, it struck me that I had just heard a piece of advice that I liked. It was the agony aunt saying that midlife is a bit like being a teenager again.

A second teen age! The angst, the sulks, the goofiness, the feeling that nothing quite fits, the urge to Do Something but you don't know what, the urge to rebel as you move on to another level. It's accepted behaviour for Young People, so why not for me?

It's a nice thought. It makes sense in a way. It cheered me up a bit.

I've since tackled Joan about what Maggie said. The cottage thing. She had the courtesy to blush. She had been at lunch with some of the friends who often join them for a day or two on the coast, and had been listing some of the people she was inviting this year. She had mentioned my name.

"But I hate folk music."

"George, that's Annie talking. You have never tried it. But I'm sorry I didn't mention the cottage to you first. I was getting round to it. You need another break. You are owed dozens of days off. Just come down to the cottage to visit us, you old fart. You can be company for my Matthew."

"And tell me, is Maggie going to be there?"

"Probably, for a day or two."

"And you don't think that she thinks . . ."

"George, she is one of the nicest divorcees I know, and she thinks that you are rather appealing, but that does not mean that I am running a matchmaking service. You are quite capable of putting her off or just hiding while she's there."

"But it's folk music."

204

"You can bring the dog, there's lots of nice countryside."

"But it's folk music."

"Justin and Sandra said they might call in."

"But it's folk music."

"Try doing something different. It's been good for you lately. You might get a column out of it."

"But it's *folk* music."

CHAPTER
TEN

SILLY? YES, THAT'S THE POINT

Anti-Style
by George Worth
14 August

Many of the simple pleasures of life provide harmless enjoyment until some trendsetter comes along and spoils things by making everyone self-conscious about being in "style". So food becomes Cuisine, clothes become Fashion and a nice walk must be part of a Personal Fitness Programme.

The fun vanishes as people concentrate more on doing it in style than just doing it. Sometimes there seems to be no escape.

And so it was entirely in the pursuit of human freedom and individual expression that I found myself drinking cider and hopping around on a packed dance floor with an astonishing mix of people high on ceilidh music at one of Britain's largest folk festivals, and wondering why this was more enjoyable than I could have imagined. And realizing that it was because nobody here seemed to care much about being in style at all.

A folk festival should be an easy target for mockery. And, you bet, I was ready to mock. There are the morris dancers. And the arts-and-crafts stalls with things made out of shells and wood. And people playing obscure old instruments that rightly went out of use centuries ago. And the morris dancers. And men in beards, many of whom are morris dancers. You can't help but think it's all a bit silly.

Then, well, maybe it was the cider, but it struck me that being unafraid to be silly was the point. These people were protecting our inalienable British right to be defiantly, awkwardly daft in our own way, and never mind what the rest of the world might think. They may look barmy, but I would rather have a drink with them than with any style guru.

Sidmouth folk festival in South Devon is one of a rolling series of summer festivals around England. Like many of August's best events, it doesn't get much publicity because a) it's not fashionable b) it has no lavish corporate sponsors and c) most of the nation's arts trendsetters are away at the Edinburgh Festival or on holiday in Provence, or Tuscany, or wherever those people think is trendy this year.

The folk community seems to be classless and age-less. Sidmouth crams hundreds of events into more than a dozen venues ranging from church halls to giant marquees. Campsites and hotels are booked out for miles around. Festival-goers were as likely to be playing as watching. Along the seafront promenade the sun shone on a weird and changing array of buskers, clog dancers, singing trios, banjo players and elderly accordionists. They weren't busking for money, just pleasure. They didn't seem to mind whether people were watching them or not and they were all smiling. You got the impression that back home their hobby might be regarded as rather suspect by their workmates — "Going clog dancing again tonight, Caroline?" — so it was their joy to be among their own kind in a town where, just for a week, folk music was actually normal.

Anyone could join a workshop to try anything from clogging to tribal drums. In the pubs, bearded and ponytailed men with guitars and fiddles improvised tunes together. In separate rooms traditional folk singers played to more earnest audiences, singing of closed mines and old ridgeways. At one pub concert I swear that I saw a woman in the audience leave her purse on her seat to keep her place while she was out of the room. Try doing that in London.

Folk bands blended musical styles: South American with Scottish, hip hop with folk, rock with country, bluegrass with ceilidh. There were performers from Africa and Eastern Europe. A comic did a farmers' moaning song and a women's corset-pulling shanty. There may have been some musical rivalries that I missed, but everyone seemed to rub along fairly well.

There was a succession of terrific ceilidh nights at the main dance marquee, and it was here that one moment etched itself into my memory as we all turned and spun to order on the dance floor. Every time I turned, there was a different kind of person in front of me. Turn, and there's an elderly man dancing with his granddaughter. Turn and there were two New Agers with braided hair. Turn and there's a middle-aged couple spinning around. Turn and there's a young couple in tie-dyed trousers and T-shirts. Turn and there are grandmas and teenagers and career types and men in shorts, all spinning and linking arms.

In England, more than in any other country I've known, the generations hardly mix socially any more. Our love for our own separate styles drives us apart. I cannot remember seeing such a mix of people at any other event. If folk keeps no other tradition alive, it can still do this.

"Could everyone stop being so bloody cheerful for a moment?"

"I'm sorry?"

"And while you're at it, once and for all, George, can you stop saying sorry all the time?"

This is Arabella, who minded the office again while various members of staff went off to Sidmouth for a few days at a time. Now we are on our first day back, we have been humming ceilidh tunes and linking arms to spin round as we pass each other by the photocopier. The occasional mock cry of "yee-hah" has been heard. From me.

"You say sorry too much, George, and I'm tired of it," Arabella says. "I know that's how one is meant to recognize an old-fashioned Englishman — stand on his toes and see if he apologizes — but you say sorry instead of pardon, and sorry instead of listen to me and sorry for sorry. So stop it. What are you so sorry for?"

"OK, I'll stop."

"Fine."

"From now on I shall cease to be such a sorry excuse for a man."

Joan is looking at us with motherly concern. It's lunchtime and there's just Joan, Arabella and me at our desks, trying to catch up with a little forward planning in these slack August days. This is called the silly season in the news department because there is so little happening of any serious consequence — no court hearings, no Parliament, no major pressure groups doing stunts. In our section, we don't call it the silly season for the simple reason that things are always silly here.

This is the moment when Arabella drops the problem on us.

"I don't want to bring you down after your tribal gathering," she says. "But I didn't want to bother you while you were away, and this is the first chance I've had to speak to just the two of you today. We have a big problem."

Joan remains quiet for a moment and then says, "Basset."

"It's awful," says Arabella. "It's quite, quite awful. And I really don't know what we are going to do."

If she says it's awful, then it is. And if she doesn't know what to do, then it's going to be difficult. We push aside the gripping suggestions on Seven Ways to Make That Summer Feeling Last All Year, The Families Who Found Their Dream Houses While They Were on Holiday and Waxwork Horrors: The Nightmare of The Home Brazilians That Went Terribly Wrong. Real life was back again.

Basset, bloody Basset. Last week, while we were away, it turns out that his squeeze was actually found crying in the toilets by one of the girls. The next day she had wept at her desk. Interrogated in the girls' favourite wine bar, she revealed that the affair was over as she had been getting "too serious" and Basset had said that she had no right to be a threat to his marriage. Like none of it was his responsibility.

That evening, Basset had wandered into the section when Arabella was on her own. He pulled up a chair and sat close. He was very impressed with her work and her dedication, he said. He had his eye on her and he could see good things ahead. He felt able to discuss important administrative issues with her. He had been taking a look at staffing levels, he said. Things were a little tight, we were going over budget. We had one remaining person on a six-month contract, which was due to expire next month. It could not be renewed. He expected that Arabella would understand.

"Let me guess," says Joan.

"He wants us to fire his ex-girlfriend?" I ask.

"He wants us not to extend her contract," says Arabella.

I ponder. "Isn't that, you know, um, discrimination or something? Is she in a union?"

"Not as far as I know," says Arabella. "Anyway, Basset says it's about the budget. And he's in charge of the budget. Joan, he said that you would understand, and that you owed him a favour about staffing. I haven't said anything about this to anyone, but what can we do?"

Pause. As a joke, Joan says, "I suppose we could go to the editor about it."

We smile ruefully. Our editor is far too busy with his endless TV appearances and his parties with the great and good to be bothered with something like this. There are basically three kinds of editor: the bully, the cerebral type and the self-publicist who is seen more often on TV than in the building. We have the third kind. When he's out networking, he probably tells himself that he is doing it for the good of the paper. We rather think that he is doing it for himself. Anyway, he likes Basset and relies on him to get things done.

For the time being, we decide to do nothing while Joan considers the situation and tries to find a way through.

There's something else. Arabella says there's some sort of buzz going on higher up, some change in the offing. Joan quizzes her on this, but it's just rumours and suspicions, nothing solid.

I hate this stuff. I'm glad that I have finally decided to leave.

I sort of decided last week. At the cottage in Sidmouth. Some cottage. Detached, a back garden shaded by trees, and seven bedrooms tucked away on the first floor and in the attic. A bedroom for Joan and Matthew, one for me, two for their student children if they ever turned up, and the rest for an assortment of friends who wandered in and stayed for a day or two, crashing on the sofa if all the rooms were taken. Open house, long breakfasts, festival visits, drinks in the garden, long dinners around a big pine table, with everyone helping out. Communal living can work so well when it's not wasted on the young.

Joan and Matthew seemed really happy, as if they had slipped back into some timeless place. And there was a timeless feel to it. I arrived by train and a long bus ride. Listening to the locals chattering on the bus, I thought how amazing it was that regional accents still survived despite all the pressures for us all to turn out the same. At the cottage, Matthew came out to greet me and, knowing of his hospital examination, I couldn't stop my eyes straying to his crotch. He didn't notice, thankfully. He showed me to my room, which had a comfy three-quarter bed and a wardrobe. I said that I would just be staying for a few days, although I had the whole week off. He said fine, whatever, come and go as you please. Then Joan came back from some shopping and said, where's the dog?

I was dogless. It's just possible that Sister Rosalind has not forgiven me for my late arrival back from Northumberland. When I had asked her about taking Ben away again she said, er, no, she was having her new friend to stay this week and she wanted her new friend to get to know Ben. So I wandered around Sidmouth without him, feeling a little exposed. I have to admit, he has become my social face, my official greeter, my better-looking friend. If you are a bloke out walking on your own and you say "Hello" to a stranger, some people look at you as if you might be an axe murderer or something. But with Ben, I felt more approachable, more normal. And less in need of company.

At first sight, the town had been occupied by a strange hybrid of the British people, who were all relaxed and smiling endlessly. There was music everywhere, different at every corner, so that it was like listening to someone tuning a radio, working through all the stations, and finding that every station was playing folk. I felt like that brigadier character in *Monty Python* who keeps wanting to stop everything because it's all far too silly.

But then, well, I started to relax. Joan and Matthew took me to watch a barn dance in the backyard of a pub and poured a couple of pints of cider down me. Before I knew what was happening, I was having a dance with Joan, the first time I'd danced since, well, I don't remember when. I can be a bit self-conscious, dancing. Disco at my age can feel odd — it's like trying to impersonate myself as a teenager, while my arms and legs don't respond in the way they once did — and the waltzes and stuff at some of Annie's office functions had felt absurd. But this was OK. Normally I'd be worried about looking stupid but that wasn't a problem here. The great thing was, nobody really minded if you put a foot wrong or went the wrong way as we linked arms and swung around, because we were all in it together and next time it might be them who tripped up or turned the wrong way. It felt good.

Oh Annie, I thought, we could have done this together. It would have been fun.

And I also thought: I did all that damn philosophy last month, but maybe all I needed was some cider and a dance.

214

Anyway, the weekend went by. I made myself useful in the cottage. I was an extra host, helping to unload suitcases, answering the phone, guiding new arrivals. The sun shone down on everybody like a merciful god. I got a bit of a tan, bought some new T-shirts to fit in with the crowd a little more, and even acquired a one-week festival pass, with my name on, worn on a ribbon around my neck so that I could wander into almost any event that still had some spare space. By the time Justin and Sandra arrived on the Tuesday, I felt settled.

Tuesday was a strange day. Thinking back, it was like some giant country dance when I didn't know who was going to catch hold of me and spin me round next. Endless music and chatter.

Sandra was big now. Everyone fussed over her, the women gave advice and men opened doors and surrendered the best armchairs. She had checked that there was a local maternity facility, just in case, and she wouldn't go anywhere without her medical details in her shoulder bag. A hospital overnight bag, with her relaxation tapes and nightie and baby clothes, stood forever ready in her room.

She was tired from the journey and happy just to laze at the cottage, so I went out with a worried-looking Justin to show him the town — the beach and the seafront, the marquees with all the various events, and along to the main area with all its stalls, a food area catering mainly for the baked potato and tofu brigade, and the assorted "workshops". Justin looked fairly stunned by the whole thing, like that first night when he arrived at my flat.

"Don't worry," I said. "You get used to it."

Then he said, "Hey, look. Tom-toms."

We had heard the sound before we knew what it was. A drum workshop for passers-by. A mostly male group were sitting on the grass, beating a rhythm with their hands, led by a big hairy bloke acting as voluntary tutor. BANG, bang, BANG, bang, bong, bangy bong.

"That looks fun," Justin said. "It's supposed to be good therapy. Let's do that."

"Er, really?"

"Come on then."

There were a couple of empty places so we found ourselves sitting cross-legged with a dozen other assorted idiots, learning how to make a beat. I'd been living with music for a few days now, so it felt almost normal to make some of my own. My hands hurt a bit but it was strangely relaxing all the same. BANG, bang. BANG, bang. It was silly but it was all right.

We were well into our tribal glory when I caught Justin's eye and we both smiled. A barrage of men making their own noise on a summer's day. A cluster of festival-goers had formed a circle around us to watch and listen. I looked up and saw that among them were Joan and Maggie.

They were grinning at Justin and me. I think I blushed. I didn't even know that Maggie was due in town that day. I lost my rhythm a bit — I may have bonged when I should have banged — then I looked down again and stayed in time with the group until the session was over about five minutes later.

Maggie and Joan were still there and joined in the applause. We all went to buy ice creams. Then — and I am not quite sure how she did this — Joan managed to lead Justin away to look at something. I was alone with Maggie.

"*. . . Change your partners and turn about . . .*"

Suddenly, it sort of felt like I was on a date. And I had no idea what to do.

She said, "You look very relaxed. It suits you."

And I said, "You look too good for this place."

She said, "Well, thank you."

It was not quite a compliment. She was dressed flawlessly — a clingy, curvy knitted top, immaculate denim jeans, a pair of those wacky coloured trainers — while all around her were merely dressed down. She stood out. It was as if she had just beamed in from another world. And there was something else, something about her face. The eyebrows? Newly plucked, lined eyebrows, I think. One of those things you might notice about someone when you are getting closer, before you get too close to notice.

Absurdly, her eyebrows transfixed me as we walked around and talked about nothing very much. I was thinking, why do women do this? Like, rip out their hair with tweezers and then pencil in an imitation? And this dragged up memories of past girlfriends from my single days, long forgotten. There was the girl who would nip into the loo and drown herself with perfume

217

every time we went to the cinema, presumably so that she would smell sweeter in proximity, but it just made my eyes sting and turned every film into a weepie for me. There was the girl who worked at a cosmetics counter, who wore so much make-up that when I finally saw her face unadorned, it was like a stranger coming out of the bathroom. And then there's the whole thing about shoes. (They say they do all this partly for men, but they are doing it for their own mental image of themselves, their own confidence, surely . . .)

Girlfriends! I once had girlfriends! Before Annie. I seized the memory. I'd been on dates, I'd done this before, lots of times. What did I do? Did I have a tactic? Flattery? Be a good listener? No evidence of that so far, with my mind wandering. Then we turned a corner and there were the festival's clothes stalls, a mini market of frocks and shoes and home-made jewellery and tie-dyed T-shirts. And I thought: shopping! Once upon a time, years ago, I used to impress women by being one of those men who was willing to wander round clothes shops with them without passing out in a stupor of boredom. Shopping!

"Hey, let's have a wander round here," I said.

"Really? I'd love to. Are you sure?"

"It'll be good. I wondered where all these people still managed to get cheesecloth shirts."

She roamed the racks, I tried on some daft hats. She held blouses against herself, I passed positive comments. She tried on a top with flared sleeves. And I saw a summer dress that would have really suited Annie.

Damn.

Sort of turquoise, which she liked. Subtle, a flowery pattern, very feminine. Part of me wanted to buy it for Annie, I'd done that a few times in the old days, I knew her size. Damn.

"George! George?" A hissed whisper.

"Hello. Yes? Sorry, I was miles away."

"Can we move on? There are a couple of people staring."

"Staring? What have I done?"

"No, not at you, George. I get recognized sometimes, you know?"

Wow, really? I knew that Maggie did a bit of TV work, the odd stand-in stint for presenters on holiday, but not exactly stardom. Still, people love celebs these days. And a couple were indeed looking at her. Not like in London, where we try to be cool about celebs and just glance at them to make sure they are who we think they are. These two were staring. We escaped.

"Does that happen often?"

"Now and again. It goes with the job and I don't really mind, but those two looked like they wanted to talk."

We escaped from the clothes area and spotted a glum-looking Justin having a coffee on his own. Joan had gone back to the cottage to meet another friend. I was a little relieved as I guided Maggie towards him. At least he would help with the conversation now. They were both going to be here for just a couple of days. It occurred to me that I found it easier to talk with Maggie in front of an audience.

"*. . . All join together and spin around . . .*"

An hour later, back at the cottage, the three of us found Sandra lazing in splendour on the sofa, sipping a cup of tea and working her way through a stack of women's lifestyle glossies. Joan had bought the magazines that day "to catch up on her reading". (Translation: to see if there were any ideas we could steal.)

Sandra looked up and smiled wearily at Justin: "I'm in heaven."

Joan emerged from the garden and joked, "Oh no, it's George. Quick, hide all the magazines or you'll set him off."

(Women's glossy magazines? Yeah, don't get me started. Great big whacking lifestyle bibles. Each one seems to contain more details on how to manage a home and a social life than would be needed by a rampant society hostess and her housekeeper combined. Adverts for skin cream that you would need a chemistry degree to understand. The drippy opening messages from the editors who like to pretend they are just like their readers, really, but living in a better world, a heaven on earth, where they know all the right things to do and say and buy. In comparison, our pages were almost reality.)

"You leave them alone," said Sandra. "I like to stock up on my fantasies now and again. Sometimes they even have a good idea."

"A reader speaks," said Justin.

"I merely think they should carry a health warning," I said. "You know, something like — half the world doesn't have enough to eat and drink, what more do you bloody people want?"

Maggie laughed. It was, I think, the first time I had actually made her laugh. Thing was, I was sort of being serious.

With Joan was the other new arrival, Chris, an earnest-looking chap who had just dropped in for the afternoon from his family's cottage down the coast. (Do all these people live the cottage life except me?) They knew each other because Joan helped to train Chris at his first paper. He was now deputy editor of one of our rivals, despite being at least ten years younger than me. He must be good at the media lunch circuit, I thought, and good at morning conference. Or he might just be good at everything. I had never heard of him, but there are lots of people I've never heard of.

Matthew, ever the perfect host, appeared from the kitchen with a fresh pot of coffee. We all settled back on the giant sofas. We looked like a lifestyle advert — media types relaxing in country residence. We got talking as a group and a rare thing happened: a discussion among journalists that was not just about what other people do but about what we do. Possibly we all wanted to make an impression on Chris, for varying reasons.

It was clear that the man was not one of my regular readers. He said, "You're not a big fan of lifestyle journalism then, George?"

Me: "I just think we tell people to want too much."

Chris: "But don't you think people want to want? They enjoy the wanting, they enjoy looking forward. It gives them the illusion of control. It's about aspirations. I mean everyone's got an ache inside them, and this gives them something to ache for."

Joan: "George doesn't have wants. His want button is switched off."

Justin: "Anyway, we give lots of warnings, George. Stories about people who have it all and it's not enough. Stars with more money than sense. And your column, of course."

Me: "Oh, bloody columnists. Waste of money."

Maggie laughed again. Then we settled into a mutual rant about columnists and how we all hated them — "not you George, of course" — as the Frankenstein's monsters of journalism. How editors originally created them as a cheap and reliable way to fill space without the messy expense of sending reporters out to get a proper story, but instead the papers ended up with dozens of overpaid professional whingers — "not you George, of course" — who write columns slagging off politicians or royalty or celebs, based on no more knowledge than the news stories that the rest of us have read anyway. Really, all they do is interview themselves. And above all there are the big-time political columnists, who bang on about how the trouble with politicians today is that none of them have ever had a proper job, when we all know for a fact that this criticism comes from men who have never had a proper job either, who went from Oxbridge to think tanks to

222

opinion writing to column writing, and got paid about the same as a government minister.

And then I heard myself say, "I'm only a part-time columnist, but I don't want to do it much longer."

Maggie: "Why not?"

Me: "Well, partly because it's lifestyle. And mostly because I just write about things I hate. That's what a columnist has to do, we have to hate things."

Joan: "But George, you're so good at it."

Justin: "So what would you rather do?"

Me: "Well, in the old days, a senior duffer like me could have looked forward to going back into the provinces for a nice weekly editorship somewhere."

Another mutual rant, about how the provincial papers had been destroyed by endless takeovers and mergers and freesheets, so that they hardly covered their territories properly any more, and the pay was buttons because there was a steady supply of desperate graduates eager for any job at any price. And the weekly editors no longer had a cushy life of Rotary lunches and Women's Institute teas but instead sat glued to their computer terminals all day, just like their staff, who hardly went out either and filled endless bland editions from publicity handouts and phone calls, and the Internet, and never met the readers. Nobody met the readers any more, we all avoided them.

Matthew: "I've just thought of a collective noun — a moan of journalists."

Joan: "You would be bored stiff back in the provinces, George."

Me: "No I wouldn't. There's stacks of stuff that never gets in our papers now. We're all so stuck on London."

Chris: "There's still a lot of regional coverage."

Me: "No, the regions get in the national papers only when there's a big accident or a juicy crime. I'm talking about things like this festival, or little battles trying to save local ways of life, and people doing little bits of good. Or just ordinary lives and real people. It's like they don't exist unless they end up in court or shag someone famous. There's still a lot of regional variety in this country. Lifestyle is convenient because it's so bland and easy, because it acts like we all want to live the same way."

Sandra: "So why on earth do you stay?"

Me: "That's a fair question."

"*. . . And change your partners again . . .*"

The day ended with me sitting on the edge of the promenade with Justin, each drinking pints of beer bought from a nearby pub, listening to the sounds of distant music and watching the moonlit sea crunching against the pebble beach. Most of the gang from the cottage had gone to watch a booked-out concert by one of the more serious folk singers, the depressed sort who cup their hands to their ears as they sing. Joan had a few tickets but not enough for us all, so Justin and I nobly volunteered to miss out and go to the pub instead. We promised to make up for it by going to the big ceilidh the next night.

Justin had been looking a bit glum again and I wanted to know what was the matter. It took a while for him to say. It was the baby. Of course, of course, just worries about imminent fatherhood. Terrific. I've spent years worrying about ending a life, and now he's worried about having started one. So I just let him talk.

"It's just going to be such a big change," he said at last. "It's daft, I know, but I have only just realized that. The pregnancy is fine, I can handle that, I'm an expert, I've read all the books. I know about the mechanics and things like the mucous plug — that's not a punk band, it's the seal that forms over the cervix — but that's while the baby is inside Sandra. There'll come a time when we are standing in our flat with a brand new real baby, and it's scary. And so permanent. I can't tell her this, I'm supposed to be easing her worries. I seem to have spent most of the past year being scared."

This was a surprise.

"I don't remember you being scared before."

"When I first came to London, I was nervous as hell."

"I just thought you were a cocky little bugger."

"Yeah, well, that's me putting on the style. We all act sometimes. Well, you don't but the rest of us do. Anyway, then I was scared of the job, and scared of losing Sandra. And scared of you."

"Oh come on."

"Guv, you've done so much stuff. And you're so disdainful of it. It's, well, it's really cool."

"Sorry, I'm cool?"

225

"In your own way," he smiled. "You've been a bit of a rock to me, George. Someone to lean on. Even that weird best man's speech, it was one of a kind. I could have drifted a bit if you'd not been there."

"I'm not so solid, Justin. You know that."

Pause.

Justin said, "Were you serious before? When you were talking about leaving?"

"Maybe. I hope so. At last." I sighed. "I've got a bit of cash tucked away, I could take a break. Or it could just turn out to be one of those things that middle-aged men say when they are on holiday."

I watched the waves roll in and out, crunching away the stones bit by bit. I changed the subject back to him.

"Are you going to be at the birth?"

"Yes, if I can. It's expected now, and I want to anyway. We've chosen not to know whether it's going to be a boy or a girl, so I'd like to be there when we find out. All the women have got their blokes with them at the ante-natal clinics and the classes. There are guys in suits, blokes in overalls straight from work, black blokes, Asian blokes, Muslims and Sikhs. Everyone is there. It's good.

"I know it's better than it used to be in the old days when blokes just stayed at work or went to the pub when their wives were giving birth. And they never saw their kids really. The children would be up for maybe half an hour when the men got home from work, and they didn't know what to say, or the mum had set up the father to deliver a telling-off. You know, "Wait until your father gets home". So they became some kind of ogre to the kid.

"It was like that with my dad a lot, really, right up to when he had his heart attack at the office. I never got to know the poor old sod. Do you know why I know so much about your generation's music? It's because that's all my dad really left of himself — his record collection. I used to listen to it when I felt sad. This was something he liked that I could still share. Some of it must have been stuff his dad liked too. That's all he left me, a lot of old tunes.

"I'm not doing it like that. Well, I've told Sandra that I won't. It's a united front or nothing. I want to play as well. I even want a turn at pushing the pram. I see a lot of dads pushing prams and pushchairs these days. It's the style. Later I want us to play computer games together."

"Oh no."

"Maybe not. Just winding you up, George."

We stood up, last drops of beer finished, and started ambling back up the lanes to the cottage. A warm night. Silence for a while, then Justin said: "Did you ever wonder how I came to study happiness for a while at university?"

"No, not really. It never surprises me what you lot waste your time studying."

"I think now, it's because I hadn't really been happy. But now I am. She makes me happy, Sandra does. I think that's the scary thing, thinking that it may have to change."

"Justin, you'll be fine."

Silence again, then: "Hey, what's with this Maggie and you? Anything happening?"

"Very difficult to tell."

When we got back, the cottage was mostly in darkness and everyone had gone to bed. Matthew was just coming out of the bathroom. When I went in to wash my face, I noticed he had left his toiletry bag behind and it was open. Just inside there was a packet bearing the name Viagra.

I closed the bag and moved it out of the way. Good for you, Matthew, I thought. At least one of us is in action.

Usually I try not to remember my dreams, but I had a cracker that night. There was a clothes rack, like in a dress shop, but instead of clothes on the hangers, there were women. All the women I know, just hanging around waiting to be picked. Arabella, Rosalind, Joan, all the office girls, even an unpregnant Sandra, and Maggie. I chose Maggie, then Justin appeared as a trendy shop assistant, handed me a Viagra tablet and said, "Go for it." We were on our way to the changing room when I noticed a sign which at first seemed to say "No refunds", but then it turned into a quote from that self-help book I read, warning how men too often choose a woman before they have worked out what they want to do with their lives. I awoke confused, but with a rock-hard willy, and the thought that it was entirely possible that what I really needed was a bloody good shag.

That morning I ambled up to the main festival area with Maggie. This time I was going to be really impressive. I was going to buy a dress. It had occurred to me that if a dress suited Annie's colouring, it might also suit young Annic, whose birthday was the next week. I tried out the idea in a phone call to Berwick and her mum told me the right size and said, yes, why not, we'll say it's all the fashion in London.

Maggie said: Who is this girl anyway? And I said: It's my niece, she's the nearest thing I've got to a kid. And Maggie said: Lucky you, I had a big party when my two finally left for university, they thought it was a party for them, but really it was for me to celebrate them going.

After a successful purchase, we stopped at one of the food tables for a coffee before heading back into town. On the opposite side of the table was a swampy-type woman with reddish braided hair and a green T-shirt. Hard to tell her age, maybe forty. For a moment, she looked at Maggie intensely.

Maggie got that panicked look at being recognized again.

"Just off to the loo, George. Back in a minute."

As she left, the swampy woman spoke.

"Is that Maggie Wotsit, the presenter? The one on TV who does that radio show as well?"

"Er, yes."

"So are you George Worth, then?"

Gulp. "Er, how do you know who I am?"

"Well, she called you George. And your voice is vaguely familiar . . ."

"Yes . . ."

229

"And you are wearing a festival pass with the name 'G. Worth' on it."

"Oh yes, so I am."

"My mum reads your column every week."

Sigh.

"She really hates you."

"What?" I laughed. "How wonderful. So why does she read me?"

"She says it helps to remind her of all the reasons why she divorced my dad. That he was an old stick-in-the-mud who would never catch up with the times. But then she is a really keen shopper, my mum."

She said this with a sudden, broad smile that changed her whole face. It was a nice, wide face, no make-up, a spray of lines around the eyes as if drawn by some hard times. The eyes were lively.

I asked, "And what do you think?"

"I don't know, I never read your paper. I don't read any papers much. But I've heard you on the radio once or twice. I think you were quite brave the other week, talking about having no sex. I'm in the same boat as you."

Um. This was possibly getting a little intimate, so I changed the subject.

"Do you live in a, er, community around here?"

"A community? What do you mean?"

"Aren't you one of the, er, New Age people?"

"Me?" She laughed. "I'm a librarian. I live near Durham. In a house."

"Sorry, it must have been the hair."

She fingered her braided locks. "I've just had this done here. I've always wanted to know how I would look. It won't last long. I'm not usually this relaxed."

"Well, me neither. How did you get to be here?"

"I'm a cloggie. Clog dancing, you know? A group of us girls came down together. It's my first proper break for a while."

She glanced behind me. "Look, here's your friend coming back. I don't suppose she does much clog dancing, does she?"

"Er, no. I don't think so."

Maggie appeared at my shoulder, ready to wander into town, ignoring the stranger. As I left, I shook the woman's hand.

"Nice talking," I said. "Sorry, I don't know your name."

"It's Caroline. I'll tell my mum you're not so bad."

On the way, I asked Maggie: What's this thing about being recognized, have you had a bad experience with a fan? And she said, No, it's not that, it's silly really, it's just that I never know what to say to them.

She knew all the arguments about why she should be nicer, that these people pay our wages, that we'd be nothing without them and so on, but really she'd said everything she wanted to say during the programmes and she didn't want to say any more.

A group of us spent the afternoon on the beach. Maggie stripped down to her costume, revealing a nicely well-preserved figure, and went for a swim. Afterwards she sat on the beach and invited me to put sun cream on her back and shoulders. As I performed the task, I caught Joan grinning and I stuck out my tongue at her from behind Maggie's back. It occurred to me that the last person I had stroked on a beach was Ben.

The late-night ceilidh. A giant marquee packed with people. Happy, throbbing, lilting music. Electric violins, tambourines, flutes, drums, guitars. We moved around at the instructions of the dance caller: turn this way, turn that way, swing around. It seemed that all human life was there and they were all happy. Moisture dripped onto our heads, and I realized that it was the sweat in the atmosphere condensing on the ceiling and dripping down.

It was Maggie's last night, and she was my main partner, weaving in and out of lines, holding hands, spinning around. Sometimes we were split up by the dancing. There was one of those dances where couples proceed in a great circle, and every few bars of music the women step forward to dance with the man in front, and on round the circle, so that you spend most of your time dancing with strangers, a different woman at a time. But she always came back to me.

Later, when we felt breathless and too hot, I got Maggie a drink and we went to stand outside in the night air, the lights of the town shining through the trees.

She turned to me and smiled.

"Do you like this life?" she asked.

"This life being . . .?"

"Just drifting around, taking your pick of what's happening, living in an open house, talking about things, putting the world to rights?"

"Oh that life. Yes, it's fine. Doesn't seem normal, but it's fine."

"I think London can be like that. There's lots of stuff to do, and the trick is to treat it like a permanent festival. The galleries and the concerts, the lunchtime lectures. I get invited to a lot."

I was thinking, she has a great voice, very warm. It's her voice I like. She's easy on the eyes, but here in the darkness, there was mainly her voice.

"So do you want to come along sometime?"

"Where to?"

"To a concert, or a gallery, or a lunchtime lecture?"

I'd done this sort of stuff with Annie. I've done London. Do I want to do it again? On a VIP ticket?

"Oh, maybe. You can't be short of company."

"No, George, I'm not short of company. That means I'm suggesting it because I genuinely like your company."

In the dark, I blushed. I seem to have stopped all the crying and started blushing instead.

"And I've always got room for another friend. And you usually say something interesting and amusing," she went on. "And we can share ourselves with the other people we meet, and you won't need to feel threatened. My ex-husband was useless at all that. People manage to like you even when you are grumpy. That's a real talent, you know."

I had never asked about her ex-husband, or her children. I had not asked about any of that stuff because I had not wanted her to ask about any of my stuff. We had just been getting on as two people with thoughts and opinions but no past. Did we have a future?

She was looking up at me.

This was the moment when I could kiss her, I thought.

I probably should kiss her, I thought. It would be the thing to do. There was a comfy life on offer here. Other men would be envious. She was very understanding.

I felt as if I was a kid about to have his first kiss, wondering how you manage that vital moment, how you lean down and glue your lips to someone else's mouth, curious to know how it could be done.

And I spent most of the rest of the evening wondering why I didn't, as I led her back inside to return to the gang, and then back to the cottage and our separate bedrooms.

I could see that, in theory, she was a very attractive woman, and maybe very interesting. But not to me. I just didn't fancy her. If I had fancied her, surely I would have done something by now. It was possible that I didn't even like her. Certainly, I couldn't put up with this strange thing about running away from real people all the time.

She was available but, romantically, it was as if she was the warm-up act and the real star hadn't arrived yet. I could have pretended and gone along with her, for the experience. It would have been a performance, not real. And that would have been using her, wouldn't it? So it was sort of noble that I didn't. Although I'm not sure Maggie saw it that way.

I saw her off the next day. She shared a taxi to the distant station with Justin and Sandra. I hugged all three.

Maggie said, "I'll call you sometime."

"Fine," I said. "Or we'll see each other at the show."

"No," she said. "I meant, I'll call you as well as the show."

"OK."

That afternoon, Joan's student son and daughter turned up at last, fortunately at a time when their rooms were available. The girl is studying physics, the boy is a mathematician, but that didn't stop them from sliding back into childhood once they were back in their old holiday haunt. They relied on Joan for food and domestic services and Matthew as a taxi driver. It was clear that they all revelled in their family life. Both were Annie's godchildren.

And they said, "Is there a late-night ceilidh tonight? Let's go." So off we went again.

I feel silly writing this next bit, considering how it turned out afterwards.

It was the same big tent, the same crowd. I was enjoying it all right, taking turns with Matthew to dance with Joan, or just standing at the side and watching, happy to play the wallflower, listening to the music.

235

And then, over in one corner, the crowd parted for a moment and there was Caroline, the lady with the braided hair.

She was laughing as she danced with a group of other women, probably her clog-dancing pals as they were all wearing black dresses, which seem to be the cloggies' uniform. In a dress, she was a striking figure, leggy and slender, her red hair shining against the black. There was something innocent about the way the women were dancing with each other, like girls at a school hop. Then the crowd closed up again and they vanished from my sight.

A couple of tunes later, I was with Joan when the caller announced that dance where the women move along from man to man, all around the circle. Once again, a succession of different women appeared before me, spun me round, skipped alongside me and then moved on. And right at the end of the dance, the woman who appeared was Caroline, so that when the music stopped we were left facing each other, panting and happy.

"Hello again," I said.

"Hello," she said.

"You must really like dancing," I said.

"In my village," she said, "you can do either dancing or jam-making. I don't like jam."

I laughed, and the music started again for a new dance, and I took her hand and said, "Dance with me?"

And she was a pleasure to dance with, and I managed not to bump into her, and after a couple of tunes I was getting tired and thirsty, and I said, let's go

236

and have a drink at the bar. And she regarded me thoughtfully, like it was a big decision, and then said, yes, all right. And on the way to the drinks area, I caught Joan staring at me with an amazed look that I found quite satisfying.

I got the drinks and there were a couple of seats at a table. Caroline gave me that thoughtful look again as we sat down. And I asked where her clogs were, as she was wearing normal shoes, and she said that the clogs were in her bag over with her friends, she had changed shoes for the ceilidh, you can't really walk much in clogs. And she asked if I was big on folk music and I said, to be honest, no, it was OK but I was really here for a holiday. And she said that was a relief, she liked the dancing but some of the real folkies were a bit overwhelming.

And I told her that this week was the first time that I'd been dancing since my wife died. And she said that this was her first holiday since her husband died, and that was what she had meant yesterday when she said that we were in the same boat.

And so there was this thing that we had in common, widowhood, which was strange, but it was like we were survivors from the same disaster and could talk about it. Her husband was a teacher who had cancer for a year. And she said at least they'd had the time to say goodbye. And I said, but you had to see him suffer. They had two children, a girl at university and a boy now in the sixth form who was staying with her mum this week, as they all lived in the same village and could keep an eye on each other. And I said, they must be a comfort. And she agreed, but said that she wasn't sure that the children would let her move on if she ever met another man.

So we talked of life and death while happy music played in the background. And she said it seemed to her that, one way or another, we all get to spend some time alone in this life. And that sometimes she went into Durham saying that she was going shopping, but instead just sat by the river and tried to sort out her memories beneath the shadow of the giant cathedral.

And I said, I like Durham, fantastic cathedral, it's where one of my heroes is buried, the first great English historian, the Venerable Bede. And I went through Durham on the train a few weeks back, on my way from visiting Northumberland and my former in-laws, and the view of the cathedral from the train was one of the most spectacular parts of the journey.

She asked if I knew that the cathedral was founded by the monks from Holy Island after their pioneering monastery had been ransacked by Vikings raiding the Northumberland coast. They had lost almost everything and wandered for years, carrying a few of their relics with them, like people in mourning, until they found the right place to begin again and start something bigger.

And I said, "It's a wonder they didn't just give up, after having lost so much. They could just have sat in the ruins. They had done a lot already."

And she said, "Oh no, then all that trouble and pain would have been for nothing. They were the survivors, they had to carry on."

Then it was as if a cloud crossed her face, and she stopped talking and looked down, and a tear spilt down her cheek. And I knew this moment perfectly well, the sudden memory, the clash of grief and life, so I took her hand and just sat with her until the moment passed. The music played on and when she finally looked up again, she smiled and wiped her eye. And she did not apologize, like I would have done. And really why should we apologize, after all, for feeling such a rightful emotion? Do we apologize for smiling?

I picked up the conversation and asked if she was interested in history. And she said, more ecology really. She was involved in a local group which attracted all ages and worked on campaigns to try to protect the landscape and ancient sites around the north-east, from Durham all the way up to Northumberland. And I said, so it's not just jam-making and dancing out your way? And she smiled and said, no, there's a bit more to life than that.

And I had another flashback to dating days, of dates that worked, when I was not thinking about tactics or what to say, but really getting involved with someone. And it was as if, behind the chatter, inside my head a bit of me had woken up and was waving frantically at her, and she was waving back. And at no point did I talk about my stupid job.

Then we just had time for a couple more dances, before she had to leave with her friends to catch the last bus to her campsite.

Outside the marquee, her friends waited diplomatically in the distance as we started to say goodbye at the exact spot where I had stood with Maggie the night before.

Only this was different. Not least because, as she stood close, I really, really wanted to kiss her. And not just that. All at once, I would have rather liked to take her somewhere, remove our clothes, discover the scent of her skin and apply gentle pleasure to various parts of her body.

Instead, I said, "Will you be around tomorrow? Can I see you here tomorrow?"

And she said, "Yes, of course."

Then she took a deep breath, reached out and touched my arm, leant forward and kissed me on the cheek, then went to her friends. In the dark, I think she was skipping.

But she was not there the next night. Nor the night after that, when the festival was over.

By then, I had begun to feel stupid looking out for her. And I was angry at myself that when I was asking her about big things such as life and death, I never asked her for any of the little details that might have enabled me to find her again. Such as where exactly she was staying, or the name of her village. Or, um, her mobile number. Or her surname. (I realize that I'm hopeless at women's surnames. When women introduce themselves, they always go straight to first-name terms, and it's just so nice and informal, that's how I think of them.)

I felt like Prince Charming, who danced all night at the ball with Cinderella but was too transfixed to discover who she really was and where he might find her again. And like the pantomime prince, I tried to find Caroline through the only clue I had — her

240

footwear. I kept looking in on clog-dancing events, endless lineups of smiling women stamping on stage in unison, all shapes and sizes, their arms hardly moving but their feet going mad, like *Riverdance* for beginners. They looked funny, all those happy feet, but none belonged to Caroline. There were a number of groups from the north but I didn't recognize any of her friends among them, and I didn't have the nerve to ask anyone if they knew her.

So I never saw her again. She was just another warm-up act.

Back at the cottage, Joan and family had instigated a seemingly endless game of Trivial Pursuit. It was a family favourite. I joined in a few times. It was very competitive. We were all playing to win and it was satisfying to beat the kids a few times. I'm quite good at the level of pointless knowledge required for Trivial Pursuit. And it seemed a fitting end to the week.

I've been thinking about all that philosophy stuff from last month, and realizing that it all needs a bit of silliness to make sense, to join it all together in a sort of theory of everything. Schopenhauer basically said that everything was silly. Montaigne basically said that people should accept that they are silly. And the God of my father had been happy for humans to live in silly innocence frolicking in the Garden of Eden.

Worth's unified theory of philosophy states: Life is silly, we are silly, God bless our silliness.

I don't think I'll be mentioning this to anyone.

★ ★ ★

Something is definitely going on at work. Not just the Basset girlfriend thing. Something else. I'm crap at office politics but I can feel a buzz just slightly. It's not a big nasty buzz, the sort you get when someone who knows someone in management has learnt that there are going to be big budget cuts or a takeover or one of those other company things. But it's not a small buzz either, not a bit of gossip about an affair or someone being poached by another paper or someone facing a libel writ after a potentially embarrassing cock-up. It's an executive buzz, something in the corridor of power, maybe a shake-up or a relaunch or maybe some sort of reorganization. That sort of a buzz.

In the pub, people talk darkly about projects being stalled, appointments blocked. Any reporters and photographers who are known to be sleeping with executive secretaries are quizzed respectfully to see if they have heard any crucial details, but they are genuinely ignorant of anything other than that Something is Going On.

There's a worrying rumour that the proprietor is behind it, that this is one of those moments when he has been reviewing all his various business interests and decided to focus on us. In newspaper land, this is a source of real terror. We feel like children who have had the house to ourselves for a while and been playing all sorts of games, and suddenly Daddy is home and is not pleased. We are reminded who is ultimately in charge.

The newspaper is looking a bit tired, the theory goes. It could be time for a shake-up, maybe a cull of senior executives. Time for loyalties to be tested, time for allegiances to change, muscles to be flexed, people to find out where they stand. Or time to keep your head down and not get in the way.

It's two weeks since we all got back from Sidmouth. Basset's former girlfriend is still with us but her contract runs out in three weeks. Joan went in to see Basset about her and came back furious. I knew she was furious because she just sat at her desk, took the phone off the hook and stared at her computer screen. When Joan is angry at work, she doesn't throw things, doesn't shout, doesn't take it out on anyone else. I really, really admire this woman.

At the end of the day, I went round and sat on the edge of her desk.

"Hello, old chum," I said.

"Hello you."

"Any luck?"

"I am ordered to fire her."

"And will you?"

"I can't renew her contract without approval. But I can hire temps and freelances on a day-to-day basis. I don't need his approval for that. I can keep her on like that."

"Have you told him that?"

"No I bloody well haven't. He'll have to lump it."

"What if he won't stand for that?"

"I don't know. I may have to go over his head somehow. I hate this sort of shit, George. This life could

243

be so much simpler if people like Basset didn't screw it up."

A pause of silent agreement.

"And what else is going on, Joan?"

She looked up at me and raised an eyebrow. "I believe the usual response to that question is, What do you mean?"

"I believe there is something going on in the corridor of power."

"Really? What have you heard?"

"Nothing. I've heard nothing. But that's because some people are keeping their office doors closed when they usually leave them open."

"That's rather subtle. So you think there's something going on because really you have heard nothing?"

"And a couple of associate editors have cancelled their holidays, according to the secretarial gossip. That usually means they are frightened of being away for some reason."

"But nothing else?"

"Er, no."

She considered my comments. "If anything happens that affects you, George, I will let you know, really I will. That's all. Don't talk it up."

"OK boss. And the Basset thing?"

"I won't budge."

And then there was the strange bit of the conversation that I keep going over in my head. As a parting shot, I said, "I'm glad I don't have your job."

And she said, "Are you? Would you never want my job?"

244

"Me? Never."

"You mean, even if my job came up, you wouldn't want it?"

"No! Certainly not. I'm not staying anyway. I've said that. And I could not stand to be here at all if you weren't in your job."

"You are a survivor, George. I'm sure you would be fine."

Next day, another strange thing happened. Basset wandered into our section, ignored Joan and Arabella completely, stood over my desk and flopped a ring-spined folder in front of me, open at a paragraph bearing my name.

"I thought this might interest you."

I glanced down at rows of numbers. There was a table with age groups and percentages and the names of some other writers.

I said, "It looks too difficult to me."

"It's our readership survey. It says you are one of our most well-recognized writers. Even though you are tucked away at the bottom of the page, a high number of readers recognize your name and read you every week. Mostly the over-35s, of course, but there's a lot of them."

"Blimey." I looked at the figures. "I'll try not to let it go to my head."

He actually touched my shoulder for a moment, then said, "I just wanted to tell you, well done."

Then he left. I realized that everyone was staring at me. I felt ashamed.

★   ★   ★

I'm sitting in the flat with the lounge window open. Ben is at my feet resting. Actually, his great head is resting on my left foot, which is going to sleep in sympathy with him. Everything feels safe. But everything is not safe.

I have two confessions. This is my turning point. I have decided. Everything leads on from this.

Confession one: I am going to do something. I am going for Basset. I can't keep my head down or stay out of the way. I can't believe what I have in mind, but if this thing does not resolve itself, I am going to do it.

This is not for the sake of his discarded girlfriend. She's a grown woman. She knew what she was doing and how awkward it made us all feel. She's old enough to take the consequences when it's over. We are all grown-ups here, aren't we?

No, this is about Arabella and Joan. Especially Joan. What did she mean when she asked what I would do if her job came up? And why was Basset being nice to me?

I think the executives are preparing to battle among themselves in some game of musical chairs, and that Basset is setting up Joan to be the one without a chair when the music stops. First he bullies Arabella to try to get her on side while we were away. Then he goes out of his way to praise me. Bullying and flattering the two trusted lieutenants, a signal to stay out of the way when the shooting starts. Somehow he's luring Joan into a showdown.

And I can't have that. So there needs to be a pre-emptive strike, something public that brings it all out into the open, stops the doors being closed. So I will walk into the showdown for her.

Confession two: I'm not such a hero. It's no sacrifice if I get sacked. I can afford to do something, I can afford to chuck it all in.

I suppose, at last, that this is my deepest secret, my most embarrassing shame. No one has ever asked me about this, but it should be obvious to anyone who thinks about it. I have tried not to think about it until now.

I don't actually need to do my job.

A man reveals himself a bit at a time. I suppose that is partly what I have done in this journal. He may start by talking about his job and the things he hates about it. Then his likes and dislikes on other stuff, movies and music and things. His romantic and family circumstances, his obsessions, his fears. What he thinks about the young/the old/women. Points of pride and his biggest mistake. His fantasies, his deepest thoughts, his "inner child" and all that stuff.

And last of all, the thing that undermines him most. The thing that, when revealed, would make anyone dislike him because really he dislikes it too.

I don't need to work.

My Annie, my businesslike Annie, my investment-wise wife, was good with money. She had long been shoring up her pension fund. She had various life policies. She had shares and savings accounts quietly building up for the future. She wasn't mean — she gave more to charity than I did — but she was prudent. She knew her business. I understood none of it. She guided me on how to invest the money from selling my parents' house. We managed to pay off our mortgage. Generally, journalists are crap at money. She was not.

I gained hugely from her death. Her pension fund paid out a lump sum and a life pension to her widower. The life policies paid out too. Apart from some personal bequests, her will transferred the stocks and shares to my name. Not only that but, without my seeking it, my car insurance company won a payout from the council whose lorry we hit.

I have touched none of it, except to take the price of our old house to buy this flat. I counted up the rest and I was appalled. This money was meant to be for our old age, maybe early retirement. She gave her life to me, I failed to save her, and the result is that I am secure for the rest of my life. It's not like winning the lottery, but I could live on the pension and the interest without much changing my ways.

But I could not stop work when she died. I could not cash in on her death and anyway, the job kept me going. I admit that. I had no other good way to spend my time. I happily sneered at the way other people spent their money, while I wanted nothing. Other people are trapped in daft jobs by the debts they have run up buying expensive things to compensate themselves for being in daft jobs. I have no such excuses.

Sometimes there are inquest reports in the paper about men who were made redundant but who kept it a secret for months or years, going out each day in their work clothes to catch the train as usual because they could not admit the truth, until more debts piled up and they finished themselves off. I feel like them, but in reverse. I have set off each day like some wage slave, and kept up appearances because I could not admit the truth, which is that I do not need to work.

It's taken a while but I faced it at Sidmouth: I do not want to do this job any more. I don't quite know what I want to do, but not this. So I can afford to take a risk, go out with a bit of a blaze.

Annie wouldn't mind me getting the sack for Joan. She was her friend. It's a noble cause, chivalrous even. Cometh the hour, cometh the man. I am Shane, I am Rick from *Casablanca*, I am Clark Gable. I can afford to ride into the sunset, alone, if I must. It's time to stop reacting, and act. After so long, it's time to stand up to a bully.

I feel like I am back in the hunt, going for the big beast. It's a shame that in modern life the hunt must take place in the office and not the wild outdoors. But this will do.

I will have to choose my day carefully, but I think that I can do it.

This is reckless. I feel like I felt when I bought that car. I've never done anything like this before. All I have to do is put something in my column that no one will spot until it's too late. Something carefully phrased that will get the right people asking questions. And I can do this, thanks to computers. It's all so wonderfully silly.

CHAPTER
ELEVEN

THE RESULTS OF SEX

Anti-Style
by George Worth
12 September

It's been a while since a politician was caught with his trousers down and accused of hypocrisy. I quite miss it. Either they have stopped having affairs or they are being much more clever about it.

Other people have not stopped having affairs. Some of them are the real hypocrites. Let's talk about them.

In newspapers, we love exposing adultery among politicians, showbiz types, and even the staff of "serious" political journals. It's hugely entertaining for everyone. As an excuse for our interest, we say that immorality among public figures should be exposed if they fail to live up to the family values that they have projected. We also say that power carries responsibility, and that a lack of morality in private life is a clue to a lack of morals generally.

Partly, this is high-handed rubbish. The way we live our private lives does not necessarily make us do our jobs improperly. A caring doctor may be a serial adulterer in private, a good businessman may be an absent father. We have all had shadows in our behaviour, and thoughts that might not look too good under the full spotlight of the media.

And think about the size of that spotlight when a big story breaks. If every news organization — every national newspaper, every radio station, every TV channel and every news agency — puts just two journalists on the case, that's a pack of up to fifty motivated, competitive professionals hunting down the details of someone's private life. Nobody else can call up such a senior squad into immediate action at a moment's notice, not the police, not the SAS, not a politician. It's a heavy responsibility. Under that sort of spotlight, anyone can be made to look bad.

Adulterous politicians may be suspected of reckless-ness, as they know the risks, but it seems to me that the real hypocrites are elsewhere.

The real hypocrites are in newspapers.

This is a trade secret. You may never guess it, but newspaper executives have been known to commit adultery too.

No, you say, surely not. You don't recall reading much about it. And yet, how strange, all the accusa-tions levelled at politicians can also be levelled at the people who run newspapers. They preach family values. Their morality is a matter of public interest. They have power — in fact, they are far more influential than most politicians and they are not accountable through the ballot box.

In my time in national newspapers, I have known of a couple of adulterous proprietors whose activities just about made it into print, and a couple of editors. Yet I

251

have also known of a few senior executives whose activities never reached public attention. At the same time, their papers gleefully reported the private fumblings of even the most minor backbencher. The newspaper code of conduct does not have a section for hypocrisy.

Does it matter? I think it does. It's not often that I get so high-handed but I think the test is whether it can be demonstrated that private immorality has been carried through into the culprit's conduct of his job. If powerful figures with shaky marriages have strayed but still conduct their duties energetically and honourably, it's probably none of our business.

But if, say, they had an affair with a member of their staff, then sought to sack the lover once the affair was over, leading to the kind of office politics that disrupts the lives of innocent bystanders, then that should be a matter for general comment and examination.

And, of course, the same rule should apply to all.

"I can't believe you did this."

"I'm not sorry."

"But George, it was so sneaky," said Joan. "I didn't know you had it in you."

"Neither did I."

When Joan and Arabella went home the night before, they left me to see our last couple of pages away, alone with the joys of new technology. All the pages had been approved from on high, there were just a couple of minor corrections and alterations to finish. It was so easy to delete the Anti-Style column that Joan had seen (it was titled "What's My Line?" and suggested a new quiz show in which panellists would have to identify celebrity guests from the inane ringtones on their mobile phones). I transposed my substitute column and sent the page to production. There's a man somewhere whose job includes checking all finished pages, partly in case of late acts of sabotage. I reckoned that the lifestyle pages would be about the last on his list and he was unlikely to read right to the end. Anyway, he would have to know about the Basset situation to make the connection properly. The page sailed through. If anyone on the night news staff read the first edition and realized what I was really on about, they kept gleefully quiet.

Acts of editorial sabotage in newspapers are rare because the computer files can always identify the culprit and, as a general rule, people are not willing to be sacked. Staff on the brink of departure are the main risk. In recent years, an opinion writer on his last day on a tabloid shaped his final article so that the first letter of each sentence spelt out "fuck off", followed by the name of his proprietor.

I figured that I would get the sack but not straight away, as my instant departure would merely draw explicit attention to the very thing I had hinted at but not actually mentioned. (It was not as if I'd said something like, For true happiness send me a large cheque, or, I'm the world's greatest lover, call me, or just, Fuck off Basset.) There would be an in-house row. The job of Basset's woman would be rendered more safe to avoid accusations that the whole thing was about her. And Basset's bullying of Joan and Arabella would become better known around the office, so that he would not dare to make a bigger move for a while. They would all live happily ever after.

I am very stupid sometimes.

It was a strange morning. When I got in, a few of the girls hugged me or patted me on the back. At the coffee machine, a couple of male colleagues silently shook my hand. Others gave me a wide berth when we passed each other in the corridor. Some people don't like to be seen with a marked man.

I ignored my phone and asked our secretary to tell any callers that I was out. Joan was on the phone quite a lot. One of the calls was a summons from the editor's office to be available for an afternoon appointment.

Joan took me out for a walk just before lunchtime. In our open-plan world, it was the safest way to have a really serious talk. If we went to a pub or a restaurant, we would be seen or overheard, so we walked.

"Do you realize what you have done?" she began.

"Yes, of course." And I explained my cunning plan.

"You can be very, very stupid sometimes," she said. "First of all, you know very well that you are not supposed to use a newspaper to slag off journalists. Second, there is no way this is going to stay in-house. From the first thing this morning, a lot of people on this newspaper, including some quite senior people, have been ringing their friends on other newspapers and *Private Eye* to tell them about it."

"That'll just be normal gossip," I said. "It won't go anywhere."

254

"No, that will be gossip with a purpose. They will make sure their mates put it in the diary columns and the media sections, hinting that this is about Basset. Some of them want this because they have been having affairs themselves and they don't want their wives to think that your article might have been about them. And some just hate Basset and want to grab the chance to get at him publicly."

I thought for a moment. "Well, that's OK. Only *Private Eye* will actually name Basset. The others will only hint at his identity. Unless they can get him to speak."

"You may be interested to know that several other newspapers have already phoned Basset. Apparently, one of them has phoned his wife. She may well be the sort of woman who knows about his dalliances, but still . . ."

"Oh fuck."

"And the executives who are spreading the gossip won't be identified as the gossipmongers. The blame will fall only on you. Do you want to be sacked?"

"Me? Sacked from my wonderful life on the lifestyle pages? I can handle that. I think it's time."

We had been walking slowly round a couple of London blocks. People passed us at London speed, full stretch, gabbling into phones, munching sandwiches, guzzling coffee, swinging shopping bags, talking loudly. Our talk was barely a murmur. Joan stopped as we turned into a relatively empty side street and stared at me. She looked very worried.

"You might never get another job anywhere when this gets out. Did you really think that you were helping me?"

"You asked me if I'd want to do your job if it fell vacant. Surely that was an admission that you were in danger?"

"But — that was nothing to do with the Basset thing!"

"What was it about then?"

Pause.

"Nothing. Something else. Maybe nothing."

"You still can't say?"

"Oh George. You've spent so long with your sad old thoughts, you've forgotten that what you do affects things, lots of other things, in ways you don't always know."

"Joan, I would never do anything to harm you. Not you. After all this time. Look, I'll put it right. I'll offer my resignation or something. Anything. This is down to me."

"Resign? Oh bugger that. That wouldn't work at all."

Then she hugged me and I hugged her. Two old friends, two of Annie's nearest and dearest, giving each other's shoulders a squeeze in a London street. Then she let go of me and gave me my orders.

"I want you out of the office for a bit while I try to clear this up."

"You mean like I'm suspended or something?"

"Call it gardening leave. It will buy time. Say, till next week. We've got some of your unpublished pieces to fill your space while you are away. I'll say that I have sent you home to think things over. That way I'll have done something and it'll look like the editor has done something too. He'll have to think about the rest of it. He takes a long time to think. Decisions aren't his strongest point. They'll have to think about whether they actually want to lose you."

"They don't need to think too seriously about that."

She smiled at me. There was a bit of pity but still some respect. And maybe some amazement too. "George, this is now part of something that's much more serious. Just keep your head down, you fool. Annie would be very surprised at you."

I went back to the office to get my bag and sort out a few things to hand over to Arabella to handle while I was away. While I was there, my phone rang and I answered it without thinking. It was Maggie, saying that my piece would make a great subject for her programme. She had even lined up a sacked Cabinet minister to join in.

I said that I couldn't make it for the rest of this month. Nothing I could explain. I was just going to be very, very busy.

It's nearly two weeks later and I am still not allowed back. I tell Joan on the phone, look, I'll resign, I want to resign. And she says, no, not over this, hang on a bit longer, it'll probably be all right to come in next Monday.

My column has appeared each week. Any careful columnist keeps a few spare, timeless articles on file, a few leftover rants, in case of emergency or a blank mind. I read these words in the paper now and it's like they have been written by someone else.

I'm not good at doing nothing. I don't think I would suit the lifestyle of the idle rich.

It's funny, I have always felt resentful when other people and things waste my time. I have always felt that, on my deathbed, I'll try to claim extra time backdated in return for all the accumulated hours I must have spent, say, waiting for barmaids to try to operate a new till. All the time I have spent waiting for computers to switch on and sort themselves out. Time spent trying to find a matching pair of socks, or the time spent waiting at the cashpoint behind someone who seems to have found a PlayStation option on the screen for all the buttons they keep pressing. All those times when I have held open a shop door for a woman, and ten more people sailed through without a thank you, as if I was a doorman. Time spent trying to get things out of shrink wrap. Time spent waiting to open the door of the washing machine after the cycle has finished.

Add to that: time spent writing a pointless list as an idea for a column that I will never write. Time spent with too much thinking, too much mind noise.

For it seems that I have been wasting my own time.

Basset was named by *Private Eye*, and some of the newspaper diaries gave dark hints. But here's a thing: Pauline, the ex-mistress, has said that she doesn't want to stay anyway, that we'd all been very kind but really she didn't want to be in the same building as Basset and she's got a job lined up somewhere else.

Nothing else seems to have changed.

Really, I'm not safe to be at large. I feel like I've been in another crash. It's as if every time I try to do something, to change things, it goes kapow, clunk. I've really mucked things up, and all for nothing.

I had a strange moment at the shops the other day. I had wandered down to Camden high street, just a few bus stops away, looking for a book, a CD, an idea or something. I found myself watching people again, surging around with such purpose. For some time, for a long time, I have thought of them as basically absurd. All this striving. Didn't they know they were all going to die one day? What was the point? Who did they think they were, anyway?

Yet I have to admit, they have a kind of reckless courage. They know that they are going to die one day, they must know it, yet they carry on in defiance of this obvious fact. I had spent a long time mocking them for it. But now, for a moment, I felt a kind of fondness, almost envy. I still couldn't believe this was my tribe but I'm impressed at how they battle on, driven by their relentless will and some sort of idea that the purpose of life must be to live it, somehow, anyhow. And what did I know about their other lives, their real lives away from the shops, and whatever miseries they had been through? Who did I think I was, anyway?

And I thought, we're all survivors really. Everyone is a survivor of endless events and coincidences we can't control. What we all want are a few shiny moments, those feel-good cliché moments, when it all seems to fit into place and we get our own scene in the big picture.

Maybe that's what the most determined shoppers want to find — something that suits them to perfection, that makes them feel just right for a moment, the star of their own movie, their defiant protest against the passing years.

Among the crowd on the pavement there was a man rattling a tin, collecting for charity, gathering up the spare change that had not been spent on things. I smiled. It could have been Dad in the old days, doing some of his charity stuff. He didn't mind rattling a tin at shoppers, reminding them that there were problems somewhere and they could still help. After all, that was one of his rules: often the best way to protest was to do a bit of good.

I know I'm not doing much good. There's no point in being tough and resilient and reserved if I'm just stuck on my own, grumbling.

Things are different at home. I am slowly losing Ben. I am not needed there either. My relationship with his owner has always been a little strained, I suppose. Rosalind has never regarded me as anyone interesting, but I don't mind that. She has seemed to lead a life free from romance, and that's fine too. But now things have changed. She has a bloke. Derek is an ambulance man, a big bloke in a proper job who generally looks at me like I'm an intruding idiot. Derek likes to be around to help, Derek often works different shifts to Rosalind, and Derek likes dogs. Three times in the past week I have asked to take Ben out, only to find that he has company already. Mutual embarrassment. It's like being a kid again, calling round at a house to see if a friend can come out to play, only to find that he is busy. Ben greets me, but he is torn. Rosalind told me that Ben and Derek were getting to know each other and that it was important to her.

I've been thinking, I'd like to travel round a bit. Get out of London, write a book. I've got an idea for some kind of a history/travel book, telling British history through places. It's sort of a plan.

In the meantime, I've tried to have an active phone life. Joan. Maurice and the family (young Annie liked the dress). Justin. He's coming over on Saturday with the still pregnant Sandra for a visit, combining a bit of work with seeing me, taking the train to the Heath. I'll be meeting them with Ben, I have permission this once.

I'd been wondering about my chances of tracing the phone number of a clog-dancing, widowed librarian named Caroline, somewhere in the Durham area. And then wondering what I would say if I found her. I might sound a little strange and desperate, a rare example of a media "personality" stalking a listener rather than the other way round.

Then, an envelope in the office's stationery arrived in the post. I thought, here we go, it's an invitation to a disciplinary hearing. But no, inside was a handwritten note from Joan saying: "Thought you might be interested in this." Enclosed was a letter to me at the paper. With a County Durham address. A phone number. A name. Neat handwriting, as if written with some thought.

"Hello. I'm not sure what to say when my name appears in a national newspaper column as some sort of crazy cloggie. Was this a punishment for standing you up, or was it something else?

"I had to leave Sidmouth in a hurry on the Friday afternoon because my son rang to say that my mum was seriously ill with a chest bug. Most of my pals left with me because we were sharing a car and the week was nearly over anyway. Mum was in hospital for a while. Since she got home she's been catching up with the papers. She's a loyal reader and doesn't like to miss anything. Finally she saw your article on the festival and showed it to me.

"I had left our evening as a good memory. For all I know, you may spend your entire private life chatting with women who have recognized you, although it did not seem that way to me. I like to think it may just be possible that you might want to talk again sometime. And I'd like that too.

Caroline."

I reached for the phone but then I thought, what do I say about what I am doing right now? Hello, I'm on suspension for trying to fix the man who once tried to screw my late wife, and I may have to spend the rest of my existence living on the money she left me.

I decided to leave it for now. See how things turn out. Get on with stuff.

In all this time off, I've had one appointment to keep, and after that I decided to do something that I had been putting off for two years. I sorted out Annie's papers. All the things I had put in a box and ignored.

They divided into three groups: photographs, letters/diaries, and money. This is a life. This is what we leave when we go unexpectedly. These are the traces of existence.

The photographs were mostly leftovers. We kept albums of the best pictures of our lives, and the albums were in my bookcase. In her desk, there had been a drawer of other pictures, mostly in those envelopes you get when you collect a film from the chemist. Pictures that never quite made it to the album, the two of us looking less than perfect, one of us blinking or windblown on a trip to the seaside, or growing tired of looking at the camera and the smile fading. It meant that they were pictures of the real us, as we truly were. As I was sorting them, two snapshots dropped from separate ends of the pile: Annie just after I had met her, and Annie towards the end. I just held one in either hand and thought how all the time in the middle was me. There was this young single girl and there was this woman approaching middle age, and this whole chunk of life had been taken up with being with me, as if there was nothing better she could have done.

The letters included none from me. I don't think I ever wrote my wife a letter. Did I never? We communicated by phone, we lived in the same city, I never took a holiday without her. But did I never write her a note just to say I loved her, except in some long-discarded valentine cards? I told her often enough but that left no trace. There were letters from everyone else, carefully kept, from her friends and godchildren. It reminded me how I had let them all down, cut them all off, since she went. There were no revelations, nobody I did not know.

Her diaries were simple and businesslike, brief notes and reminders of domestic life, short mentions of daily events so that she could announce, as she often did, that this time two years ago we had been in St Ives, or Brittany, or wherever. (Of course, if we'd had a home computer all those years, maybe she would have done her diaries on it and I wouldn't even have these, something in her own writing, something she touched.) Each diary ended with a summary of the year's events, favourite books, best films, high points, low points. I knew she did this, I helped to vote on the best and the worst. Each diary began with resolutions, which she often confided. An organized woman, my wife, a creator of caring habits. Often her resolutions were about other people, things she would do for relatives and godchildren, take them to a special place, remember to ask them about a new interest.

And one resolution about me, at the start of the year when I bought the car: "Must shake George out of the doldrums."

Lastly, I sorted out the money.

It was tempting fate for Justin and Sandra to come to visit me, and for Justin to leave me to look after her while he did a spot of work. Bloody Young People.

I waited with Ben by the brick cafe near the tennis courts, to watch for Justin and Sandra walking up from the railway station. I spotted them easily — Sandra was huge in a voluminous summer frock, and walking very carefully. She was due in the next week or so. When Ben saw Justin, he woofed and ran down to greet him. Ben never forgets a friend who fed him.

We had a coffee at an outside table, Sandra easing herself into a seat as if testing it for strength.

"I'll never look at a fat person in the same way ever again," she said. "It's like carrying around your own prison."

"How's everything?"

"It's weird. Usually the big events in your life are Out There somewhere. A new job, a new flat. They're places you go to. This is already here. There are four human beings at this table. This is going to come out of me."

Justin and I stared at her stomach. It is absolutely impossible for a man to contemplate giving birth. No matter how empathic we are, no matter how hard we try to imagine it, we simply cannot do it.

"We've had a few false alarms," said Justin. "Sensations that turned out to be nothing yet."

"How do you tell the difference?"

"Who knows?" said Sandra. "Some twinges are just twinges, some mean it's on the way. I keep thinking it's time to get my hospital bag, then I realize it isn't. I nearly didn't come along today, then I thought sod it, why not?"

Justin was fiddling with a snazzy new mobile phone that could apparently play movie clips, music and games, tell him the news, take photographs and hold half a book if required. (He said it was his last boy toy before all the toys he would have to buy for the baby.)

265

The phone bit seems increasingly irrelevant — who wants to speak to anyone when you've got all that other stuff to do? — but he was waiting for a tip-off. He was working on a lifestyle feature about the new home of a semi-retired pop star in Highgate village, and the interior designer had granted permission for a photographer to enter the exalted premises. Justin was waiting for a call from the photographer to meet outside the house so he could go in with him and look around. He reckoned it would take about an hour at the most.

While we waited for the call, we all took a careful walk part of the way up Parliament Hill, Ben racing ahead, Justin and me trying to slow down to Sandra's pace. Near the top, we actually pushed her up.

Justin and I started to laugh.

"Bloody men," she said. "It's not funny."

"Is this really wise?" I asked.

"Dunno, don't care," said Sandra. "Justin said this was a good view. I want to see it. I'm not a bloody invalid."

London looked restful in the September sun. Down there people were battling for money and parking spaces and refugee status and sex and shopping. Up here it was just a silent view, from Battersea Power Station across to Canary Wharf. Sod London, I thought, it doesn't impress me.

I remembered the last time I was up here with Justin and Ben, when I had told Justin my tale of woe. Sandra sat on the bench where we had sat that night.

"How are things, really?" he asked.

"Better. I'm OK."

"Any news about work?"

"I'm back on Monday. I'll sort it out then. You'd better tell me the gossip when you get back from your star's home. We'll have a meal."

Back down the hill, the neighbourhood was strangely quiet because roadworks in the village had blocked off most of the traffic that usually comes our way. Justin got his phone call, kissed Sandra on the cheek and said, "See you soon." We arranged to meet at a restaurant. I said, "Don't worry, I'll look after her." Then he headed up the lane.

As he walked off, Sandra said, "I'd like a rest now."

"We'll go and sit in the back garden. Or you can come up to the flat if you can make the stairs. You can see where Justin slept."

She smiled. "That seems a long time ago now."

She looked sweet and stately as she ambled along the pavement, a gentle mother figure carrying part of the future inside her, something she would teach to walk and talk, something to share with the world . . .

And then, of course, she stopped suddenly at my front gate and said, "Oh fuck."

Pause. The world revolving. Maybe something big happening. Oh fuck what? You can't be serious. Just wait an hour, please.

"I don't think that walk was such a good idea," she said. "Or looking at it another way, it's done the trick. I think my waters just broke."

Me staring at her. Her staring at me. Ben perhaps noting an unusual smell but not sure quite what to do, just hovering between us, facing her.

267

"I really think they have, George."

"OK, right. Um, you know, I've never been quite sure what that means."

She was standing with her legs apart.

"It means, it bloody means, that the life-support pod inside me is breaking up and the passenger is preparing to launch. It means that the contractions I have been ignoring today were real and they are happening more often. It means I want to sit down. It means I want to get to a fucking hospital fairly soon."

She slumped on the front steps, breathless. My turn to speak.

"Right, OK, right. Stay here. There's a hospital just up the hill. I'll go and look for a taxi."

"OK. Good luck."

I ran to the corner of the street. Sometimes you can get a taxi right away, on its way back to the city centre from a Highgate drop-off. Saturdays aren't good though. Not so many on a Saturday. And today, none at all. Bloody roadworks.

I waited a minute. Two minutes. There's a body language of a Londoner desperately looking for a taxi. Glaring in all directions, like a hunter, turning at every sound of a diesel engine, stepping forward hopefully at a possible sighting in the distance, standing on tiptoe, dropping back disconsolate when you realize it's just another damn 4x4 people carrier. I went through it all, then I ran back to Sandra. She looked wretched, clutching her stomach with one hand, stroking Ben's head with the other as he sat beside her.

She said, "Now I think I've had a show."

A show? How did she mean, a show? Somehow I didn't think she meant at a theatre or an art gallery. I should know more about this stuff. I'm supposed to be the older generation here.

"No sign of a taxi," I said. "We can phone for one. Or an ambulance?"

"But they might take bloody ages. And the ambulance people might think I'm not urgent unless the head is almost popping out. Oh God! I just want to get there and feel safe. Haven't you got a car? Oh no, you haven't, sorry. Isn't there anyone else? This is an emergency, we're in London for fuck's sake."

Then she said, "Whose car is that?"

She pointed to Rosalind's old Metro in the driveway.

"It's my neighbour's. Ben's owner. She walks to work. She's there now, at the hospital, oddly enough."

"Can you get into her flat? Do you know where she keeps her car keys?"

"Yes, I think so, they're on a hook in the kitchen with her other keys. But even if we could take the car, you can't drive in your state."

Pause.

"No, George, I can't drive in my state. But you can."

"Me? But I don't drive any more."

She looked at me. Ben looked at me. It felt like all the world was looking at me.

"George, I know that you have been through a lot and I wouldn't ask this if I wasn't desperate but I think I'm going into labour sometime soon and you are all I've got."

I stared back.

"It's only up the hill, isn't it? Your neighbour's a nurse or something, surely she'll understand, won't she? Please, George, just-fucking-get-me-there."

The last bit would have been a shout if she wasn't so breathless with panic and possibly pain. Instead it came out like a sob.

I stopped thinking and just acted. Don't think, I thought. Just do. I took Ben into his flat, told him I would be back soon and that I hoped this would not get me banned from ever seeing him again. Or arrested for car theft. I came out with the car keys, loaded Sandra into the passenger seat, got into the driver's seat. And sat frozen.

God, don't let me screw this up, it's such a short way, I'll give up anything, I'll give up Ben, I'll give up the job, just let me get this right.

"Key in the ignition," said Sandra, breathing in and out between each few words. "Check gear, turn ignition, select gear, handbrake off. Remember? I'll talk you through."

"Why are you doing that — making that panting noise with your breathing?"

"These are my breathing exercises. They are supposed to calm me down."

"Can I do them too?"

"Yes, fine, great (*pant, pant*). I'll talk you through the driving, you do my breathing exercises. Fine."

I looked at her and looked at my reflection in the rear-view mirror. We were both pale. We were both sweating. We were both scared. We would both have preferred it if she did the driving and I gave birth.

270

The car lurched forward.

"Stop at the kerb! (*pant, pant*). Now then George, which way are we going? Right or left?"

"Right (*pant*), left (*pant*), then right (*pant*)."

"Look both ways (*pant*), pull out slowly (*pant*)."

We edged up the road to the corner, turned, then edged to the next junction. Gently does it. Both staring ahead. I was turning right and risking a change of gear when a bus came up on my left. I braked.

"Well done George (*pant*). We may all make it alive (*pant*)."

"Are you sure this might be labour (*pant*)? Are you having more, you know, thingies, contractions (*pant*)?"

"Yes (*pant*). I have never felt like this (*pant*). Can we get moving again (*pant*)? Or I'll be having the baby here."

I moved out and up the lane, somewhere between the speed of a novice L-driver and a pensioner out for a Sunday tootle. I was going so slowly that the car stalled on the way up the hill. I started it again and risked a little speed.

"Now where (*pant*)?"

"Up to the cemetery (*pant*)."

"Terrific (*pant*)."

"Turn right, left through the housing estate, left and right, then left on the main road and we are there."

"Go on then (*pant*)."

Behind us, a snazzy-looking Highgate car blasted its horn. We ignored it. I hugged the centre white line until the turning. I couldn't believe how crap I was at

271

driving. I risked more speed. Then we hit the speed bumps.

"OK (*pant*). Let's slow down (*pant*) on this bit. I'm shaking enough (*pant*)."

Two more corners and the final stretch. The dark mass of the old Victorian hospital rose on our left.

"Can't we stop (*pant*) and go in here?"

"Sorry, no (*pant*). There's a giant security wall all the way round. There's only one entrance."

"Terrific (*pant*). You've brought me to a prison."

Highgate Hill was full of diverted traffic. I edged out. No one gave way.

"Hit the horn (*pant*)."

"I can't (*pant*). I need both hands on the wheel."

"OK (*pant*). Let me."

Sandra reached across and played an insistent beat on the horn. People glared but a bus actually stopped. We squeezed through and I edged around half a dozen cars and into the hospital entrance. I looked for a place to park.

"Sandra (*pant*)?"

"Yes (*pant*)?"

"You can stop doing that with the horn now. We've arrived."

"Gear in neutral, handbrake on, switch off engine."

"OK. Now what?"

"Help me out (*pant*)."

She leant on me, legs awkwardly apart, and we staggered through the nearest doors like the last runners in a three-legged race. Inside the receptionist was busy but a security guard came into view.

"Maternity!" I shouted. "Where's maternity?"

He grinned, like we were not the first people who had been through this. I found a hospital wheelchair, loaded her up, then we were off again.

The maternity nurse had also seen this before.

Sandra in a cubicle. Me outside while she undressed. Nurse puzzled why I was being shy. Me explaining that I was not the father.

The father.

"Sandra, we haven't called Justin!"

"Oh no! Justin! Can't think why we forgot." She laughed. "You can come in now, George."

She was lying on a bed, looking more relaxed, in a green smock. A more senior nurse arrived, possibly a midwife. How would I know?

"One minute," Sandra told her, then reached into her handbag. "George, you have been wonderful. Please can you do two more things? Here are the keys to our flat. Can you go there and get my overnight bag? It's in the hall. Get the Tube or something. You don't have to drive."

"Thanks, great, OK. And the other thing?"

"Here's my mobile phone. Go and ring Justin. He's on memory in the address list, it just dials him automatically."

"Great. Just one problem."

"What?"

"How do you use the phone, exactly?"

"Oh George, you're amazing."

"I hate to interrupt," said the midwifey person. "You can't use a mobile in the hospital, they interfere with equipment. There's a payphone down the hall."

I said, "But I don't know the number of his new mobile."

Sandra said, "And I can't remember it. It's all in my phone."

As the midwife prepared to examine her, Sandra tried to tell me what to do, then finally just said, "Good luck, George."

"Good luck, Sandra." We smiled at each other and I fled.

Outside the hospital there were the usual clusters of smokers and people on mobile phones. Twice I tried punching the minuscule buttons on Sandra's phone, and twice I failed. I couldn't even find Justin's number, let alone dial it automatically. Nearby a young man with an earring and a stud in his eyebrow had just finished a call on a similar-looking phone and was starting to check his text messages. I asked him for help, which I suppose was pretty much an invitation to be mugged. He looked at me as if I was an idiot, took hold of the phone and started the call, then handed it back. Apparently they work much better when they are switched on.

"Hello?"

"Justin, where are you?"

"I'm sitting in a designer lounge, sipping something interesting and . . . Why? What's happened?"

"Sandra's going into labour. She's at the hospital on the hill."

"You're kidding. But I've only been gone about half an hour."

Was that all?

"I'm going to your flat to get her bag. You get down to the hospital. She's in maternity."

"Well, I'm glad it's not geriatrics. Did you get an ambulance?"

"No, I drove her."

"You what?"

"I'll tell you another time."

"Thanks George, I'm on my way."

I was wondering if I should call into casualty to find Rosalind, and interrupt a few dozen life-saving treatments and a weekend queue of about one hundred patients while I told her about the car. Then I saw the ambulances parked nearby and I wondered if Derek was about. Wonderfully, he was there on standby, large as life. Funny seeing you here, I said. Where do you think I'd be, I'm a paramedic, I work here, he said. Look, I said, and I started to blather about the car. He looked at me like I was barmy, like I'd offended him personally by not calling an ambulance, and suggested that I should return the car soon. I told him that I'd just got a quick errand to run by Tube.

Almost two hours later, I was back at maternity. At the reception desk I explained that I had brought the bag for Sandra Smith who urgently wanted her relaxation tapes and her nightie.

"It may be a bit late now, she's in the delivery room. You wait, I'll go and see."

I sat down. After a minute, the nurse returned

"Things are a bit advanced. I can look after the bag if you want to leave."

"Er, no, thanks, I'll wait."

So I sat there, like an expectant father. Life went on around me. It was a nice experience to be in a part of a hospital where people were at the start of life and not at the end. There was another panic arrival, visitors came and went, babies cried in the distance. It was strangely reassuring. I was exhausted. After a few moments, I must have dozed off.

When I woke up, Justin was standing over me.

"Hello, George."

"Hi. Anything happening?"

"Yes! I'm a dad."

"Is Sandra all right? Is the baby all right?"

"They're fine. It's a girl. I've got a daughter."

Then we both burst into tears. I half stood up, he hunched down and we hugged each other. A shared, shiny moment of real life.

Men.

"Sandra told me about the drive here," he said. "Amazing."

"Oh bugger. The car!"

"What?"

"It's still outside, if it's not been towed away. Are you doing anything right now?"

"No, they're both asleep."

"Well, would you drive me home? Then would you help me with a spot of grovelling to the car's owner if she's there? Then maybe we could have a drink."

He beamed at me.

"George, that would be fine. And can you do me a favour?"

"What, another one?"

"I need somewhere local to stay the night."

"Again? Oh all right then."

CHAPTER
TWELVE

LOST AND FOUND

Anti-Style
by George Worth
(*hold for publication date in October*)

Older blokes don't like to throw things away. We're hopeless at it. We keep music albums that we no longer play, clothes that are worn out, books that we will never read again. Some men even hoard old bits of wood and broken radios, just on the off chance that it might all come in handy one day for something other than Bonfire Night.

We are sentimental that way. If something has served us well, it seems unfair to just chuck it in the bin without a good reason. This may be why changes in fashion are less appealing to us. What's the point of reinventing yourself with a whole new style when you haven't finished with the old stuff yet?

Life is just too short to worry about fashions, surely? Life is just too short anyway. So much to do, so little time, so much to remember. You get the hang of a few things, learn how to order the right wine, get the bank cashier to recognize you and maybe treat you with a little respect then, bang, you realize you can't remember the name of the wine you liked last time and you have forgotten your pin number and it's like you are a stuttering teenager again. There is junk in our minds too, it's like a giant lost-property office in there and sometimes it gets too full to take in any new information.

Soon everything seems to go on without you. People die. Babies get born. The dead people once knew everything. The babies know nothing. It all goes round again. Maybe male junk and female fashion are just two different ways of fighting the passage of time. Hoarding stuff is a way of pretending that the years haven't changed, fashion is a way of pretending that you are keeping up with the years and maybe even getting a season ahead of time.

Blokes like to keep things because the things have been landmarks of our lives. In our prehistoric days as hunters, we always needed to know where we were and where we had been. We liked to check the perimeters and know it was safe out there. (These days checking the perimeter has been reduced to locking the front door at night and surfing through all the TV channels just before we switch off.) Clinging onto the past makes a kind of sense. It helps to know where we have come from. The path of life may be short but there are ways to make it feel bigger and more solid under our feet, and one way is to look back and know that we were not born yesterday.

This does not, of course, help us to know where we are going or what will become of us. The truth is, at the bottom of an older man's respect for old junk is a fear that one day he may become a piece of junk himself. Like that old timber or the broken radios, just lying around, possibly of use if the right situation arises, if someone needs it. Otherwise, just junk. Or like some appliance that has gone just a bit wrong but isn't worth repairing in this throwaway age, so it simply gets junked and replaced before its time.

This fear is why middle-aged men commit sudden, rash acts of protest against the years, and chuck it all in, or run off with the barmaid or buy a bright red sports car. The weight of the junk gets too much, the perimeter gets too familiar and we are not good at subtle changes.

I am having a bit of a clear-out myself at the moment. For a start, I am chucking this column. You have put up with my thoughts on the lifestyle world for nearly three years and you will never know quite how much it has meant to me in its way. Thank you for all your thoughts and comments, but it is time for change. This is my last appearance here.

I am going hunting in new pastures, looking for new prey. Maybe we will meet along the way. I'll be the one with the new winter coat and the faraway look in his eyes. Just think of me as a fashion that's changing. After all this time, you can do that, if I can.

A new editor! The newspaper has a new editor. So that's what was going on. An old editor squeezed out, a new one dropped in. Simple, really.

"I'm sorry," said Joan. "I just couldn't tell you. There was a bit of a battle. It could have gone either way. It was better that you didn't know."

"That's OK," I said. "I'm not good at plotting. Take me for a drink at lunchtime and tell me what it all means."

This was Monday, the day I returned to the office, not knowing what was going to happen to me or what I was going to do. No wonder I hadn't been called in for a bollocking from the editor during my time off. He must have been far too busy negotiating his severance pay to be concerned about me.

The news came through at the very start of the day. Our old boss had already gone, cleared his desk at the weekend, leaving an email for his secretary to spread around, thanking us all for wonderful times together, urging support for his successor, who was on his way into the building as the news was announced.

I still didn't want to stay, but I couldn't quite manage to leave until everything was sorted out.

We looked to see the name of the new man. It looked vaguely familiar to me, Christopher something or other. Then I realized it was Chris from Sidmouth, Joan's friend.

The man who listened as I slagged off every trend in the entire newspaper industry. That Chris.

His appointment did not get much news coverage. Editors change about as often as football managers, but no one cares as much about them in the outside world. I doubt if 10 per cent of readers can name the editor of their daily paper, despite all the power involved. Really they should be analysed as much as a new Cabinet minister, but few journalists are going to write an aggressive, warts-and-all analysis of someone they may one day need to ask for a job. Our direct rivals might give a few sneers in their media pages, usually written by ousted editors. If an editorship is changed too often it's portrayed as a sign of panic, and if the same editor has been around for a while, like our guy, it's supposed to be a sign of the paper being tired. Ho-hum.

I expected that my return would give me some vague, comforting sense of purpose, back in the old routine, but it didn't. So I helped the girls with a collection to buy a gift for Justin's baby. I noticed Basset a couple of times on the other side of the office. I like to think that he was avoiding me — I can brazen this out if he can — but I expect that at the moment he's simply too busy trying to ingratiate himself with the new man. There was no excitement over the change at the top, just a lot of weary tension. Changes of editor make people feel insecure. For years they have been acting on unwritten promises of promotions and opportunities from one guy, then he's gone and all bets are off. A whim of the proprietor had shifted the editor, so no one was safe. Time for change. Time to shake things up, especially the share price.

"So what's really been happening?" I asked Joan at lunch. The wine bar was buzzing with small groups of hacks from the office trying to work out what it all meant and how they should adjust their thinking. Journalists have easy-wipe minds. We have to. Things that may be terribly newsworthy one moment are often superseded within hours or minutes. Stories that were desperately important get dropped and we must just walk away with a shrug. A new editor must mean new priorities. We just have to know the new direction and if we can live with it.

"It's simple enough," said Joan quietly. "I've known Chris for years and we've always kept in touch. When this paper started trying to poach him, he rang me to find out what things were like here."

"So you've been briefing him. Told him a few ideas that might impress our beloved proprietor. Pointed out a few weaknesses. On the unspoken understanding that his arrival might just be good for you."

She smiled and looked at her glass of wine. "Well, I might have helped a bit, but not much. He's a smart guy. He had a few ideas of his own, he just wanted to try them out on someone. I didn't say anything that could be seen as disloyal."

"And how many people knew that things might be changing?"

"Just a few at the top. They know when the skids might be under an editor. There are angry phone calls from the owner. The big money goes into abeyance. Nobody talks too much, they are too busy trying to use their knowledge for themselves."

"And knowledge is power." I poured her another glass. "So this is what you meant when you hinted that your job might be changing. You might be going up, not out. I tried to be your Sir Galahad and really I am just one of the ignorant rabble."

She put her hand on my arm. "George, if I need a champion I know that you would come through somehow. I know what you did to get Sandra to hospital."

"Justin's going to miss all this now he's on paternity leave. I must call in on him later in the week."

"I doubt whether any changes will reach as far as him."

"And how far will they reach? And when? Is the new man going to settle in first or hit the ground running?"

"Running, I think. Better to get the tension out of the way, yes?"

"And do you know what's happening to you? Or me?"

"He is seeing a few executives today or tomorrow morning. I'm going in this afternoon. I don't know anything for sure. He is his own man. Really, anything could happen."

I spent much of my afternoon sorting out my desk and wading through a few weeks of internal emails. There was a short one from Basset that just said: "You write crap after all."

My resignation letter was in my pocket, undated.

It was early evening before Joan got her call to go to see the new man. It must be strange to hear your destiny from a chap you knew as a raw recruit. After half an hour she still had not returned, and I had to leave to get to another appointment. I would just have to catch up with the news the next day.

Tuesday. Office politics are quite funny when you don't care about them any more, when you know that you are out. I'd been planning a farewell column about how men never throw anything away, but I wasn't sure whether it would ever get printed, whether it would be modern enough for the new chap. He must be a modernizer, surely, they all are. Aiming for those young professional readers who the circulation boys always describe as vital. More stuff about pop stars and fashion, more Internet things, less of the mundane stuff about the realities of life and when reality does stray in, dress it all up like a romantic novel or a thriller as if it all makes sense somehow.

Joan wasn't there. She left a message that she was up with a designer on another floor, working on some ideas for the editor. She would not be coming into our section that day. But the editor might want to see me.

After polishing the same old winter-fashion page a dozen times in the afternoon, I got the call from the editor's secretary. Would I like to come and meet the man for a few minutes? So I wandered across the main floor, and people could see where I was heading, well away from my usual territory, through the newsroom, beyond the potted palms, into the corridor of power, down to the big door at the end.

I'd never been sacked before.

He was sitting at his desk as the secretary showed me in. He looked so bloody young. No tie, sleeves rolled up, pages in front of him, afternoon conference due to start in ten or fifteen minutes. Just time to squeeze in old Worth. This won't take long.

"George, take a seat," he said. "This shouldn't take long."

"Thank you," I said. "Nice to see you again." I tried a smile. He didn't smile back.

"There's a little matter outstanding," he said. "That article about Clive Basset. Rather an unwise thing to do, yes? Although Joan filled me in on the background.

"The thing is, George, I have to say, I am not sure that you are really executive material. If people are doing executive jobs, even junior executive jobs, I want their hearts to be in it. It struck me that a man who would connive at something like that would be better using his talents elsewhere."

Pause. I cleared my throat. Elsewhere?

"Elsewhere?" I said.

"There's some people I'd like to bring on, give them a chance." He was looking straight at me. "There are some people who really like working in lifestyle. People who would like your position there. Do you really enjoy it?"

"You know I don't. I've had no alternative."

And I'm thinking, this isn't the sack, it's taking too long. But what is it? And finally, he smiles.

"Well, there's your writing. Just the writing. You were quite a good reporter in the old days, I'm told."

"You want me to go back to reporting?" Demotion of the worst kind. Shame, embarrassment, scorn. An old hack skivvying for newsdesk, facing rivalry from young reporters. No thanks.

"No, good Lord no," he said. "I just want you to do a column. A different column, which would need some of your old skills."

A columnist. A proper columnist? Promotion to phoneyland. No way.

"This isn't promotion, let me make that clear, we should not call it that after what you did. But I want to take you out of lifestyle and let you rabbit on somewhere else. Instead of at the bottom of a lifestyle page, put you at the top or the side of a proper features page. Give you more space."

His voice dropped a little, as if confiding in me. "The thing is, well, whatever I do, I am going to be accused of being too modern, of alienating older readers. You are one of our more popular writers with the older lot, so if I give you a bigger display, it will reassure them."

"But what would I be writing about?"

"Well, we discussed this, didn't we, in Sidmouth? I don't want you to be topical, I don't want you to attack public figures. I just want you to be grumpy with a good heart. I seem to recall you talking about the stuff you think that the national media always miss. The little local battles and the forgotten Britain? Ordinary life? Anything you like, within reason. Go out and find it.

"The thing is, George, it's just possible you might be onto something. There's a feeling that some of the purely aspirational, lifestyle journalism may have had its day for a while. A lot of people are just spent out. They're broke. It's always impossible to say what readers really want, but some surveys are showing that they want us to connect more with everyday life. Families, work, communities and so on. They feel a bit left out if it's all fashion and celebrity scandals, all frocks and shocks. There might be a bit of a trend against that."

Pause. Then I spoke.

"So you are saying that I might be a bit of a trendsetter? In a non-trendy sort of way."

He smiled again. "What do you think?"

I said, "It sounds, um, interesting."

287

"Right." He had turned to his pages again and began putting them into piles. My time was up. "Think about it overnight, and come and see me again, er, late tomorrow morning. I'd like to get this sorted out. I'd like to hear some suggestions from you, to see if this can work, to make sure you are not running out of ideas. Thanks for coming in."

Outside his office, assorted news executives were waiting to come in for conference. I tried not to catch anyone's eye. Keep them guessing.

Good grief, I thought. Blimey. Part of me was thinking my big mouth had got me into another challenge, like when I said that best-man speeches are easy, or that time on the radio when I said that the twentieth century had not invented very much. This time I'd said that newspapers don't reflect ordinary life enough, and someone was saying OK, you go and do it then.

I tried not to grin as I wandered back through the newsroom. I seemed to have got away with the Basset thing, like I'd got away with driving Sandra to hospital. Maybe I could get away with this new column. More, this might be something that I actually wanted to do, at least for a while. It might be good for me, travelling around, talking to real people in real neighbourhoods.

I'm not so stupid that I can't see a second chance when it is presented to me, maybe a chance to see things differently, listen to other voices for a while. In the old days, before everything had to be glamorous, this sort of coverage was called down-your-way journalism, finding out what was happening where the

288

readers lived. I used to enjoy this stuff. Now it was a new idea? Had I become unfashionably fashionable?

I could still be grumpy, but on behalf of others. It would be like being let out of prison, a suspended sentence, probation with community service. Just to see how I could cope.

I went for a walk outside to have a think. Once again I found myself watching the crowds of people, and I had a bit of a rush of blood to the head. OK, I thought, maybe I'm going to remind myself what you all do when you're not shopping for a lifestyle, and I'll see what makes sense.

London was not the centre of the universe. Somewhere else, I could find local heroes rather than just national villains. Bits of protest, bits of pride, differences worth celebrating, joyful bits and strange bits in modern life. I could go to places a bit, well, grittier than just the likes of Northumberland and Devon. Maybe I could find some other, older voices. Perhaps the power of real protest starts around middle age, and it's up to us to protest when so many Young People seem too busy worrying about work and debts and parties and shopping.

This could even be interesting. If we are not all going to hell in a shopping cart, I suppose that something has to improve. We have to want better lives, not just better things. We all have to slow down. I know there are people out there still doing something, perhaps just one thing each, to make it better. If I could help a little bit, that could be my one thing. I've not been any use sitting on my own trying to solve problems like Age and

Death, so I could go out and do this instead. Just being grumpy isn't enough.

It would be a risk, it could all go wrong, but maybe I could feel like I was in the right tribe again. If I could feel connected and involved and useful, I might even feel happy. I might feel I deserve it.

Then I went back to my desk.

There was a small pile of letters on it. I said to Arabella, "What's all this?" She said, "That's your readers' mail for the past week or so. Joan hasn't had the time to sort it yet and possibly she won't ever have the time again. You're a big boy. You do it."

I was thinking, she looked unusually smart, even for her. Positively shining. She was just turning off her computer terminal. I said, "Going anywhere interesting?" She said it was her turn to see the editor.

So I sifted through the mail. I'd seen bits of it before, the nicer bits, people agreeing with me, people with ideas for subjects, people describing funny things that had happened to them.

I had not always seen the letters saying that I should get a life, that I was an old fart, an idiot, a leftie, a puritan or a snob. Letters in green ink or red ink and with words underlined. Letters saying that I was trying to put people off buying things, damaging businesses and the economy, or that I was obviously picking on them personally. Who did I think I was? Even lifestyle drivel can be a touchy subject when you tread on people's dreams. I put the letters in piles for standard replies from our secretary.

290

Of course, when I said that I was going to meet the public, to meet actual readers, that did not mean I had to meet *all* of the public, not *every* reader, did it? Not everybody would greet me with open arms.

Then I thought about another letter, lying on my desk at my flat.

Men have three kinds of fantasy, I remembered. There was the adventure fantasy. Well, I had rescued a damsel in distress on Saturday. Then there was the sports fantasy, and what are office politics if not a bloody game? And then there was the other kind of fantasy . . .

So when I went home, I rang Caroline. If nothing else, I needed to come up with a list of things about everyday life that a real person might feel were often missing from the papers.

We spoke for about an hour.

Maggie had been wrong. Sometimes it's good to speak to people who recognize you. There are other things to say.

Wednesday: there's Joan, Arabella and me, sitting at our desks. We were a strange triumvirate to have been packaging lifestyles to fill people's dreams. Clearly the team was going to change. None of us was saying how.

First thing, I polished off my male junk article with a new ending. Joan was looking at me brightly. Arabella was getting on with a page about the vital controversy over whether kitten heels or spike heels would be the must-buys from the latest choices in women's boots.

How could I give up all this? How could I have stood it for so long?

"Anything you want to discuss?" said Joan. "Anything at all?"

"Not yet," I said. "How about you?"

"I can't yet."

"How about you, Arabella?"

"Me neither," she grinned.

"So neither can I."

The call came just before eleven o'clock. Joan looked up from her screen and said, "Go get them, tiger."

I took the long walk again.

"George, welcome," said Chris. This time he was on his feet, walking me to the chair before going behind his desk. Yesterday was the softening up, this was clinching the deal.

A bit of blather at first. I would get a desk in the main features section, near Justin. My salary would be unchanged, which was fine considering the drop in duties. I might do other features but mainly I'd look out for ideas from regional papers and national organizations, and just go where I liked. He expected me to be out of the office quite a lot. I would be a columnist who went places and met Joe Public.

"I think I can do that," I said.

"So, what are the first possibilities?"

He'd been worried that I might run out of ideas. I had to prove otherwise without worrying him that I might go crazy with freedom. I cleared my throat: "Well, um, attitudes to death, and attitudes to birth, and everything in between. New estates where kids

292

moan they have nowhere to go and entire towns where grown-ups have nowhere to go except the shops. Village community centres that seem to offer nothing more than jam-making and clog dancing. Little local charities that help the poor and homeless, the ill and the lonely, and the problems they face. Local campaigns that have saved a local institution, and why it was in danger to start with. The historic sites that get ruined to make them accessible to tourists. The people who think getting a breath of fresh air means driving to a beer garden, and the glories they miss on the way. A day in the life of a long-distance footpath, or a road-crash patrol, or a cemetery, or a giant DIY store, or a provincial lap-dancing club, or a church that is still the centre of a community's life, or a library, or a village fête, or a local activity group struggling for lack of volunteers. Trying to buy old-fashioned gifts for children instead of all the film-related stuff. University courses that are obviously a waste of everyone's time.

"I could do some stunts: join a protest somewhere; learn something New Agey like meditation; or stand outside a big electrical retailers and ask people a) do they believe in global warming and b) if so, why have they just bought a TV for the third bedroom? Actually, there are a lot of questions I want to ask. Like, how much time do people spend on idle shopping and pointless Internet surfing, and what would happen if a fraction of that time was spent on helping with something in their neighbourhood? Or do people get less involved in their neighbourhoods because they are

293

always dreaming that they will soon move somewhere else . . .?"

Chris was starting to look a little apprehensive. Perhaps he'd guessed that I'd probably done damn all for my own neighbourhood. Perhaps he thought I might get myself into trouble, or that I was asking too many questions. But I'm curious now. I've got more of my old curiosity back. I really want to know this stuff. I ploughed on.

". . . Do people still have normal hobbies? Do we really have busier lives than previous generations, or do we just feel more pressured in our heads? Why do all Young People seem to want to be famous? Why do construction firms still keep building new office blocks that stand empty for ages? Are there any pubs that still hold sing-songs? Is it good or bad for an area when the first cappuccino cafe opens? When people chuck out furniture and household stuff because it's out of fashion, even though it's still in good condition, why is it so hard to find a way to give it to the poor, or do even the poor insist on being fashionable now? What's the effect of every greetings card being either obscene or moronic? Why isn't there a magazine for men who already know what a naked woman looks like? Why are modern philosophers no real use to anyone? Why do scientists waste their time on stupid things when there is so much important stuff to do, like at least coming up with a fashion shoe that women can walk in? Why don't the generations mix more in Britain? How do regional accents survive when people move house so often? Will we miss notes

294

and coins when plastic is virtually all that's left? What are people's rules of life? What are the real symbols of Britain, say, the twenty places where anyone would need to go to feel that they understand the nation's history . . .?"

"George."

"Yes?"

"I think some of those will work just fine. You've convinced me. That's enough for now. I hope you find some answers."

"OK," I said.

There were a couple of other points I wanted to mention. If he was keen to get us writing about real family life, I'd got an idea for an occasional column for someone to write in my old slot. And second, I needed to know what was going to happen to some other people. Just between us. I needed to know who I would be working for.

He looked away for a moment. He sounded tired when he began to speak; he was thoughtful, measured, like a man trying to pull a lot of strands together. For a moment I was envious of him, envious of his power to walk in and change everything, wave a wand and make everyone fit in with his imagined world. But I knew that I could never do it. Not really executive material, at the end of the day. He was right about that. I had feared that he might be my executioner, but instead he was like the prince who comes on at the end of a Shakespeare play and sorts out the lives of those who are left standing.

He finished with only a few interruptions from me. "So, how about it, George?"

"I thought you might want to see this," I said, handing him a printout of my column on junk. "I've got a couple of leftover Anti-Style articles that can be run first, and this could be my last."

He sat and read, smiled two or three times, reached for his pen to make a couple of marks that improved the odd sentence, then got to the end with a grin on his face.

"That's fine, George. Thank you."

I got up to go, we shook hands, and when I was halfway to the door he spoke again.

"George, one other thing. If you pull a stunt like that Basset article again, I will sack you."

"Yes. Of course."

When I got back to our section, I put my column in front of Joan, kissed her on the forehead, then left to have an early lunch on my own. When I got back she had left for an afternoon of meetings, but there was an email waiting for me.

It said: "Welcome back to the human race. Of course, you realize that these days we like our roving writers to be contactable by mobile phone?"

I wrote back: "No chance!"

In the afternoon I had to go to see a designer to look at possible ideas for the title of my new slot. They had tried a range of wording. "For What It's Worth". "Worth: A Visit". "Worth's while". There was a plain one that just said George Worth in firm, friendly letters.

I like that one, I said. It's as if I'm a brand.

★ ★ ★

On the way home, I called in to see Justin and Sandra. They both looked exhausted. The flat felt totally different to my previous visit. It was not that the decor had changed much, but that the decor clearly no longer mattered compared with the new arrival sleeping in a cot in the corner of the bedroom. There was a pile of babycare books on the coffee table, where Justin's style magazines used to be. There were baby clothes spilling out of a new cupboard in the corner. Classical music was playing.

"Is that Mozart?"

"Yup," said Justin. "It's supposed to help their brain development. She cries if I play my stuff."

"Good for her."

Sandra laughed a tired laugh and said, "We play Brahms at night. It sends us all to sleep, but not for long."

I stared for a while at the baby, who looked the same as all babies except that I felt connected to this one. There had been three of us in the car last Saturday, after all. I looked into her face and imagined saying to her, "Welcome to the world. There's lots of heartbreak ahead, but it's too bloody late for you to turn back now." She was to be called Lily, a name from both their families. Two Young People get to name something completely new, and they pick an old favourite. Typical.

"So how does it feel?"

Sandra answered first. "It's like finally meeting a neighbour you've heard banging around next door for months but never actually seen. And you find she's not too bad, not like anyone you've been afraid of."

Justin added, "When you have a baby, they call it settling down. I don't know why. It's the most unsettling thing I've ever known. And we're going to start looking for somewhere bigger to live. Once I know everything is going to be all right at work. Is everything going to be all right?"

"Yes," I said. "I rather think it is. For a while, anyway."

So I told him about my new job. And how I would be working directly for the new Assistant Editor (Features). And how it would be announced tomorrow that the new Assistant Editor (Features) would be Joan, as the previous incumbent, one Clive Basset, had left the office with a big pay-off that morning, unseen by anyone.

"Blimey, guv, is it your fault that he's out?"

"No. Far from it. I may even have been in danger of stopping it. They wouldn't have wanted his removal to seem like a result of my article. But his time was up. He was too connected with the old regime and maybe he was too busy with his private life to keep up with what was really happening.

"Arabella will be the new lifestyle boss. Good for the paper's image to have her there and she's more than capable. The editor is bringing in someone from his old paper to be her deputy. Life goes on."

Sandra asked, "So you're not going to leave, after all?"

"No," I said. "I'll see how this goes. It might be a terrible mistake, but a chap likes to feel useful, you know. Maybe it will all go belly up in a month. Maybe

298

Basset will come after me with a brick, though I doubt that. I just think the good times don't happen that often, so we may as well enjoy them."

I decided it was time to leave them to it. On the sofa, Sandra nudged Justin in the arm and he spoke.

"We'd like to ask you a favour."

"Oh no, what is it this time?"

He looked embarrassed. "We're thinking about the christening. The thing is, we'd like you to be a godfather. If you don't mind. You've helped out from the beginning. It seems right."

They looked at me hopefully. I was thinking, a dutiful godfather has to keep in touch for years and years. There might be endless more favours. Bloody Young People.

"Thank you," I said. "I don't mind. Not at all."

At the door, as he showed me out, Justin asked, "So, are you going out somewhere to celebrate all this?"

And I said, "Not tonight. I'm going home. There's something I'm supposed to write . . ."

Dear Annie,

I'm trendy. I'm cool. I'm modern. Maybe I'm even post-modern. Grumpiness is the new irony, ordinary is the new special. For a fleeting moment in media land, I am in fashion. I'm wanted. Stand still long enough and the world turns to the right place.

And you are not here to see it. Damn.

I did not want to write this letter but I'm told it's a good idea, it's therapy, so I'm trying. (I realized last month that I never wrote you a letter in all our time together. I've spent most of my adult life writing stuff but never to you.) We were together so long that I felt you already knew anything I wanted to say. Now I want to say more and I have to accept that you are gone.

I had a good day today. One of those great days when I would come home with things to laugh about. We should crack open a bottle and celebrate. The great moments don't come often and no success is ever final, but I have got a chance to get out of my prison and I must take it. And in a way, that means saying goodbye to you and some of this stuff inside my head. So my first letter to you is also a letter of farewell.

For a long time, you were the best of me. The very best. I never had to ask myself where I was going, I was going home to you, even though at times I may have seemed indifferent to it. The mistake I made was that you became everything, all I had left. When you died, it was like I was no longer a real person. To survive, I suppose I knew that I would have to become someone new, someone different. But really, I didn't want to be anything at all. And I think I lost you at just the wrong time.

I have been keeping a journal. Yes, seriously. It's been more like a prison diary. I'm stopping it now, finishing on a high point. This letter will be the last entry.

In the past couple of weeks I've had two appointments with the grief counsellor who suggested the journal in the first place. I can barely admit I went back to him but I've been stuck for so long, I just needed a little help. He greeted my return with a look of earnest delight. I read him bits of the journal, gave him the overall picture, and said, well, what did he think?

The trouble with these people is that they are so damn non-judgemental. It's all phrased in questions. Did I feel that by coming back to him now I was finally willing to seek "closure"? (Maybe.) Did I think that I had now thoroughly experienced all the feelings evoked by my loss? (God, I hope so.) Did I know it was possible to over-idealize the dead — you, my dad — which just made it harder to move on? (But you really were ideal!) Did I find that I had been in a sort of mourning for myself so that, at my age, it had all become part of facing up to my own mortality with an unconscious search for meaning? (Oh, get on with it.) That sort of thing.

He was kind enough to say that I had managed very well for a man with no support system and no sense of purpose in my work. He reckoned that my recovery had begun when I "reached out" and helped the homeless Justin, because learning to accept yourself means accepting others, or something like that. All the rest was about learning to cope. Apparently, people who are bad at coping with change and uncertainty have big problems dealing with grief. And another thing: daft behaviour can be a sign of someone breaking out of the inertia of depression and finding the energy to act again.

So, I said, all right, all very interesting, now suppose I am needing "closure", how do I do it? And he said, well, some people with long-unresolved issues find it helps to have a final conversation, to say everything they want to say as if the dead person was there. And I said, where? And he said, in that chair over there, speak to her as if she was there. And I said, er, no, give me another idea. And he said, well, writing a letter can also work.

The trouble with "issues" is that they change all the time, and maybe it's taken me this long to think of them all. There's a point where the effects of a bad event are only as bad as you allow them to be, and I had allowed all this to be pretty bad. Here's a big thing: I have forgiven myself about the damn car, but I still feel guilty about the money so I am going to resolve that now.

Thanks for the money, Annie. I don't need it all. As it's yours, I have tried to think what you would do with it if I wasn't here, and that makes it simple. Some should be kept for a rainy day, of course, but I am going to keep in better touch with all your godchildren and if there's something they really need that their parents want help with, then they'll get it. I have a godchild of my own now. And I'll always keep in touch with young Annie and the family.

As for the car-crash money, I am going to find a charity that helps kids with no chance at all and I will give it to them in your name. You were a sucker for charities like that. This way, maybe there will be a new playgroup in some inner-city dump, or a classroom in Africa, that's there because you lived and died, and it will make a kind of sense. And I will do all of this with love, with pleasure. Dad would be pleased with that, thank God.

I can't escape the thought of Dad at the end, scribbling away in his darkness, trying to narrow down some simple rules of life before it ended. And I think perhaps I have been like that. Maybe we all are. He managed to come up with, what, fifteen thoughts that I found? I can hardly think of any. Shouldn't everyone be able to come up with, say, ten? To show that we have all lived and learned? Maybe one rule is, try to do things you wouldn't normally do. And, helping someone helps you to feel needed — sometimes you can help just by being around; take risks and be silly sometimes; never get too comfy; take stock every month; don't live in London longer than twenty years; get involved with other families if you don't have your own; mix the generations; er, save the planet? That's still only nine. I know: regrets are pointless unless they change you.

I found myself writing something this week about life being a short path and how we need to look for ways to make it seem bigger. I have been thinking about that tonight. We can make the path wider with friends and experiences, make it seem higher and deeper with knowledge and music and our thoughts, make it start further behind us with history, but how do we change the horizon ahead, how do we make the path worth travelling on? The past is no use without the future. Our history has to lead us somewhere or it is just bones. I had been thinking of writing about the past, but for now I'm going to try the present, where the future starts. We get there from here.

I find I am wanting things again. Not the things I am meant to want, but things I choose to want. (Like, I may get myself some new shoes for Christmas, but they will be hiking boots. And I might get a health check-up.) I want my new job to work. I want a future. I want to smile more. I want to look up some people from my address book, and I want to speak to people other than bloody journalists. Maybe I'll meet someone wise. Maybe I'll be able to help with things that are worth getting grumpy about. I'll give it a year. I want to travel round, probably by train and bus. I'll be able to listen to people that way. I don't miss driving now, cars are so isolating.

I want to start to like life again. Not lifestyle, but life. I've had a few flashes lately and living is not a bad idea. I feel as if a stopped clock has started ticking again. I could find more things that I actually like, more that I can believe in. It is exhausting to keep pushing it all away. I've got some of my old confidence back, largely because I've got away with doing some fairly stupid things lately.

And I think, finally, that I want some romance. Something tentative and long-distance might be wise. I don't think for a moment that romance is the point of existence, but it's an expression of it. It's one of the ways to share. I may grow back into it.

I'll keep the flat for the time being, though things are changing here. My downstairs neighbours are planning to move away to somewhere bigger. I will still go for walks on the Heath sometimes. I will never forget you.

304

It is a shame that you don't know me now, you might like me better. We should be doing this journey together, instead I must start a second life without you. But thank you for the first life. Thank you from the depths of my recovering heart.

George

Afterword: A STRANGER IN THE NIGHT

Daddy Cool
by Justin Smith
20 November

WAAAH! Forget about a good night's sleep. Waaah!

Postpone that touring holiday in the States.

Waaah! Never mind about a social life.

It's 2a.m. and it's my turn to feed the baby. It should be me who is crying, instead of my daughter. Yet I stagger out of bed to hold her and comfort her with a weary kind of wonder. Whatever I have lost, I have gained this wonder.

But I don't feel much like I'm Daddy Cool.

The idea for this new occasional column is to provide a frontline report on what happens to a faintly groovy young man about town when he suddenly becomes a dad. How does he feel? Can a man really change for the better?

Right now, fatherhood feels a bit like being called up for action as a rookie recruit. No one actually shaves off your hair, takes away all your belongings and sends you to boot camp far away from your old life, but they might just as well.

According to my wife Sandra, a surprise pregnancy is like suddenly finding yourself in the Marines when you have not even volunteered. But in the middle of the night, I think that a weary new parent has more in common with a member of the bomb-disposal squad — handling something very delicate while nervous and exhausted.

It is just as well that little Lily does not yet judge by appearances, as I look awful. And this brings me to my first fashion point — clearly, new parents need a combat uniform. There's not much point in wearing my trendy clobber when it just gets crumpled and covered in various forms of baby goo. I'm thinking that something nice in a camouflage pattern would be much more practical, maybe with detachable epaulettes to soak up the sick. A uniform could also help to identify me to the world at large as a man who is dangerously short of sleep and possibly carrying a loaded nappy.

But can men really alter? Well, yes, of course we can, given the right cause. When readers last heard from my colleague George Worth, the previous occupant of this bit of the page, he was somewhere in the northeast, grinning as he stood shoulder to shoulder with a bunch of Green types in pouring rain, protesting about a new shopping complex near some sacred historic site. If George can do that, I can do this.

Let's put it this way. There was a new film opening in London last night and until recently I would have said it was important that I went to see it. Not merely interesting, but "important". I don't feel like that about anything very much now except sleep and baby Lily. It may not last but it's an entirely new sensation.

It's just possible — and only a possibility, that's all I am saying — that the trends and seasons of passing fashions are a pale imitation of the seasons of life. And if that's the case, then this is the real thing. On the other hand, it may just be that when you are on a real high, or a real low, you stop wanting things for a while simply because your brain is full and it needs to be rewired.

Some of my wants will come back, I know, but some of them will be replaced by wants for her. Eventually I am even supposed to help her to learn things: how to talk, how to walk, how to stop pooing her pants. These are the great social skills we all owe our parents, whatever else they got wrong.

There's a lot I didn't know or hadn't thought about. The lads' mags don't prepare you for this, even though fatherhood is the destiny of most men and the natural result of the very activity that the magazines keep going on about.

I didn't really know that babies arrive with such a great part of the human will already wired in their heads, right from the beginning, a little bundle of wants. She is relentless.

And there's an amazing thought about a daughter: she came out of a woman, who came out of a woman, who came out of a woman, and so on, all the way back to the beginning of time, and she can continue this Russian doll effect right into the future. This endless line of family is my last weary thought tonight.

One of the duties of new parenthood is showing the baby to her grandparents, and listening while the older generation discusses which part of the family she looks like, remembering some part of the past that has been renewed in her.

It's as soppy as anything but I may as well enjoy it. As I return Lily to her cot and watch her sleeping and almost visibly growing, it seems to me that life is in a constant state of renewal. We can ignore it, or resist it, or work with it or try to control it, but it will happen one way or another.

Renewal, it's all about renewal. And that's the best I can say for now.

THE END

Author's Note

This book is a work of fiction. I don't think that I'm George Worth (although like Justin, I have spent longer than expected in George's company). The workplaces and the people in this story are all imagined. Many lifestyle journalists are really quite normal, considering, and some columnists are positively inspiring.

There are some things it was not necessary to make up.

The strange impracticality of women's fashion shoes gained its own anthem in 2000 with "In These Shoes?" (MacColl/Glenister) in which the late Kirsty MacColl sang of a succession of adventurous suitors inviting her to make love on a mountain top or to go horseriding, only to find that her footwear prevented her from making the romantic journeys. "Fairytale of New York", recorded with the Pogues in 1987 and re-released several times since, is a Christmas anthem of lost hopes and dreams, and might be just the sort of thing that George yearns for in chapter 2.

A suggestion that buying new boxer shorts can help to change a man's life was the second of 52 life-improving ideas in the 2004 New Year edition of

Men's Health (usually among the least daft of the men's lifestyle monthlies). It recommended: Find out how looking smart underneath your clothes makes you feel smart all day. Improving your relationship with your father was 12th, trying a religious service was 19th, voluntary work was 37th and talking to strangers was 47th.

The speed of the Earth in Worth's 12th rule is our planet's individual orbiting speed around the Sun. I am aware (so please don't write in) that our entire solar system also moves around the centre of the galaxy at about 490,000 mph and that our galaxy is also rushing onwards at more than 2 million mph, and so on. It's just a number, OK?

The Northumberland coast path is among the many wonderful parts of Britain's historic countryside; more than 80 per cent of Britain is countryside, and Northumberland is England's least populated county. St Bride's remains the London journalists' church. The Sidmouth folk festival is also very real, as are the briefly mentioned farmers' moaning song and the corset-pulling shanty, performed by Sid Kipper.

And I'm sure that I did once see a shop poster advertising "New shoes for Christmas" somewhere in London, but I can't remember where.

The self-help book read by George in chapter 7 is clearly based on Steve Biddulph's definitive *Manhood* (Random House). Many men probably need to put this book on their reading lists at some time in their lives, to work out where they stand. I thank the author for his permission, and sense of humour, for it to be parodied here. It's just possible that George might achieve all the seven steps in the end.

In the world of ideas, George must have experienced many influences, from John Cleese onwards, but the responsibility for any conclusions lies with George. He is his own man.

Some people would argue that the Sermon on the Mount (Matthew 5–7) is the fullest list of rules in the Gospels; others would say that the Sermon is more about attitudes than actions. The chateau tower where Montaigne did his thinking still stands in the French countryside, between Bordeaux and Bergerac. (You can probably also visit old haunts of Schopenhauer somewhere but, as he might say, what would be the point?)

If you read this book after autumn 2007, you should probably not try to catch the Eurostar from Waterloo, as the service is supposed to be switching to St Pancras station. And if you don't want a hefty bill, it is never advisable to just abandon a car outside a London hospital unless a nearby ambulanceman keeps an eye on it for you. The hospital in the story is not meant to have any significant resemblance to any real hospital that happens to be in the area.

In past years I have worked as a sub-editor in offices at most of Britain's national newspaper groups. George's office is not based on any in particular, especially not *The Times*.

Possibly this story could have been set in many other major world cities but London is especially well-qualified as the British are champion shoppers. We may score badly in many European quality-of-life surveys but we know how to spend money. The British are by far the biggest users of credit cards in Europe, with the greatest amount of personal debt — one in five adults has unsecured debts of more than £10,000, not counting the mortgages on their homes. Including the home loans, Britons personally owe a total of well over £1 trillion.

In the late 1970s, more than half the population belonged to local community groups of various kinds; the figure is now less than 20 per cent. An ICM poll for the BBC in September 2006 found that half the population thought that life had worsened in the past couple of decades and only a quarter thought it was better. Another poll found that nearly a quarter of the population was worried about feeling depressed. And a survey of personal regrets for UK TV Gold in October 2006 found that 44 per cent of Britons in their twenties regretted that they were not yet famous. Britain is said to be 41st in the world happiness league.

A widely reported study by MORI for the BBC in August 2002 singled out the 35–54 age group as the

314

most doubtful about modern life. Compared with older and younger generations, they were the least positive about politicians and the state of public services, the least likely to think that the people in charge know best, the least likely to expect fulfilment from success at work and the least likely to be impressed by brand names. (This helped to form the basis of the popular BBC series *Grumpy Old Men*). It was not so well reported that these midlife rebels were also far more likely to continue to believe that public protests are "signs of a healthy social system". And according to research by the Charities Aid Foundation, males aged 45–54 are the generation of men who give most to charity. They may be grumpy but they are not hopeless.

Special thanks are due to Laura Longrigg at my agents MBA, to Simon Taylor and the team at Transworld, and for various reasons to Amy, Katie, Jack, Carol, Michael, Annelise, Sheila, Royston, Paul & Lorraine, Kirsty & Rob, the Susans, Sarah, Charles & Liz, Kathy, Michael M, Jaya N, Frank, Cathy, and to the Bristol gang: Life goes on.

David Wilson
London 2007

Also available in ISIS Large Print:

Laying the Ghost

Judy Astley

Have you ever wondered what your ex is up to?

When Nell was a student, she and Patrick were a serious item. They were inseparable, and she really thought he was The One, despite their tempestuous relationship. But then Alex came along . . . He seemed the safer, more restful option, and thanks to her over-controlling mother she opted for him instead.

Now nothing is going right. Alex has left her to live in New York with a younger, blonder woman. Escaping to the Caribbean for a recuperative holiday, Nell is mugged at Gatwick and her bag is stolen. It's crisis time — and she makes two decisions:

First — she will takes lessons in self-defence. Second — she will try to find Patrick again.

Is she trying to put her past behind her — or setting out to ruin her future?

ISBN 978-0-7531-7916-1 (hb)
ISBN 978-0-7531-7917-8 (pb)

Fifty is Not a Four-Letter Word

Linda Kelsey

Funny, wise — I wish I had written this **Cathy Kelly**

Funny, wise, true and not just for women of fifty!
Wendy Holden

Life begins at 50 . . .

Well, it certainly does for Hope, though not at all as she had planned. She reluctantly hits her half-century on New Year's Day, and within weeks she has lost her job, her husband, her mother — and her last shred of self-esteem.

But Hope has guts — and a sense of humour. By the time she reaches 51, she has acquired a taste for designer underwear, climbing mountains — and the memory of one perfect night in Paris.

ISBN 978-0-7531-7928-4 (hb)
ISBN 978-0-7531-7929-1 (pb)